"This is sumptuous, lavish writing. Get a copy of *Loving Søren*, grab a cup of tea, sit down by the fire, and prepare to be carried away to the time and place so deftly evoked in this beautiful first novel from Caroline O'Neill."

— THOM LEMMONS,
author of *Sunday Clothes* and coauthor of *King's Ransom*

"A beautifully written love story that reminds us that love has always been complicated. Caroline O'Neill writes about what we think of as a simpler time. But affairs of the heart and conflicts of faith are never simple. The trials and passions depicted in *Loving Søren* are very much with us today."

— DEBORAH NORVILLE,
anchor, *Inside Edition*

"Caroline O'Neill's stunning sense of time and place provides a captivating backdrop for an equally compelling story. In the midst of the darkness that so often enshrouds us all, she provides a sparkle of the hope love holds."

— NANCY RUE,
author of *Pascal's Wager* and *Antonia's Choice*

Loving Søren

Loving Søren

Caroline Coleman O'Neill

a novel

Nashville, Tennessee

13-digit ISBN: 978-0-8054-3089-9
10-digit ISBN: 0-8054-3089-X

Published by Broadman & Holman Publishers,
Nashville, Tennessee

Dewey Decimal Classification: F
Subject Headings: ROMANCES
DEPRESSION (PSYCHOLOGY)—FICTION
PHILOSOPHY—FICTION
EXISTENTIALISM—FICTION
KIERKEGAARD, SØREN—FICTION

1 2 3 4 5 6 7 8 9 10 09 08 07 06 05

To my father, for bringing us up
on Søren Kierkegaard.
To my mother, for not.

Author's Note

This is a work of biographical fiction. All of the epigraphs, letters, and journal entries in italics—except the two letters in chapter 36—are authentic, as is some of Søren Kierkegaard's dialogue.

Regine Olsen told her side of the story to several people who recorded it in the second and third person. In the epigraphs, I have taken the liberty of returning her words to the first person.

The portrait of Regine Olsen on the front cover was painted by Emil Baerentzen in 1840. It now hangs in the Copenhagen ByMuseum.

Contents

Copenhagen, May 1837

1

The Fork

"I saw her for the first time at the Rordams."

SØREN KIERKEGAARD

"Mr. Kierkegaard called on the Rordam family and the liveliness of his intellect made a very strong impression on me, which I did not reveal, however."

REGINE OLSEN

Regina Olsen perched on a red sofa in the Rordams' Chinese-style drawing room, adrift amid a sea of glamorous ladies. The scent of beeswax rose from the veneered floor, mingling with the aroma of coffee bubbling forth from the inflamed samovar. Soft flakes of spring snow whispered against the leaded windowpanes, pressing toward the sea green damask curtains. The long twisted tusk of a narwhal lay on a squid-shell table. Beside it, a silver bird took flight, its mother-of-pearl feathers glistening in the snowlight that draped through the windows.

"It is so very hard to find good *help* these days," the widow Rordam said. "Everyone who presents himself is so very *unsuitable*." Encased in black, the widow sat in a regal chair of red silk. A smile hovered on the corners of her once beautiful lips. The three other young ladies nodded.

Regina hoped the widow's maid wasn't listening in at the keyhole. She fingered the edge of her gown, wishing she had chosen a different one. Although it was May, she had worn a winter white dress, unconsciously echoing the colors of the snow-laden sky. The whiteness of the dress and its intricate ivory stitchwork highlighted the darkness of her hair and eyes and echoed the pale luminescence of her moonlight colored skin. At home, the dress had seemed beautiful in its simplicity, but here in the Rordams' large drawing room on the outskirts of Copenhagen, beside the mourning taffeta of the widow and the brightly colored dresses of the three other young women, Regina's dress seemed dull.

Just as Regina began to lose herself in an elaborate daydream about Fritz Schlegel, her new history teacher, a door opened. The maid mumbled a name, and a thin young man strode into the room. His blue eyes, defiant and questing, had one of the most intelligent expressions that Regina had ever seen. He held his lips in a tight, compressed smirk that quivered slightly at the edges. A knee-length black coat that he wore over a black waistcoat and cravat had a shiny, threadbare look at the elbows. The huge collar of his starched white shirt nearly buried him, and his blond hair seemed to leap from his head. The man's face had the nervous intensity and delicate beauty of an artist. His whole body, Regina decided, radiated an inner zeal. She sat up a little straighter.

As the widow Rordam made the introductions, the young man's blue eyes prowled over the three fifteen-year-olds on the red sofa—Regina and her schoolmates, Eline Sorenson and Thrine Dahl. Regina blushed and lowered her gaze to his dark shoes. She looked up with a small smile, but the young man had already put his back to her and was greeting Bolette Rordam, the eighteen-year-old daughter of the house.

Regina sighed. Yet another person who was going to pay no attention to her. It was going to be a long morning.

"Please," the widow told the young man. "Have a seat." She pointed toward a plush velvet armchair. He seemed not to notice the direction of her hand and chose instead a hard, straight-backed chair to Regina's right.

Bolette approached him again, this time holding out a silver tray. "Pastries?"

The young man leapt up to examine the contents of the tray, and then recoiled as if Bolette were trying to poison him. Regina suppressed a giggle at his melodrama. The others stared at him as if he were the strangest man they'd ever seen.

What was his name? Regina wondered.

"How I love pastries," he said. "I am drawn to them, as if by magnetic force."

Was it Søren?

"So which will you choose?" Bolette asked. "The tray is getting heavy."

Søren what?

"None." The young man waved her away and sat again in his hard wooden chair.

"Very well. But I'll leave the tray here beside you," Bolette said, "in case you change your mind."

Regina didn't know how the young man could refuse Bolette anything. She and her cousin Thrine Dahl were the two most beautiful girls in all of Copenhagen. Regina coveted Bolette's narrow gown of pale pink silk, its high waist and puffed sleeves edged in dark pink velvet. Bolette's hair, as gleaming and polished as everything else in her mother's house, lay coiled in golden braids around the top of her head.

A pink silk ribbon perched on one of the braids. Her full lips were as red as the Chinese flowers that wound their way up her mother's wallhangings.

"I missed his name," Regina whispered to Thrine.

"Søren Kierkegaard." Thrine's finely sculpted lips barely moved. Her tone suggested she didn't think much of the man. But then her sharp cheekbones and regal demeanor had an icy coldness that suggested she didn't think much of anyone.

"I thought you said you loved pastries Mr. Kierkegaard," Bolette said, a flirtatious smile on her lips.

"Yes. And that is precisely why I must refuse them," Søren said, accentuating his point by grabbing a silver fork off of the platter and jabbing the air with it.

What a curious philosophy, to refuse the thing he most wanted. Perhaps he didn't like pastries as much as he claimed.

Bolette persisted, her rosebud mouth in an almost circular pout. "Surely one small pastry would do you no harm."

"Miss Rordam," he said, "it is just such small evil choices, made over the course of a lifetime, that doom one to perdition. You wouldn't want to be responsible for sending me to my doom?" The young man's gaze roamed to the young ladies on the sofa, then he looked away again.

"According to your father, Mr. Kierkegaard, you've done a fine job of putting yourself on that path." The widow spoke in a voice that would, in a younger woman, have been flirtatious. "And I will thank you not to call my food evil."

Transfixed, the younger girls stared at the profligate before them. He didn't look particularly wolfish, except for a certain predatory gleam in his eyes. Regina guessed he was about twenty-five—ten years older than she was. His skin was pale and soft, but Regina noticed he had a faint pink bloom in his cheeks.

"Søren calls on my cousin Bolette almost every morning," Thrine whispered to Regina, "even though she's already engaged to Peter Kobke, one of his fellow philosophy students."

"No," Regina mouthed back.

Thrine nodded, her eyes as glittering and sharp as two sapphires.

"But why would he call on her if she's already engaged?" Regina whispered. "Is he arrogant? Or does he have some sort of death wish?"

The widow whirled round in her red silk chair. "Young ladies should not whisper."

"Especially," Søren said, with a wicked grin, "when it is obvious you are talking about me."

Regina blushed.

"Perhaps," he continued, leaning back with a satisfied air, "one small pastry would not make much difference in the grand scheme of things." He pounced on a pastry and took a generous bite. "Delicious," he said.

"I knew you'd give in," said the widow.

Søren ignored this. "Pastries are," he went on in an innocent voice, "far less dangerous than becoming engaged—an enterprise my father advocates as a way of reforming me."

Bolette and her mother exchanged glances.

"Yes," Søren cried, as if someone had violently disagreed with him, "the commitment of engagement is one I shun."

Regina didn't believe him for a second. *He's just trying to interest Bolette by appearing disinterested,* she thought.

"As the widowed mother of four unmarried daughters, I can assure you that such views are frowned upon here," Mrs. Rordam said.

"Good. Good. I love being frowned upon," Søren replied, rubbing his hands together.

The widow Rordam gave him a withering glare, but Regina smiled. Søren glanced her way.

"Why do you shun engagement, Mr. Kierkegaard," the widow asked, her face twitching as she remolded it into a polite mask. "Most people make it their aim in life."

"Precisely why I spurn it."

The widow looked annoyed. Regina was intrigued. She had expected an uncomfortable morning call on glamorous stiff people, and instead she found herself in a room gripped with tension. She glanced at Eline, whose mouth had fallen open as it always did when she was concentrating on something. Thrine was also staring at Søren, her expression laced with disapproval.

"I think, Mother, that Mr. Kierkegaard is teasing us," Bolette said.

"Of course," the widow said. "I knew that." She turned to Søren. "Tell us, then, the real reason you're not interested in becoming engaged."

Eline poked Regina. Regina focused her eyes at the far end of the room, pretending not to notice.

"Because no Christian should marry," he said.

"I've never heard such poppycock," the widow said. "The human race would die out."

"Good," Søren said.

Regina stifled a laugh. Again, she didn't believe him. And yet she felt drawn to something in the extremity of his position, something in his disregard for the opinions of others, something she longed for but had never dared voice.

"Nonsense," Mrs. Rordam said. "Why would God create man in order to die out?"

"Saint Paul says marriage is only a concession to our, shall I say . . . passions," Søren said.

Regina squirmed. Bolette looked out the window as if fascinated by the spring snowfall.

"Saint Paul was an old stick," Mrs. Rordam said.

Regina was shocked. *No,* she wanted to say, *no. Saint Paul was beloved of God. He was God's mouthpiece. You cannot discount his words just because you don't like them.* She clamped her lips tight.

"Ah," Søren said. "You must be paying attention in church. They teach all kinds of heresy there these days."

Regina had to bite back her reply. *Quiet,* she told herself. *Let the widow handle this. You can thrust and parry at home.*

"Heresy—" the widow began, but Søren interrupted her.

"Heresy," he said. "And why should I want to marry? To make children who look like me? No, thank you. I'd spare them that if I could—at all costs. To put more sinners in this world? Hardly. From the Christian point of view, the marriage ceremony is a funeral ceremony."

Regina started to laugh again, but stopped herself.

"Oh, for heaven's sake," Mrs. Rordam said.

Søren's eyes sparkled.

It's almost as if he relishes her look of disgust, Regina thought.

"Besides," Søren said, "it is said in polite society that the commitment of engagement is as strong as that of marriage, is it not?"

"Absolutely," said the widow, giving Bolette a significant look.

"To break an engagement would cause a scandal," Søren added.

"Yes."

"And yet the goal of proposing is to make another happy."

"Ye-es."

"But you cannot know what it is like to become engaged unless you try it," he went on.

"Now there I must—"

"And so if I will not know until I am engaged whether I will make a girl happy, and yet I should not become engaged unless I can make a girl happy, and once I am engaged I may not become *dis*engaged, then I abhor engagement."

Regina longed to argue with him, to throw herself into the lion's den. Søren gave her another quick glance.

"Although," Søren mused, "happiness is an illusion anyway."

The widow narrowed her once lovely eyes. "I would not go that far."

"But you must," Søren insisted. "You must go that far and farther. It is the only way to progress—by taking the most extreme position possible." He waved the fork with one hand and seemed to grip the air in front of him with the slim fingers of the other. To Regina, it looked as if he was not merely daring someone to respond, he was begging for it, begging to be rescued from the extremity of his position. Her lips itched to answer. She pressed them shut.

There was a silence.

The silence grew painful. Regina's lips trembled and then opened, releasing the words that pressed against them. "If happiness is an illusion," she said, "then you might as well become engaged and not worry about whether your fiancée is happy."

Søren laughed, and Regina felt her small body relax.

"Ah," he said. "To be so young and yet so practical."

Why did he speak as if he were an old man? "It is hardly my fault I am young, Mr. Kierkegaard," Regina said.

Regina could feel her two companions on the couch stirring, uneasy at the way she had launched herself into the conversation. Regina's right hand gripped the small gold cross at her neck. When she placed her hand back in her lap, she noticed she had gripped the cross so tightly that the edge of it had made a small imprint in her thumb.

"Miss Olsen, was it not?"

She nodded, surprised that Søren had remembered her name.

"I can see nothing wrong with you at all," he said, his eyes gleaming. "Young or old. But what if there were another world? A world we cannot see except in rare glimpses, like the lamp of a carriage in the distance, passing in the night?"

As he spoke, Regina recalled how, as a child, she used to have imaginary conversations with her heroine, Joan of Arc. She did not often see Joan anymore, but every now and then Regina would turn a corner and come upon a memory, a place where Joan still lived, the way the smell of snow would remind her of the magic of Christmas. Was he talking about such fairy tale magic? Or was fairy tale magic itself only a foretaste of Søren Kierkegaard's other world?

"Because, if this physical world we see before us were the only reality," Søren continued, "then it would certainly be better to be young. But if . . . ," he leaned forward and jabbed the fork in the air again. "Rather *as* there is another world—a spirit world, a more important world, indeed the only important world—being young or old is irrelevant. The only thing that matters—the only thing at all—is that the eternal spirit inside of you is constantly in touch with the eternal presence of God. Because feeling God's presence buoys you through life, like the joy of falling in love."

One of Søren's hands, delicate and vulnerable, gripped the chair beneath him.

"I'm sorry you didn't enjoy the pastry," Regina told him. Søren stared at her. She saw, with a feeling of satisfaction, that he had finally put down the fork. "Because if the physical world doesn't matter, then you couldn't have enjoyed the pastry," she said.

"Touché, Regina," Bolette said, laughing.

Something in Søren Kierkegaard's gaze made Regina look away.

The widow Rordam rose to her slender feet. "It is time, Mr. Kierkegaard, for my youngest daughter to accompany me on my turn about the house. Before her *fiancé* arrives."

A slight jolt seemed to course through Søren.

You asked for it, Regina thought. *You brought it on yourself.* She stiffened as she wondered if Søren would accept the widow's dismissal. After a painful pause, Søren rose and bowed to each lady in turn. It seemed to Regina as if he avoided meeting her gaze. Had she offended him? The moment the door closed behind him, and Bolette and Mrs. Rordam had strolled into the kitchen, Thrine eased herself off the sofa and rolled her eyes.

"My eldest brother knows him," Eline said, drawing her long lips together, "and he says that Søren Kierkegaard is a sarcastic, annoying, and vain young man."

Regina knew Eline's eldest brother, and had often thought the same of him.

"Søren Kierkegaard made fun of *my* brother in school, so my brother and his friends stuffed Søren into a desk and closed the lid." Thrine rapped the arm of a chair. "That was the end of his sarcastic comments."

With a pang of empathy, Regina pictured the young man she had just met being stuffed into a desk by a pack of less intelligent boys. "He seemed merely passionate to me," she said. "Someone who gets carried away by his ideas, who likes to take an extreme position in order to stimulate discussion."

"He certainly seemed to stimulate your discussion, Regina Olsen," Thrine said.

Regina didn't know how to answer her. It struck her that ever since the young man had left, the light inside the room had become as flat as the snowlight outside.

It is lucky, Regina thought, *that I am already in love with Fritz Schlegel.*

2

The Frozen Garden

"He who has borne the weight of his father's melancholy from childhood on is like a child who has been taken from its mother with forceps and who always bears a physical trace of the mother's pain."

SØREN KIERKEGAARD

"My own father suffered from melancholia."

REGINE OLSEN

When the morning call finally ended and the hired carriage rolled away through the icy ruts in the snow, Regina stood for a moment outside her front door in her white fur-lined hat, cape, and boots. The spring snowfall had transfigured Copenhagen overnight, whitewashing the streets, the churches, the bridges, and the roofs of the houses and palaces for as far as Regina could see. Regina's home, the second in a row of town houses known as the Six Sisters, lay on a finger of land stretching out to the sea. Dark, tense waves lashed at the pier that edged her street. The air smelled sweet and sharp, like spring rolled up in winter. It was the sort of morning on which every young girl imagines, just for a moment, a prince on a white horse charging toward her through the snow, with marriage on his mind.

But the street was empty.

Head bent low against the falling snow, Regina pushed open the front door of her family's town house and listened. She heard her sisters, brother, and mother laughing together in the blue sitting room to her right. She heard Anna, the housekeeper and cook, humming in the kitchen beyond. But the one voice she strained to hear was silent.

She knew where her father was without having to climb the wooden staircase. Although a Councilor in the Finance Ministry, he had not emerged from his room to go to work this morning. She imagined his body having made a double of itself, an imprint in the down mattress, a heavier, depressed self that held him captive to his bed. Regina longed to go to him, to raise him out of bed by his shoulders, to drag him downstairs and make him laugh until tears came into his eyes, but she knew that his door would be locked.

She slipped through the narrow hallway and out the back door into the tiny garden beyond. The snow swirled around her, seeming to change the color of the air. A layer of glassy ice trapped each branch and leaf. Regina sat on the bench in the middle of the frozen garden and looked out on the canal behind the house.

She prayed. She prayed for so long that she felt as if her prayers must be frozen in the air around her. *Lord, let my father choose life. Lord, let me be an instrument of thy peace.*

The door creaked open behind her.

"I feel as if I am looking at a painting," the Councilor said, seating himself beside her. He wore only dark trousers and white shirtsleeves, the twilled cloth of the shirt stretched tight over his stout stomach.

"Frozen Girl on Bench," Regina said, trying to hide her surprise at his appearance. *That was fast, Lord.* "Are you cold, Father? Shall I fetch you a coat?"

What she really meant was, "Are you well? Are you alive?

Can you think of anyone but yourself?" She glanced at his face. The edges of his eyes slanted down into two thin wrinkles, as if he were permanently amused. But she knew better than to trust the irony of the mirthful outer sweep of his eyes. It was the bewildered look within his brown eyes that moved her and challenged her to wield her most engaging brushstrokes.

"Suffering," he said, "is an illusion." His eyes glimmered, a light dusting of snow now coating his brown hair and sideburns.

"Of course," Regina responded. "It only looks as if we are frozen. On the inside, we are burning up."

The Councilor smiled. And as he smiled, Regina felt her shoulders relax.

Thank You, Lord, for allowing me to be the instrument of thy peace, she whispered silently in her heart.

"I'm glad you came to rescue me," she said out loud. "I was beginning to feel a little sorry for myself out here all alone." She usually didn't voice such thoughts to her father, for she had learned by watching her mother that her mission was to cheer, charm, and entertain him.

"Loneliness, like suffering, is good for you," he told her. "I rejoice when my children suffer."

"Of course you do. Because loneliness, like suffering, is an illusion."

"How is it," he asked, "that you're able to accept and challenge everything I say, all at the same time?"

Regina grinned. She observed her father's eyes again to see if his melancholy lingered there, like a cat sleeping in an alleyway. He looked tired, but she could tell by the way he was taking her in, the way he was enjoying her gentle quips, that the depression had released him from its all-encompassing grip.

And with that realization, Regina felt freed. She felt freed to dream her own dreams, to desire her own desires, and she allowed herself to ask the question that was burning in her mind.

"What do you know of my new history teacher, Fritz Schlegel?"

The Councilor looked out at the softly falling snow. "A promising young man, by all accounts. His father was well liked before he died. What do you think?"

"He will do," Regina said, speaking the language her father had taught her—the language of understatement, of using words to say only part of what she meant, while she let her heart-shaped face and the spring in her small, soft body suggest much more.

"Although . . . ." The Councilor shrugged. "I have always found the Schlegel family rather . . . ordinary."

Regina pictured Fritz Schlegel's tall eager frame, his earnest eyebrows, and his kind brown eyes. The image dulled, slightly, in the shadow of her father's words.

They sat in silence, the snow falling all around them. The silence grew too much for her. Her shoulders tensed, notching tighter and tighter. She felt she must fill the open space between them, bond him to her. She heard herself say, her tone light, "I am glad you are with us again."

The Councilor did not move his body, and yet Regina sensed his spirit withdraw from her, the way souls are depicted as departing from corpses at the moment of death in medieval paintings. Attuned like all children to the silent language of her parents, Regina felt her own body freeze. By speaking of her father's depression, by mentioning the unmentionable, she had given it a power he abhorred.

He didn't answer, and pain slipped back in behind his eyes. Desperate to change the subject, Regina began to chatter about Mrs. Rordam, Thrine, and the young man with the fork. She tried to undo with words the damage her words had done. She babbled. He did not respond.

The door banged behind them. Regina's three older sisters approached, all buxom, all small. While the image of one almost glowed with warmth, and the second with sweetness, the third seemed as cold and stiff as the frozen branches of the garden. Regina tensed up further, waiting for the assault from Olga, the eldest.

"There you are." Olga stamped the snow off her shoes and took her father's arm with an officious air, as if she already knew that Regina had failed in her duty. The Councilor stood up.

Marie, the second oldest—a pretty, merry girl—laughed and took her father's other arm. "Come," she said. "What could you two possibly find to do out here in the cold?" Cornelia, the third, creased her kind eyes in concern.

Their father laughed an over-hearty, fake laugh, but it was still a laugh. Regina exhaled in relief. Only then did she realize she'd been holding her breath.

"All right, all right," the Councilor said, "I'm coming."

Before following her sisters, Regina looked back at the garden. The snow muffled all sound except the faint murmuring of the iced leaves of the holly bushes. In this magical world, a world in which her father's revival had given her permission to hope, she'd begun to dream again about Fritz Schlegel. She thought about the way his lips parted slightly when he listened to her, as if—she could not help but think—he was waiting for her to kiss him.

Lord, she prayed, *if only You will give me the desire of my heart, I know I will be happy. Let Fritz Schlegel fall in love with me. Let him want to marry me. Let us have beautiful, laughing children together. Grant me a miracle.*

She imagined her words rising from her mouth and mixing with the swirling snow around her. And as she surrendered her prayers to her dreams, a small, precious part of her self broke off and departed with it, so lightly, so easily, that she barely even felt it go.

3

A Gentleman Caller

"There was a teacher from my school days to whom I was very much attached, and I believed that he also cared for me."

REGINE OLSEN

"[R]eligiously understood, I was pre-pledged early in childhood."

SØREN KIERKEGAARD

Just over a year later, Regina's prayer began to come true.

The moment she finished the Daughters' School, the moment the teacher-student relationship was behind them, the moment Fritz had been hired into a promising position in the colonial office, he sought out Regina one summer Saturday at a scavenger hunt in the country. And he let her know by the way his eyes sought hers after every one of his jokes; the way his smile expanded every time he looked at her; and the way he took her arm so gently, so carefully, to help her across the treacherous, muddy lawn during the hunt, that Fritz Schlegel had embarked on a quest, and Regina Olsen was his quarry.

"And now that you have finished school," he asked her at the end of the hunt, "what will you be doing with all your free time?"

Waiting for you to call on me.

"Many things," she said, longing to soften the earnest lines of his pointed nose, his sharp chin, and his bony cheekbones.

"May I pay a morning call on your family?" Fritz asked. "Would you mind?"

"No." He was so tall, so masculine, that she found it almost painful to look into his face. She glanced down at her delicate ceylon slippers peeking out from beneath her long, striped ceylon skirt.

"No?"

"I mean yes," she said. She lowered her eyes.

"Yes, you would mind?" he asked. His voice was grave, but she looked up again and caught his brown eyes twinkling, their softness accentuated by the swirling browns and yellow of his cravat.

"Now you're teasing me," she said.

"Yes," he said. "Yes, I am teasing you. And yes, I will call on you. If you don't mind."

"No," she said. "I mean yes." He smiled, and every line in his angular face softened, like a chalk drawing suddenly blurred by an artist's finger.

So Regina waited at home every morning after the scavenger hunt. Five days later, she was still waiting.

The moment she woke up on the fifth day, she fell to her knees besides her four-poster bed. *Did I imagine it, Lord?* she begged. *Did Fritz Schlegel really seek me out? Does he really care for me? But why hasn't he come then? Why?*

The seagulls cried outside her open window, as the damp summer heat poured in. Women along the pier called out the delights of shrimp, of watercress, of flowers.

Let Fritz visit today, Lord. I can't bear to wait any longer.

A breeze lifted her yellow curtains like a woman's skirts. A voice cascaded inside her head like an echo in a cavernous place. *If Fritz Schlegel does not call on you, you are nothing, you were never anything, and you will never be anything.*

Maybe it was time to read her Bible. She padded in her white nightshift and bare feet across the thick wooden floorboards, marionette-like, so she wouldn't disturb her brother Jonas who slept in the room below and always complained about her slightest move. She sat at her worn wooden vanity and opened her Bible. *Find me a verse, Lord,* she prayed. *Speak to me.*

She closed her eyes, flipped the pages, and pointed with a blind finger. A verse rose up out of the book like a sword. "Set a guard, O Lord, over my mouth."

Oh, Lord, she sighed. *Did You have to remind me about my impetuous mouth? Today?*

So she prayed. She prayed until her guilt about her mouth dissipated like a polluted river that runs, runs, runs until it runs clear. She felt confident that today she would restrain herself. Her words would be seasoned with salt—wise, holy, and pure.

Four hours later, while Regina sat with her family in the large, green drawing room on the left of the front hall, Anna announced the arrival of a Mr. Fritz Schlegel. Regina froze. Jonas gave her an eyebrow-raised, elder-brother look, and she glared back at him. *Shhh,* she motioned. Jonas grinned, his elegant cheekbones, his slanting eyes, and the curl of his dissatisfied lips all laughing at her for being so transparent.

Anna, shorter and rounder than any of the Olsens, ducked her head, buried her chin in the white shirt points of her gray dress, and withdrew. A moment later, Fritz strode into the room, and Regina's frown tilted into a smile. He wore an elegant blend of browns: a light brown vest, a neat brown cravat with white polka dots, and a brown coat that fell to his knees, revealing camel colored breeches, ivory stockings, and shining brown shoes.

Regina smiled and wondered why she'd ever doubted him. She surveyed the scene with pride. The family portraits seemed to gleam with pleasure from the gilded green walls. The blue and yellow flowers on the carpet looked like a wedding canopy. Surely even the canaries in the cage by the window sang more joyfully. Herald, the family's wizened greyhound, walked stiffly over to Fritz and nuzzled his whitened face against Fritz's outstretched hand.

Fritz greeted the rest of Regina's family with the ease and elegance that she had expected. "What a lovely gown," he remarked to Mrs. Olsen about her new blue silk muslin. Cornelia and Marie ducked their heads as Fritz complimented their needlework. He asked Jonas about the meeting at the stock exchange later that afternoon. Even Olga gave Fritz a warm smile.

"No wonder he's gone into politics," Jonas whispered to Regina. She jabbed him in the side with her elbow, and he grinned.

"What a lovely room," Fritz told Mrs. Olsen.

It was a lovely room. Inherited from Regina's grandparents, the furniture whispered of ancient trees toppled in their prime, lovingly split and severed, carefully fitted and yoked. A dignified mahogany tea table with a pot of pink begonias stood in front of two upright green sofas. The sofas' rosewood arms curved outward like the proud prows of Viking ships. Stately but comfortable green chairs were paired in conversation-inducing clusters. A glass-fronted cabinet held Mrs. Olsen's best china figurines, and a desk and birdcage stood before the far window. A ceramic stove rested quietly in its niche. By the entrance sat an upright piano, its gleaming wood the chestnut color of Regina's hair.

"Miss Regina Olsen," Fritz said at last, settling into a green armchair beside her. The space between them seemed to contract. "I wanted to come sooner. Believe me. Nothing would have kept me away except my mother."

Regina smiled and formed an instant dislike for Mrs. Schlegel.

"I had to leave town on a business matter for her," Fritz went on. "Otherwise, I would have been here four days ago."

"Has it been that long?" Regina asked. Behind Fritz, Jonas rolled his eyes.

But even Jonas's teasing ceased to matter as eleven o'clock faded into twelve o'clock, and Fritz accepted Mrs. Olsen's invitation to stay for lunch.

⊠ ⊠ ⊠

Later that afternoon, Regina was still floating in a daze of happiness.

Thank You, Lord, she whispered in her heart. *Thank You for answering my prayers. Nothing could pierce my joy now.*

The front door banged open. The Councilor strode by, mounted the stairs and thundered upward. Without a word, Mrs. Olsen rose from her soft wing chair and followed him. Their children heard muffled shouting, then silence.

In silence, Regina swept charcoal over her thick paper, trying to evoke the delicate curves of the pink begonias. Olga practiced her scales on the piano, up and down, over and over again. Cornelia and Marie sat in a far corner, their heads bent together over their sewing. Jonas sprawled on the sofa beside Regina in his red and blue, military-style coat. But over them all lay an anxiety that sapped their energy as mercilessly as the humidity that pressed down upon them.

"Regina! You'll be late for your music lesson!" Mrs. Olsen's voice floated down the staircase into the drawing room, halting Olga's ponderous piano playing, and making Regina jump.

Regina began to tuck away her drawing materials when she noticed Fritz Schlegel's profile staring back at her from one of the flowers in her picture. *How had that happened?* Her pencil had taken turns unexpected, uncontrolled. She flipped the paper over so no one would see it, and dusted the charcoal from her fingers.

"Look at Regina." Jonas grinned, still sprawled on the sofa. "Too love-sick to make it to her music lesson."

"Stop it, Jonas," Regina said, springing to her feet.

"Oh, Mr. Schlegel," Jonas mimicked in a high voice. "Has it been four days? I've only been sitting here all week, every morning, waiting for you to call ever since you flirted with me so outrageously at the scavenger hunt." Jonas twirled his long fingers in front of his face and fluttered his eyelashes. Olga snorted with laughter from the piano bench.

"You're late for your meeting, Jonas," Regina said.

Jonas leaned forward and whisked Regina's drawing off the tea table. He stared at it then burst into laughter. "Look at this, Olga. She's drawn Fritz Schlegel's face in this flower. Clear as day."

"Give that back. Now."

"Jonas," Marie said. "Leave poor Regina alone." Cornelia murmured sympathetically.

Jonas held the paper away from Regina, and Olga sprang off the bench to look at it over his shoulder. "Schlegel will appreciate your artistic skills," Jonas said, "when I show him this."

"Jonas," Regina said. "Give it back." The humidity seemed even more oppressive. Olga took one look at the drawing and burst into staccato laughter, like the sound of a gun *pop pop popping*.

"Father! Father!" Regina ran to the base of the staircase. "Jonas is late for the stock exchange meeting!"

"Regina," Jonas hissed. "Don't."

Above them, footsteps echoed on the narrow stairs, then the Councilor's voice exploded, harsh and condemning. "Jonas?"

"Thanks a lot, Regina," Jonas whispered, his face twitching with anger.

Oops, Regina thought. *What happened to that guard I set on my mouth? He must have fallen asleep.*

"Jonas!" the Councilor roared.

Jonas skulked into the hall in answer.

"Get out of this house at once," the Councilor yelled from the landing at the top of the stairs. "Are you a fool?" The words came out like he was spitting. "Didn't I teach you anything about your responsibility to your profession?"

Hardly, Regina thought, her eyes downcast. She counted the pattern of black and white diamonds painted on the hall floor.

"You, too, Regina!" The Councilor's voice lashed out, making her jump.

"Me? What did I do?"

"You're thoughtless, both of you. Get to your piano lesson. Why do I have to bother with such fools?" Each insult struck Regina like a slap in the face. "Making your poor mother have to come and remind you about your responsibilities."

Poor mother, nothing, Regina thought as she lifted her poke bonnet from the closet beneath the stairs and trod a funereal march toward the door. *He's only upset he had to get out of bed himself.* Still, the Councilor's words continued to reverberate in her head. *You're thoughtless. You're a fool.* The words seemed no more, no less, than she deserved.

Her mother caught Regina before she could escape the house. "Wasn't Mr. Schlegel kind to call this morning," Mrs. Olsen said, descending from the landing. "What a nice young man."

Regina refused to meet her eye, refused to thank her for this feeble rescue. When Jonas opened the door, a fresh wave of humidity and heat rolled over them. It was so strong that it almost pushed Regina back into the house. Mrs. Olsen bustled forward and forced an umbrella into Regina's hands.

"Daddy is tired today, darling," her mother whispered, leaning down to engulf Regina in her large, soft body. Regina returned the hug, but her mother's warmth seemed hollow, as if she'd handed Regina a present wrapped in the most beautiful paper, but it had nothing inside.

"I don't need it," Regina said, handing the umbrella back.

"But it's going to rain," Mrs. Olsen said.

"I don't care," Regina said. She turned her back on her mother and joined Jonas on the street.

They walked along the narrow cobbled road, past the stretch of pastel town houses and toward the redbrick stock exchange building. On their right, a haze of heat hovered over the water beneath the pier. A muscle twitched in Jonas's cheek.

"Sorry, Jonas," she said. "But it's your fault, anyway. You should have been at the meeting."

"So, little Regina, shall we expect an engagement announcement soon? A Mr. and Mrs. Fritz Schlegel?" Jonas's voice was mocking.

"He just paid a morning call," Regina said. "That's all." She paused. "Don't be mad at me, Jonas. I'm sorry."

"Of course you're sorry. You're sorry you got in trouble, too," Jonas said, and then he ducked into one of the dwarf-sized wooden doors of the stock exchange without looking at her again.

The moment she was alone, the air seemed to shift and change as she descended into her hurt.

4

The Summer Storm

"I learned from my father what father love is, thereby getting an idea of the divine father love."

Søren Kierkegaard

"Søren always reproached himself over his relationship to his father."

Regine Olsen

Regina kept walking, moving by instinct rather than by sight. Unfanned, the flame of the Holy Spirit inside of her waned. Unhooked from the source of forgiveness and love, she threw up against the cave walls of her mind a shadow image of her father, her mother, Jonas, and Olga. Their faces were so ugly, their features so exaggerated, that it made her think there was something she'd forgotten to do, something forgiving. But the caricatures of her family gave her a grim, powerful sense of satisfaction, and she settled into her quiet rebellion.

It wasn't until she reached the door of her teacher's apartment that the red-roofed town houses, the black street lamps, the ruddy-faced, overheated people, and the panting dogs suddenly veered back into focus. She felt as if she'd been walking through a darkened tunnel without any ceiling or floor. An opalescent, blue-gray mist quivered in the air above her. The sky held a rich, water-bound intensity. She longed for the storm to hit, the rain to fall, and a refreshing sweetness to lighten the heaviness of the air.

Regina could hardly stand to go to her music lesson, though she'd been going twice a week, at the same time and place, for years. She trudged up the narrow staircase and went in. Miss Wad, a gaunt spinster with a rough voice, lifted her watch from the chain around her neck and shook her head. Regina smiled to try to placate her, placed her hands on the yellowing ivory keys of Miss Wad's piano, and began to play.

The humidity made the middle C stick, and Regina focused her attention on striking the errant key just right. She had to force it to spring upward like the others. She had to stop it from interfering with the music she could hear in her head—the way the music was supposed to sound, but wouldn't, no matter how hard she pounded the sticking key.

"Regina," Miss Wad scolded as she paced behind Regina, the wooden floorboards creaking beneath her. "Stop focusing on that sticking key. Focus on the entirety of the music." Regina tried, but she couldn't ignore the sticking key. She just couldn't.

At four o'clock Regina walked out of Miss Wad's apartment and immediately felt a change in the air. A coolness was descending from above, swirling and mixing with the heat. She hurried down the narrow alleyway, trying to outpace the storm. Just as she reached the place where the street opened into the broad expanse of Nytorv Square, thunder cracked and rain whipped down. The rain startled the heat that had gathered and lingered on the cobblestones throughout the past few days the way a splash of water scatters a sleeping dog, and a blast of hot air rose up around Regina's face.

Exhilarated, she glanced around the square to make sure no one was watching, and then she stopped and lifted her face to the rain. She basked in the contrast between the hot humid air and the cool water. The rain felt marvelous against her skin. Even the sudden clamminess of her clothes felt refreshing.

An ox tethered to a fountain raised its head in protest. The rain matted its brown hair into pointed dark tufts. The ox flared its nostrils and lowed.

Regina looked up over the muted green, blue, pink, and yellow town houses of the square and saw a jagged line of lightning strike the horizon just as another clap of thunder erupted overhead. She reminded herself that the synchronization of lightning and thunder meant she was standing in a dangerous place, in the very center of the storm, and that she could be hit by lightning at any moment. She forced herself to stand still and let chance determine her fate.

She imagined herself flat on her back, her hair standing on end, and she pictured Fritz Schlegel's face as he stood over her. "So young," he would sob, "and so pretty. How I wish I'd proposed. If only she knew how much I wanted to marry her."

"This is no weather for young ladies to stroll in," a stern voice said.

Regina spun around with a start and looked up into the face of an old man in a tall, black top hat. He had a coarse, round face and blue eyes with heavy lids. Wearing a velvet cape over a homespun coat, he seemed such an odd mixture of peasant and gentleman that Regina couldn't help staring. She felt as if she'd seen him before, but these eyes looked down at her as if she were a stranger.

The old man introduced himself as Mr. Michael Kierkegaard.

Kierkegaard, she thought. *Kierkegaard. He must be the father of that young man with the fork.* She had frequently passed Søren Kierkegaard in the streets of Copenhagen over the past year.

She'd passed him so many times, in fact, that it had begun to irritate her that he never engaged her in conversation.

"You must shelter in my home until the worst has passed," Mr. Kierkegaard said, raising his voice to be heard over the storm. He pointed to a large house next to City Hall that towered like a gravestone over the square.

Regina opened her mouth to say no, but the door of the grand house beckoned her. She was curious to see Søren's childhood home. *It is raining, after all. And the door is just here beside me.*

She followed him in. Mr. Kierkegaard led her into a sparsely furnished room in the front of the house and rang a handbell to summon a servant. "I'm sorry. I have no wife or daughter left to fetch you a fresh shawl," he said.

Her host stood almost too far away from her, as if afraid of something. She couldn't help wondering if he found her attractive. Several plain wooden chairs stood about, but the old man did not sit, nor did he ask her to. They faced each other across a distance.

Trying to hide her awkwardness, Regina looked around. The house had an empty, neglected feeling. What was wrong? Was it the spartan furniture? The crumpled papers scattered across the bare floor? The truth hit her with a sudden clarity. There was nothing feminine. There were no flowers, no warmth, no light, delicate touches. Regina's fingers itched in a way they hadn't during her piano lesson.

"You see," Mr. Kierkegaard said. "Every woman who enters this house seems to die."

Maybe it was time to leave.

The old man grinned, wrinkles spreading outward from his mouth. "I think you will be safe, at least for a few minutes," he said. Then his face hardened again. "God has spared me only two sons." He spoke with anger, as if God had taken his other children and wife as some sort of punishment. "Of course, it's probably two more than I deserve."

Regina stared at him. Something in his tone sounded off. *What is it, Lord?*

And with the quick, piercing intuition that sometimes transfigured her with its perfect truth, Regina understood that this man was suffering from guilt. She wanted to tell him that whatever his crime was, God's own Son had already died to atone for it.

Quiet, she told herself. *It's not your place.* "I am acquainted with one of your sons, I believe," she said instead, her warm brown eyes begging, *Don't think of God that way. Please, don't.*

"Which son?" the old man asked. "The smart one, or the one who thinks he is smart?"

"Mr. Søren Kierkegaard," she said, finessing his question.

"My youngest son is lucky to know such an attractive young lady. I am not sure he deserves such luck."

"I'm sure that he does," she said. She was surprised at herself for speaking up for Søren. Her face grew hot.

The old man stared at her. He seemed to be evaluating her relationship with his son. "He's not here, you know."

"I didn't . . . I wasn't . . ."

Mr. Kierkegaard continued to watch her with the unblinking appraisal of a hunting owl.

"Thank you so much for your hospitality, sir, but I must . . ." Regina looked out the window, desperately willing the rain to stop.

"He moved out," Mr. Kierkegaard said. The rain made a chattering noise on the windowsill. "I don't blame him anymore. What father can blame a hot-blooded young man for finding his Christian home oppressive?"

Regina didn't blame Søren for finding this home oppressive either. She smiled as slightly as she could. She disapproved of a father speaking of his son this way, and she wished him to discern her disapproval through her veil of politeness.

"In the heaths of Jutland, where I grew up, it seemed as if the rain fell on me this hard every day while I tended sheep. I didn't thank God for it. In fact, I envied the sheep their matted wool." He eyed her. "Perhaps that is why I became a hosier, supplying people with woolen products."

A servant as old as Mr. Kierkegaard shuffled through the open door. He was dispatched to fetch a hot drink even though Regina protested that she didn't need anything. She did not want to be beholden to this man.

"Please, sit down," he said as if he'd suddenly remembered his manners. "And forgive me for the sparsity of the furniture. You must use your imagination. Furnish the room as lavishly as a fine lady such as yourself requires. Velvet cushions, purple cloths, thrones of gold. Whatever you like."

Despite her resolve not to like him, Regina couldn't help being amused.

The warm tea, when it finally came, tasted good. She sneezed, and Søren's father commanded that the carriage be readied. She protested, but he wouldn't listen. "What is the use of having a carriage if one cannot use it?" he asked. Regina smiled, genuinely amused, and Mr. Kierkegaard seemed to grow younger before her eyes.

She felt relieved when he finally led her out of the house to the carriage. The rain, with the usual short-lived intensity of a summer storm, had already cleared up. She repeated that she didn't need a ride, noticing with longing how steam rose from the cobblestones. She wanted to walk away from the uneasiness she'd felt in this home, from the inappropriate comment she'd made in defense of Søren, and to absorb instead the sights and smells of the storm's cleansing.

Søren's father insisted. He reminded her that such a mercurial storm could return as quickly as it had departed. He insisted that she wrap a blanket over her dress, as the carriage hood would not protect her completely from any lingering raindrops.

Regina determined to write a thank you note as soon as possible to relieve herself from all obligation to the old man. The servant cracked a whip. She leaned back against the worn leather of the seat, her view obscured by the black sides of the hood just as blinders restricted the vision of the horse that pulled her. The servant sat straight and silent on the open wooden bench in front of her. They passed the forlorn ox, still waiting by the fountain. As the surrey swayed from side to side, Regina let herself be lulled by the steady *clip clopping* of the horse's metal shoes against the empty streets. A grayness now clouded the air, but the houses and streets seemed cleaner than before.

Regina closed her eyes and breathed in the sweet, soft smell that followed the rainfall. She wondered what Søren's childhood had been like in the home she had just left, and she suddenly felt very sorry for him.

5

The Exhibition

"Who knows, perhaps it was her pride that made her prefer me."

Søren Kierkegaard

"Kierkegaard understood me."

Regine Olsen

A few weeks later, Regina met Fritz in front of a painting of a pink palace. "Like two magnets," Regina whispered, "drawn together."

Fritz smiled down at her, his brown eyes kind and inviting. "Will we attend every art opening here together—when we are married?"

"Shh," Regina said, her eyes widening with pleasure. "We cannot speak of that until I am confirmed!"

"Why not?" Fritz asked. "I enjoy speaking of it—you look so beautiful when you're shocked."

"What a dreary picture," Mrs. Schlegel said, coming up behind them with her two large daughters in tow.

Was she referring only to the painting? Regina watched Fritz's face crease into a gentle smile as he looked at his mother. He didn't seem to have caught her innuendo.

Nearby, Mrs. Olsen and Olga gazed at the other paintings in the gallery. Visitors swarmed through the empty spaces of the airy cupola room, the largest room of Charlottenborg Palace's exhibition hall. The ladies wore narrow, high-waisted dresses with little capped sleeves, and the gentlemen wore long-waisted coats over breeches or even the newly fashionable trousers. Around their necks the men wore elaborate pieces of silk or muslin, some starched upward into sharp points that hit the cheeks, some folded down into complicated, twisted knots.

"Look," Mrs. Schlegel said, pointing out of the nearby French windows. "It's that friend of yours, Fritz. Søren Kierkegaard."

Fritz knew Søren?

Regina followed the direction of Mrs. Schlegel's voluminous puffed sleeve and spied a frail, sodden figure entering the courtyard from the direction of the garden. Søren carried a cane, and his legs were so thin that he reminded Regina of one of the wooden soldiers that marched, expectant but forlorn, in a dusty corner of a nursery. *Why does he look so unhealthy,* Regina wondered. *Maybe he puts all his energy into his brain.*

"Well," Mrs. Schlegel said, her voice poised for attack. Olga forced her way into their circle. Fritz's two sisters, as sweet and gentle as placid cows, looked at their mother. "I hear that despite his father's death, the youngest Kierkegaard has been promenading on the streets as usual."

"His father's death?" Regina repeated. The old man she'd met two weeks ago was dead? Impossible. If only she'd been kinder to him, if only she'd thought better of him.

"Yes," Mrs. Schlegel said, rounding on Regina. "Did you know him?"

"I just met him," Regina said. "I had no idea he was so close to death."

"It happened only two days ago. But you'd never know it from his youngest son's behavior," Mrs. Schlegel continued, her voiced laced with disapproval, her body tense. Olga leaned in closer, soaking up Mrs. Schlegel's words. "Everyone's talking of it. They say Søren went to the opera the night after his father died and then on to Mimi's. I myself passed him yesterday, and he stopped and greeted me as if it were the happiest of mornings. When I tried to express my condolences, he cut me short, made some entirely unsuitable joke about how the only thing changed was that now he had to study to be a priest since he could no longer torment the old man by refusing, and then he changed the subject."

He probably cries at home, Regina longed to say. She compressed her mouth into a careful straight line.

"How shocking," Olga cried, her already small eyes narrowing still further with pleasure. Fritz's two sisters nodded in agreement.

"Who could expect any less from a man who leads such a dissolute lifestyle?" Mrs. Schlegel asked, raising her thin eyebrows. "It's a good thing for him his father was one of the richest merchants in Copenhagen. He needs all that money to support himself."

"Don't believe a word of it, Mother," Fritz said, shaking his head. "Søren is beside himself with grief. I'm sure of it."

Regina nodded. That had to be right. Fritz was so understanding, so compassionate.

Mrs. Schlegel looked annoyed. "Then why doesn't he act like it?"

"Mother," Fritz said. "You're forgetting that Søren has had to watch almost every member of his family die off, one by one. His mother and five of his six siblings all died before Søren reached the age of twenty-one. That sort of experience must do strange things to your head. It would make anybody act in ways that other people, without the same experience, could never understand."

"The poor man," Regina said.

"At least one woman in this party has a soft heart," Fritz said, smiling down at Regina.

"My heart is as soft as goose feathers," Mrs. Schlegel snapped. "But I still don't understand why the man has to go around trying to shock people."

He has to shock them because he's trying to hide his pain, Regina thought. *His pain must be very, very great if he goes to such lengths to conceal it.*

"He can't help himself, Mother," Fritz said. "It's sort of his mission in life—shocking people. He hates complacency, you see."

"Humph," said Mrs. Schlegel. "I like my complacency, thank you very much."

Regina laughed, and Mrs. Schlegel gave her an approving glance with her tiny sharp eyes. Maybe Fritz's mother wasn't so bad.

"He sounds dreadful," Olga said, eagerly.

"Oh, Mother," Fritz said. "You know you like Søren. Remember how hard he made you laugh the day he introduced himself to us at the opera? Right after we'd left the Olsen's box?"

Had Søren followed Fritz on purpose in order to talk about Regina? It seemed unlikely, and yet there was something in Søren's smile when he passed her in the street that made Regina feel sure he liked her. A slight ribbon of vanity rippled through Regina.

"Don't you remember?" Fritz asked. "You laughed so hard that tears came into your eyes."

"Tears came into my eyes because the man makes me cry," Mrs. Schlegel said. She looked at the Olsen sisters. "Do you know Søren Kierkegaard?"

Olga shook her head. "Thank goodness, no."

"We have met," Regina said. Fritz glanced at her.

"He sounds mad," Mrs. Schlegel said. "I can tell you, if he ever becomes ordained and finds a placement, that is one church I will never attend."

"Perhaps you will not be asked to, Mother," Fritz said, his eyes twinkling.

Regina looked away to hide her smile.

"That's enough, Fritz. Take me into the next room," Mrs. Schlegel said. Fritz moved so quickly to take his mother's arm that he almost knocked Regina over.

He didn't even ask me if I'm coming, Regina thought. *Of course, it's Fritz's duty to humor his mother*, she chided herself. *You shouldn't let your pride be so easily wounded.*

Mrs. Olsen and Olga followed the Schlegels, but Regina lingered in the cupola room. She didn't want to look as if she were following Fritz around like a puppy. Especially when he was with his mother.

She wandered around the gallery alone. The paintings seemed so flat, so two-dimensional. Why hadn't Fritz taken her with him? She stamped her foot softly, quickly. Several people wandered past. They seemed to be staring at her. As an excuse for standing all by herself, she turned to look at the nearest painting. A tiny card mounted on the wall explained that the painting showed a bridge the moment after a woman in despair over an unrequited love had thrown herself off.

Unrequited love? Who would throw herself off a bridge for that?

In the painting, a crowd of people ran along the bridge, lit by a luminous moon. Regina looked closer. The bridge seemed to lean out of the painting, drawing her in, enticing her to step onto its wooden rails. A couple peered over the side of the bridge, their faces curious, questing. What could they see? Had the rescue begun? The moon cast a pale ghostly glow over the scene.

For the first time since entering the exhibition, Regina felt interested in the art.

"Did you know that moonlight is only reflected sunlight, Miss Olsen?" The sound of Søren Kierkegaard's voice in her ear startled her.

She kept her eyes straight ahead, focused on the picture. "I did. But I always need to be reminded." The quietness of Søren's voice conveyed a feeling of intimacy, as if they were the only two people in the exhibition hall, as if this picture of the moonlit bridge was the only painting in the gallery.

Should she mention his father? She glanced at him. He stood beside her in an ill-fitting black coat, his spectacles slipping down his nose and his light blue eyes gleaming. But in his eyes, behind the veneer of impishness, she saw deep pain.

"I just heard about your father," she said. "I'm so sorry."

"I am more devastated than I can say."

Ha! Regina thought. *He isn't trying to shock me the way he did Fritz's mother.* A strange, dark feeling of power coursed through her.

He smiled sadly. "I am sure it will take a long time for my grief to awaken. But when it does, I may never recover."

"I understand exactly," she said.

He leaned closer. "Don't tell anyone, but I am learning to imitate my father's voice. So I can comfort myself when I am lonely."

She smiled at him. "Perhaps you should seek comfort elsewhere."

Inside, she kicked herself. It sounded like she was offering herself up for the job. "Your father sheltered me from a storm two weeks ago," Regina blurted out, trying to cover the dreadful implications of her comment. "He was . . ." She searched for the right word. "Kind."

"You were in my home?" Søren asked. "You met my father?"

"Yes," she said. A pit formed in her stomach. Had he guessed there'd been no escort? "Is something wrong?"

"No," he said. "No, no. It's just such a coincidence." He paused. "Although . . . there's no such thing as a coincidence if you believe in God."

"No," she said, "I suppose not." For her pastor had just explained from a passage in Acts 17 that before the foundation of the world God determined the places we would live and the people we would meet.

The people we would meet.

She leaned forward to examine the painting, knowing that Søren continued to watch her.

"Do you like it, Miss Olsen?" he asked.

Was he talking only about the painting?

"Yes," she said. She felt a silence hovering and blurted out, "What do you think the people on the bridge are looking at?"

"Would you like to know what I think, or what other people say?"

"Are those two things so very different?" She looked at him and felt startled at the way his solemn blue eyes stared straight back at her.

"What other people think, and what I think, are almost always very different things, Miss Regine Olsen."

Regine Olsen. Her formal name in his mouth sounded like someone she didn't know, someone she would like to know. She smiled. "Then tell me what you think."

"I see a painting that suggests another world, the world of the spirit. And only the people on the bridge are aware of it."

"And they are so entranced by eternity that they've forgotten all about the woman who jumped off the bridge?" Pointing at the notecard, she raised her eyebrows.

"Eternity has that effect on people," he said. "The temporal ceases to matter at all." He smiled at her, and he looked, for a moment, so happy and free that she felt the warm, soft breath of what had to be the Holy Spirit.

Was this why You wanted me here, Lord? To save him from himself? And she felt as puffed up as Mrs. Schlegel's sleeves.

"Look," she said, casting about the room for something else to please him with. "It stopped raining."

"It stopped raining some time ago. Didn't you notice?"

"Regina?"

Regina spun round and found Olga staring at her. She quickly made the introductions.

"Did you say Mr. *Søren* Kierkegaard?" Olga asked, giving Regina a significant glance.

Søren bowed with a grand flourish of his thin hands. In that bow, Regina saw him slip back into mockery. She felt a secret thrill of pride that she alone had seen the real Søren Kierkegaard, the vulnerable, kind, intimate Søren Kierkegaard.

"We've all been looking for you, Regina," Olga said.

"I commend you for your concern about the well-being of your sister," Søren told Olga. "The perils of being exposed to art, unaccompanied, at an impressionable age, cannot be underestimated."

Olga frowned at Søren. Regina was amused, knowing Olga despised irony.

"I thought your sister's name was Miss *Regine* Olsen," Søren continued.

"Her *closest* friends call her Regina," Olga said with a disdainful tilt of her tiny nose.

"Ah. Then perhaps I will one day earn that privilege."

"Perhaps," Olga said in a voice that suggested it highly unlikely.

"Perhaps sooner than you think," Søren said. "My friend Fritz Schlegel has asked me to accompany him to your family's weekly open house. Unless you bolt the door on me of course," he added mischievously. Olga looked as if she'd been contemplating that very thing.

Søren was coming to their open house? Unexpectedly, disobediently, Regina's heart leapt. Søren glanced at her.

"Until we meet again," he said. He made a deep bow to each sister, in order of age, and departed.

The moment he left the cupola room, Olga's lips curved into their usual downdraft. "Regina! Wasn't that the very man Mrs. Schlegel just warned us about? The crazy one whose father just died? How right she was. He certainly didn't look like a man in mourning. What was he talking to you about, anyway?"

"The paintings. Olga, didn't you just visit that cathedral?" Regina asked, pointing to a large painting of Ribe Cathedral on the wall. "Is it a good rendering?"

"No," Olga said, turning toward it. Regina sighed with relief. "It is called artistic license, Regina," Olga continued in her most pedantic voice. "The artist has removed the organ in order to change the play of light along the walls. Personally, I abhor artists who take such license with historical fact."

Regina sighed and tried to look as if she were paying attention. Through the long French windows, she spotted Søren Kierkegaard walking alone through the courtyard beneath them, toward the garden in the back. He moved with a slow and measured pace, and, from where Regina stood, he looked like he was smiling. She wondered what he was thinking about. *Probably me.*

"Regina." Fritz sped eagerly into the cupola room ahead of his mother. His face came within inches of Regina's. "I missed you, my darling," he whispered.

As Regina smiled back at him, she noticed, for the first time, that his ears were unusually large.

6

The Parsonage

"Kierkegaard sought me out more and more."

REGINE OLSEN

"The period of falling in love is surely the most interesting time."

SØREN KIERKEGAARD

Two days later, Søren walked into the Olsen's open house behind Fritz. Regina smirked. The poor man was obviously besotted.

But somehow Regina never got a chance to speak to him. Every time she turned around, he was talking to her parents, her brother, or her sisters. Whenever Regina joined the conversation, thinking, *Poor Søren. I should be kind to him,* Søren melted away. At first she thought it a coincidence, then she wondered if he was angry at her, and finally it dawned on her that he was ignoring her on purpose. *Wretched man.*

This went on for a year. Not only did Søren accompany Fritz to every single Olsen open house, he also seemed to walk the same routes through the city that Regina did. She saw him when she crossed bridges, when she walked through open squares, when she strolled in the parks.

He really should stop coming to her house. What was the point, if he wouldn't talk to her? He was beginning to disturb her peace. She had to work so hard in her times alone with God to achieve that peace in the first place. But the way Søren Kierkegaard seemed to circle in closer and closer to her conversations was getting under her skin. Sometimes she even had to double her time with God just to stop thinking about how annoying Søren was.

It was all his fault. He wouldn't talk to her, but he seemed to take in every detail of what she wore, who she spoke to, and whether she was bored or happy. She could tell by the hungry way he watched her across the room. And Søren seemed to charm her parents so much that Regina found herself trying to overhear what he was saying to them instead of listening to whatever Fritz was whispering in her ear.

In the summer, after Marie's wedding to a wealthy, self-satisfied banker named Johan, the Olsens went to the country to visit friends. One gray Wednesday afternoon, Regina took a stroll alone down a country lane in Lyngby. As she walked, she lifted the skirt of her pale blue gown to keep the hemline clear of the mud. Hedges in need of a trimming sent thin, skeletal arms spiraling down on her. Stinging nettles lurked at the base of the hedges. Wan white wildflowers wilted beside the nettles, their petals lacerated by the recent rains. Every now and then, through a gap in the hedge, she caught a glimpse of meadow sloping down to the stream by Sorgenfri Forest. She kept having to tilt her chin to admire the view from beneath the brim of her straw bonnet.

The brim was as wide and round as a duck's bill. A sky blue satin ribbon encircling the crown of the bonnet matched the sky blue satin ribbon encircling the high waist of her gown. The gown came to a V in front, and had narrow white ruffles around the neckline and its short puffed sleeves. Anna had pulled the dress off of the laundry line this morning and ironed the ruffles so that they made soft, undulating ripples in the wind. From the way the dress wrapped itself around her,

Regina was aware that it accentuated the strengths of her figure as few dresses ever do. It really was too bad that no men were around.

A flock of sheep clattered down the road toward her. Bleating, they blocked the narrow dirt lane. "Sorry, miss," the farmer said. He wore ancient, shapeless brown trousers and an open-necked, cornflower blue shirt that billowed around his arms. Thick wrinkles punctured his deep leathery brown skin. He showed touching respect, Regina thought, by looking down as she turned into Pastor Ibsen's churchyard to let the sheep pass.

Regina eyed the churchyard with disdain. She took in the gray stone parsonage, the muddy pond, the wan grass, the tall, yellow and pink flowers sagging by the church wall, the moss-covered bench beneath a row of sallow linden trees, the goose droppings liberally spread across the ground, and she pitied the wife of the parson who lived here.

A scuffling noise made her spring round. Søren Kierkegaard came bounding toward her from the gap in the hedge. The ducks and geese began to quack and flap their way into the murky pond water. Regina tucked one stray hair beneath her bonnet and looked away. Mossy fronds moved gently from the rocks at the water's edge.

"Miss Olsen," Søren cried.

"Mr. Kierkegaard. What a surprise." *You annoying man.*

"No surprise to me," he said.

"Really? Did you follow me here, then?" she asked with sugary charm.

"Of course," he said. He stared at her, his pale, fine face melting into a vulnerable expression.

Regina's mouth dropped open. She quickly snapped it shut again. "Oh," she said. "Oh."

"Didn't you guess? I follow you everywhere."

"Please don't tease me," she said. Suddenly she wished her dress did not cling quite so tightly, that the ruffles did not undulate quite so wildly. The dress spoke a language that undermined the frostiness of her tone.

"I'm in earnest," he said. "I've been following you for years. Didn't you think it strange that you ran into me so often?"

"Yes. No. What are you talking about?"

"How you saw me everywhere, but I never spoke to you."

"You seem to have changed your tactics," she said. She tried to look stern, but his confession made her feel so wonderful she couldn't help grinning.

"I know," he said. Then he paused and tried to look sheepish. "But I must confess. I didn't really follow you. I come to Lyngby every year. I rent rooms at Bleach Farm, as do my cousins."

She was ashamed. For a moment, she'd believed him. "That was cruel," she said. "I told you not to tease me."

"I'm sorry," he said. "I won't tease you again. You see, sometimes I just can't help myself." An emotion bearing a suspicious resemblance to pride quivered on his face. "May I accompany you?"

"In my turn around the local duck pond? If you insist."

He held out the crook of his elbow. For a second, she hesitated. What harm could it do? She took the elbow he offered her.

Instantly, his body became as tense as a taut wire. He pinned her hand against his side. "Miss Regine Olsen," he said.

"Please, call me Regina. Everybody does," she said, trying to pull her hand loose. He squashed it tighter against his side. She'd have to yank her hand away to get it free.

"Not everybody, Miss Olsen. Not everybody."

She looked at the duck pond, embarrassed. She'd never seen such a change. For a year he'd ignored her, and now this?

"How do you like this pastoral scene, Miss—Regina—Olsen?"

"It's pastoral," she said.

"Could you see yourself here?"

"I am here," she said, tilting the huge brim of her bonnet so that she could see his face. What an infuriating bonnet. It was completely in her way. She could see the delicacy of his skin, how smooth his face was, how expressive his lips. But she could not see his eyes. She buried her face beneath her bonnet. Who wanted to see him anyway. He was toying with her. *The cad.*

She tried to pull free again. He tucked her hand in closer and said, "What I mean is, could you see yourself here as the wife of a country priest?"

"That would depend, Mr. Kierkegaard." Dragonflies soared around her, seeming about to hit her but always swerving at the last moment in their weighted elegant way.

"On what?" Without meaning to, the motion as quick and supple as a snake slipping through the grass, she twisted her neck to scan his face again. His eyes, bright and clear and brilliantly blue, stared back at her.

"On the country priest, of course," she said.

He laughed, and his eyes danced with false modesty. "What if the priest were handsome? Intelligent? Thoughtful, but secretly—only to those few he loved?"

"A parson would have to love everyone," she said, a blush rising to her cheeks. *Don't let him make a fool of you again.*

"That's the problem," he cried, leaping forward with such excitement that he dragged her along. She pinned her bonnet down with her free hand to prevent it from sailing into the water. "That is exactly the problem—loving everyone! I have wrestled with it!"

"I'm sure you have," she said. "Isn't that the problem for all of us?"

An image rose before her of Søren Kierkegaard in a black frock, standing at the door of a little country church, with ducks quacking and geese flapping their wings, and of herself standing at his side, nodding her head demurely to their parishioners. She would be the perfect wife of a country priest. Perfect. She could advise all the women in the congregation with her godly, wise thoughts. She could bring Søren hot tea while he wrote his sermons. She could even add a few insights of her own.

Regina tried unsuccessfully to yank her hand free again. She had to get away from this man.

"The trouble is, so few men have a true religious need," he said. "Their miseries are purely of this world. I would be bored sick."

She raised one eyebrow. "Aren't their physical needs important, too? Jesus didn't just preach. He healed people."

"All symbolic," Søren said, waving one hand. "The thing is to love people in the abstract—the idea of them."

"Perhaps, deep down, you don't really want to be a priest."

His eyes darted sideways. "Miss Regina Olsen," he said, inclining his head to the side. "Over that stone wall, I hear a flock of Olsens about to descend upon me, and I must speak my mind quickly." Regina heard them then, her father's hearty, almost fake laugh, her mother's pleasant voice, and Olga's sarcasm. She suddenly wished they would go a different way.

"I stand at the beginning of my life—of my essential life," Søren said, speaking in a low, urgent tone. "I have just passed my theological exams. Before I begin my dissertation—on irony, of course, of course—I am going to embark on a pilgrimage to my father's birthplace. It is my prayer that there I will find the idea for which I can live and die, that I will find what truth is, and whether I shall . . ." He paused and looked down at her. "Shall I marry?"

Strange creatures—larger than the dragonflies, or even the ducks—seemed to cavort in Regina's stomach. Was he going to propose?

If so, would they live together in his bachelor apartment? Or would they move back to his father's house with Søren's brother, Peter Christian? It could be such a beautiful home. If she put in some flowers and changed the color of the . . . *What was she thinking?* Horrified by the insidious turn her thoughts had taken, Regina shook herself back into the present, outside the parsonage—a world where she had an understanding with Fritz Schlegel.

Søren scanned her face and seemed satisfied. "May I call on you, Miss Regina Olsen," he whispered, "when I return?"

"You may no longer want to," she said, trying to disguise how his words had made her feel as light as her blue dress fluttering on the clothesline that morning, "after all that soul searching in Jutland."

He giggled, a high-pitched, schoolboy giggle. "True! True! But if I still want to . . . , may I?"

Regina Olsen gave Søren Kierkegaard something she had already given. "Yes," she said. "You may call on me."

Søren took her hand from beneath his elbow, turned it over, and pressed his lips upon her palm. She shivered, despite herself. "Today is Wednesday," he said, as he released her. "I will revere Wednesdays always."

Then he scuttled down the incline toward the hedgerow. His black coat flapped around him, and his arms swung at his side. His joints seemed so loose that she wondered if they were attached at the sockets at all.

Just as Søren reached the gap in the hedge, he lifted his hat and nodded in the direction the farmer had gone with his sheep. "I shall try to avoid following the flock," he yelled.

"As always," she called out.

He cackled—a thin, high, happy laugh—and she smiled back. Then he disappeared. Her eyes retained the image of him standing in the gap for a few seconds longer.

She turned back to the parsonage. The sky shone with a deep blue brilliance. A pastiche of billowing white clouds soared above, each backlit by a stream of sunlight. The stones of the parsonage glowed with a chalky gray purity. The wind rippled through the fields beyond, making the translucent green stalks dance and shimmer. The stream carved a magical ribbon toward the distant forest.

Regina raced around the parsonage yard. The ducks were adorable, simply adorable. The pond was so quaint. The linden trees were stately, marvelous. The parsonage was a beautiful place, a wonderful place. What a lucky woman Mrs. Ibsen was to live here.

Above the hedgerow she could see the top of Søren's black hat bobbing in and out of sight. *Dreadful man*, she thought.

And on her fingers, she began to count the days until their return to Copenhagen.

7

The Open House

"My family held open house one evening a week."

REGINE OLSEN

"Geniuses are like a thunder storm: they go against the wind, terrify people, clear the air."

SØREN KIERKEGAARD

In early September, the Olsens held their first open house of the fall. Regina stood beside her father in the green room, trying to look as if she were giving her father her complete attention. Every time a door opened, she jumped, hoping it was Søren. Her elderly cousins were chatting to the canaries. Thrine Dahl, Bolette, and Bolette's husband were peering at the tea table, admiring the ham and Edam cheese beneath the silver candlesticks. Just as the hall clock struck eight, Søren Kierkegaard and Fritz Schlegel appeared together in the open doorway.

Thank goodness the French hairdresser came this morning, Regina thought. She ran her fingers through the smooth curls that framed her face.

Fritz strode toward her, confident and happy, but Søren stood in the doorway and observed, a brooding look in his eyes. Regina longed to go over to him, take him by the hand, draw him in to her family circle, and make his eyes shine with laughter. She fingered one of the black, opalescent earrings that dangled against her neck.

"My dear Regina," Fritz said, hurrying to her, his claret-colored coat as neat and tidy as always, his back stiff and straight. "Councilor Olsen." He nodded to Regina's father in his earnest, happy way. Seeing Søren still hovering in the doorway, he beckoned to him.

Søren slowly walked toward them. Regina smiled, then flattened her smile, then smiled again.

"I see nothing has changed since my last visit," Søren said. "Except Regina's hair."

"I thought she seemed different," Fritz said.

"Do I sense Mr. Kierkegaard's disapproval of time wasted on fashion?" Regina asked, looking at the gilded green wall, then the empty piano bench, and then, only then, at Søren. His blue eyes bored into hers, and she knew she hadn't imagined Lyngby.

You are beautiful, Regina thought, looking at Søren's face and wishing he could hear her thoughts. *You are beautiful.*

Something shifted in Fritz's countenance.

"I don't disapprove exactly," Søren said. "But I have learned more about women during one hour at a fashion designer's boutique than years spent studying them in the streets."

Studying which women? Regina wondered as Bolette and Thrine strolled by. Søren and Fritz simultaneously stared at the two blue-eyed, blonde-haired cousins.

"Regina tells me you've just made a pilgrimage to your father's birthplace," the Councilor said to Søren. Fritz glanced at Regina. "How was it?"

"Evocative," Søren said.

The Councilor laughed. "There's an evasive answer. Evocative of what?"

"Many things," Søren said. "There was a certain peace. The peace that invades you the moment you cross one of Copenhagen's bridges and leave the presence of the monarchy. A sort of simplicity. It was tempting to picture myself living there, a country priest, confined to obscurity, teaching my flock with words they do not understand."

"With a little wife?" Regina asked, looking at the green wall again.

"I can't," Søren said.

"Can't what?" Regina looked straight at him.

Beside her, Fritz shifted his weight from one dark shoe to the other.

"I can't become a priest—one day, and then the next—I feel I must."

Regina's hand fluttered up to the cross around her neck.

"Ah! The crisis of youth," the Councilor cried. "What to do with your life."

"But why can't you become a priest?" Fritz asked in his practical way. "You've been studying for it."

"To become a priest is to condone the Church's abolishment of Christianity," Søren said, hurling out the words as provocatively as a man throwing down a gauntlet.

"I see. Not the crisis of youth, but the crisis of conscience," the Councilor said. "Will Søren Kierkegaard work within the system, or will he work from the outside?"

"You think the Lutheran Church is *abolishing* Christianity?" Fritz parried, looking around as if for someone to second him. "Aren't you exaggerating, Søren? Just a little? Surely you think at least the priests believe in Christianity?"

"Those untruths in velvet? A man who cannot shave himself can still set up shop as a barber for others," Søren said, unsheathing his blue eyes on Fritz, his mouth drawn in a sharp line.

Fritz rolled his eyes.

"Are you a Christian, Fritz?" Søren asked, thrusting his face close to Fritz's.

"It's getting hot in here," Fritz said, tugging at the paisley silk cravat wound around his neck. "Turn the microscopic glare of your eyes elsewhere, Kierkegaard."

"Are you?" Søren persisted.

Why was Søren persecuting Fritz?

"Of course I'm a Christian," Fritz said. "We all are. We're born into the Lutheran Church."

"I can't watch," Regina said, shutting her eyes. "He's going to skewer you now."

"Søren? Skewer me? He wouldn't dream of it. I'm one of his few friends. Regina, is that real Brussels lace on your gown? It is lovely." Fritz leaned forward and touched the edge of Regina's sleeve.

Regina stood still and withdrew from his touch at the same time.

"To me, your words are like a bell tolling the hours between a death and a funeral," Søren said.

"I warned you," Regina said to Fritz with an eagerness that suddenly struck her as inappropriate.

The Councilor clapped Søren on the back. "This is exactly the sort of talk that makes me open my house once a week. Keep going, young Kierkegaard. Don't hold back."

"No fear of that," Regina said.

Søren shot her a quick glance, then rounded on Fritz. "That position, Schlegel, makes you a liar," Søren told him. Fritz scowled. He seemed to be holding himself back from lunging at Søren. Søren's face lightened, came even more alive. "Basing your eternal happiness on an external event is comical,"

Søren continued. "We are tricked into thinking that we are Christians just because we are baptized, confirmed, taught, and buried by the Church. Those things have nothing to do with being a Christian. Nothing. They are external, objective. This is what the pastors should tell us, but they do not."

"They'd be putting themselves out of a job," the Councilor said, laughing, but keeping a careful eye on Fritz.

"Precisely," said Søren. "They should tell us that they can do nothing for us, that existing as a Christian means being alone, utterly alone before God. It means finding your identity—your one true self, your name, your very existence—in worshiping the Creator, not the things He has created. Finding your identity in anything other than God is sin. And you have no existence because you are but a slave to your senses."

But only in listening to you, Søren Kierkegaard, Regina thought, *do I feel alive.* Her senses quickened as she stared at the softness of the skin beneath his eyes.

"So you think the Church ought to be abolished because it misleads us?" The Councilor's dark, restless eyes studied Søren. "You think that's the answer? Teach a child to read, hand him a Bible, and let God do the rest?"

"I don't actually have a position on the Church," Søren said. "I'm not interested in externals at all. Only in the internal. Only the essential."

"Of course not," Fritz said, a muscle twitching in his cheek. "You have no interest in anything external. Not your fancy cigars, your long carriage rides, your rare books, your fine wines, or even your rather substantial legacy from your father."

"All completely irrelevant," Søren said. But he looked at the floor as he said it, then glanced up defiantly. "You could take it away—today if you like," he added with a grandiose flourish of his hands, "and it would not matter. Not. One. Bit."

"Well, even if Fritz takes away your dinner," the Councilor said with a wry smile, "I believe my wife and the marvelous Anna will feed you, at least for this one night. But go back to the Church. You tell me that you have no opinion on the Church, but you also say that it's useless? How can you possibly defend such a contradictory position?"

"I am prophesying," Søren said, his eyes boring into the Councilor's. "Christianity is dying in Denmark. Mark my words. This is 1840. The day will come—in the not too distant future—when the only time people in this country will go to church is for funerals."

"Isn't it a little late, then?" Regina asked, looking at him and thinking, *Smile, Søren. Smile.*

Søren smiled, and Regina felt herself inflate into her true self. *I am Regina,* she thought. *And I am beautiful when I am with this man.*

Fritz was watching Thrine, who passed by again in a blur of blue chiffon. "Look, Søren," he said, turning slowly back to them. "Don't use me as your straw man. You know perfectly well what I meant. Your question embarrassed me. I didn't want to talk about it. My religion is private—between me and God."

We are so different, Regina thought, looking at Fritz across the expanse of the circle.

"That sounds like an excuse," Søren said, "for a lack of faith."

"I haven't seen you in church lately, Søren," Fritz countered. He compressed his lips. He jiggled his left leg. He looked at the wall.

Fritz is furious, Regina thought. *I've never seen him so angry. I didn't even know he could get this angry.* Her muscles felt as tense as if her father were yelling at her.

"My faith is irrelevant," Søren said. "Completely irrelevant. I am like Socrates. Just a midwife who gives birth to the ideas of others."

"And that attitude—that fake, 'I'm not really here, I don't count, I'm just an outsider, an observer'—that sounds like an excuse to me, Søren. For a lot of things." Fritz bowed so sharply it cut at Regina's heart. "If you will excuse me," he said to the Councilor. He walked out of the room, his eyes averted from Regina. The claret cloth stretched tight across the back of his evening coat made her want to put her hand on his shoulder and assure him she hadn't meant to hurt him. But every muscle, every sinew, every gravitational force compelled her to stay beside Søren Kierkegaard. She watched Fritz leave, and only a tiny part of her regretted it.

"Hmmm," Søren said, making no move to go after his friend. "That didn't seem to work. His type of illusion—that you're a Christian only because you've been raised in a church—is not easy to remove. Of course, I will continue studying to be a priest. But maybe next time I will say *I'm* not a Christian. The thing is to get myself out of it completely."

"You can't," the Councilor said. "It's impossible. The messenger is always bound up in the message."

"Not this messenger," Søren said, watching Bolette. She turned, caught sight of him, and kept walking with hips swinging beneath the narrow skirt of her dress. "Try to grasp hold of me, and I disappear completely. Like this." He waved his fine, thin hands in front of his face, then swiveled on his heels to follow Bolette.

Come back, Regina thought, wanting to grasp hold of him herself.

The Councilor shook his head as he watched Søren chase Bolette. "He likes the dramatic, that one. But I do think you should have gone after Fritz, Regina. He looked extremely upset."

Regina glanced down, flooded with the embarrassment that comes when your father tells you a truth you already know.

"I'm back," Søren said, appearing beside her. Regina saw that Bolette had joined her husband, Peter Kobke.

Ha! Regina thought.

"Søren," the Councilor said. "I'm worried about you. You take too hard a line. You'll end up rejecting everything in this world if you take such a hard line."

"The ideal picture of what it is to be a Christian judges us all." Søren's face shone with a zealous light.

Regina longed to quench that light. She longed for his face to shine like that for her, and her alone.

"But you'll drive people to depression if you hold them to such tough standards," the Councilor persisted.

"So?" Søren shrugged. "I'm already depressed."

"This conversation is making me depressed," the Councilor said.

"Ham," Regina asked, "or cheese?" Neither man looked in her direction.

"It's good you're depressed," Søren told the Councilor. "You're on the right track as long as you do not mistake the essence of your depression. That mistake will lead to suicide. No, you must understand that the real source of your depression is not my boring conversation, or the weather, or even the fading beauty of your youngest daughter, but that the eternal in you longs for the divine. Depression is a blessing, you see. I would rather have heard the howling of the wolves in the night and learned to know God. You must stay with the pain."

"Perhaps," the Councilor said, dark storm clouds sweeping in behind his eyes. "Perhaps that is the source. Most days I think it is my stupidity. My failure to advance further in my career. My shortcomings as a parent, as a husband."

"It is! It's because you've centered your life on things whose nature it is to cease to be! You're wrinkling your brow—that is good. I want to upset you, to give you insomnia, if I can."

Regina leapt for the piano. "Why don't I play for you two," she said. She rifled through the sheet music looking for the most distracting, most beguiling piece she knew. Where was it? Where? She thrust a Beethoven sonata onto the holder and began playing even before she'd sat down. Her mother, her senses as finely tuned as Regina's to the insweeping of melancholy on the Councilor's face, rushed over and whisked him away.

"Did you know," Søren said in an undertone from behind her, "that in Vienna, young ladies were not even allowed to listen to Beethoven's music because it was deemed too passionate for good taste?"

Was he implying that she was trying to beguile him by choosing passionate music?

Regally, she ignored his comment. "By the way," she said, "did you say my *fading* beauty?"

"So you were listening," he said, turning the page for her, a satisfied smile playing on his serpentine lips. She wondered, for a moment, if Fritz would come back.

8

The Leap

"My heroine was Joan of Arc, and . . . for a number of months I dreamed of a similar task for myself."

Regine Olsen

"It is said that the dancer's hardest task is to . . . stand there in the leap itself."

Søren Kierkegaard

"The rose blooms need pruning," Mrs. Olsen announced to her daughters at the breakfast table the next morning.

Regina's feet felt heavy as she followed her mother and sisters out to the small garden behind the house. Bees murmured sleepily from the moss-covered brick wall around the garden. The lavender—dusky purple flowers floating on stems of dusky green—gave off a languorous scent. The wrought iron gate leading to the canal sagged on its hinges. Mrs. Olsen bent to pull weeds from between the bricks of the garden path. Regina longed to be alone, to savor her thoughts and relive the open house in peace.

The Olsen women clipped the dead roses just below the buds. The Councilor strolled into the garden and seated himself on the bench to watch.

"The roses were so beautiful this summer," Mrs. Olsen said.

"Don't worship their beauty, girls," the Councilor said.

"Yes, Father." Olga, Cornelia, and Regina called out their practiced, singsong refrain.

"Roses have thorns, like all false idols. They'll disappoint you, and, in the end, they'll come to enslave you."

"She was enslaved by a rose," Regina said in a dramatic voice.

"That's enough, Regina," the Councilor said. "I'm serious. I'm talking about all roses–the brown-eyed as well as the blue-eyed varieties."

"Yes, Father," Regina said, wishing she could stop herself from blushing, wishing she didn't have to hear the same lecture over and over. She already knew all about false idols, for heaven's sake.

"Fritz Schlegel is such a nice young man," Mrs. Olsen said.

"Then why does he hang around with that dreadful Søren Kierkegaard, that's what I want to know," Olga said. "And why does he have to keep bringing him here?" Dead roses fell all around Olga's large feet.

"Your father likes him, Olga," Mrs. Olsen said. "As do I. But where was Fritz last night? I missed him."

"He left early," Olga said.

Regina turned away to hide her embarrassment. "Excuse me. I'll be right back," she said, abandoning the roses and ignoring Olga's sarcastic, "Of course you will."

Regina slid into the empty hall. The narrow staircase above beckoned her, calling her name in a soft seductive whisper.

I only need a moment by myself, she thought. She crept upstairs, the narrow wooden stairs creaking. She passed her parent's bedroom, its door open, the bed empty. Jonas's door was shut. He was probably still asleep. *The sluggard.* She rounded the corner, went higher, and passed the girls' rooms. She kept rising. Finally she reached the little dormer room at the top of the house, the one beside Anna's bedroom.

The room didn't belong to anybody. It was where the domestic business of the house was accomplished. It was intimate and cluttered, warm and quiet. Two black irons lay warming on the potbellied stove. Laundry that needed ironing lay in a pile on a shelf. Some sewing sat on the old wooden school desk by the window. This was not the elegant embroidery engaged in by the ladies of the house; this pile contained stockings that needed darning, trousers that needed patching, and sheets that had ripped.

Regina sat at the desk, the attic ceiling sloping down at a sharp angle above her. She was extremely happy, perhaps happier than she had ever been in her life. She reached up and touched her cheek. It felt soft. She realized that she was smiling and, fearful someone might walk in and see, she told herself to stop.

Full of nervous energy, Regina wanted to do something this very minute—dance or sing, she didn't know which. Staring at the crystal punch bowl set, carried here so that Anna could file down the chips made in the rims of several of the fitted glasses, she imagined herself and Søren at a ball. He was offering her more punch, passing the glass to her without taking his eyes from hers.

Some nagging portion of her mind tried to force Fritz into this imagined scene, but she could not fit him in. The image of Søren was so much stronger, so much more intense. And yet, with a feeling of inevitability, she resigned herself to the fact that she most likely would end up staring at Fritz Schlegel across a crystal glass of punch.

She turned away and faced the tall, narrow, leaded window. The sun streamed in, and she turned the handle to open one side of the window. Cool air rushed in. There was something glorious in the contrast between the heat of the sun and the coolness of the sea breeze, both caressing her at the same time.

She peered out the window and looked down to the street and sea below. It was a long way down and she wondered, idly, what would happen if she jumped. Not that she wanted to jump, but the mere fact of being so close to the open window, so high up, so near to danger and yet feeling so removed from it, caused her to wonder what would happen if her sense and reason and everything she had ever been taught were completely wrong. What if she were to step out of the window and instead of plummeting to her death she floated gently down, her fall broken by the wind and air itself?

The idea that she could think this disturbed her. She closed her eyes. After awhile, she felt happy again, very happy. She felt that if she could only drink up the sun, absorb it into herself, something wonderful waited for her inside of it—something entirely satisfying that she had not yet found but knew existed.

It must be God I'm hungering for, she thought. *Only He can satisfy me in the way I want. I won't think of Søren Kierkegaard again.*

Regina began to sing softly and she imagined Søren Kierkegaard somewhere in this city, sitting beneath another rooftop, listening to her with his head cocked to one side, thinking what a marvelous singer she was.

The sun began to feel too hot. She shifted in her seat and leaned back. She felt dissatisfied. She imagined herself sharing these thoughts with Søren. He would surely understand her strange dialectic with the sun. She wondered—and it seemed now an innocent thought, a perfectly innocuous thought—if she could make the corners of those wild eyes crackle with laughter.

She closed her eyes and forced herself to pray, to bring her Father back into her thoughts. *Lord, help me dispel this demon of longing. Erase Søren from my mind.* She opened her eyes, expecting an immediate answer. But Søren's presence seemed to linger in the air around her.

Why, Lord? she asked to the open window. *Why don't You answer my prayer?*

The sun continued to pour in and the sea, dangerous and enticing, shimmered in the distance. The only solution was to avoid Søren completely.

"Regina!"

Regina jumped and raced downstairs to hear her mother's instructions.

No, she didn't mind accompanying Cornelia to the haberdashery. Yes, she was sorry she hadn't returned to the rose garden. As she tied the ribbons of her bonnet under her chin, Regina caught herself wondering if she would run into Søren along the way.

Danger beckoned from every street corner.

9

The Touch

"I know that her soul is losing interest in everything else."

SØREN KIERKEGAARD

"I had to confess to myself that he gained great power over me."

REGINE OLSEN.

One week later, Regina prepared herself for another open house. She parted her hair in the middle, combed it smoothly down toward the sides, curled it, and arranged the rest in a simple coil high on the back of her head. She walked into the drawing room to discover Søren talking to her mother. For the first time, Fritz was not with him. A thrill rippled through her.

Regina watched Søren through the crowd as he leaned over her mother. His forearm rested against the molding that ran along the middle of the wall, separating the green paint below from the gilded green diamonds above. Her mother sat in a simple but comfortable wooden chair, her large frame encased in what Regina thought of as her native garb—a huge swath of russet silk trimmed in red and green braid. Her mother's cheeks were ruddy, shot through with fine grains of sharper pink. Søren commented on something, and her mother smiled and responded. When Søren tilted his head to answer, he looked straight at Regina, exactly as if he expected her to be there.

When he looked away, she felt as if they'd just had a conversation, and that he had invited her to talk further with him later that evening. She turned, elated, not quite sure where to go, but excited because now she knew that it didn't matter what she did or where she went; she would end up talking to him.

Then a quick, sharp jab of guilt about Fritz shot through her. *It's all right to be excited,* she told herself. *Søren's a nice gentleman. He's interesting. You just want to help him.*

Regina pushed away the thoughts that crowded in on her, the thoughts of how she wished everyone else in the room would disappear in a puff of smoke; how she wanted Søren to run to her side, now, this instant, and talk only to her; how she was already rehearsing all the fascinating stories she would tell him and how she would be annoyed to waste them on anyone else.

As Olga sat at the piano and began to play a ponderous, complicated piece, the idea came to Regina, silent and swift, that Søren had driven Fritz away on purpose, that he'd come early today because he knew that Fritz was sulking. For a moment, she had an image of Søren seated beside a chessboard, moving the pieces with a smile on his face.

She erased the image from her mind. Of course Søren was not that calculating. Of course he valued his friendship with Fritz.

Søren left Regina's mother and brushed against Regina as he went by her, the thick black cloth of his coat rubbing against the raw silk of her sleeve with a rustle, a whisper, a promise.

Once, about a half hour later, he passed her again, and, as there were many people close by, each pressing to go in a different direction, he touched the small of her back, silently suggesting that she make an adjustment in the angle of her torso. In order to direct her, he stood very close, and when he touched her back she felt as if he had pressed the spring lock on a box; she responded immediately. She moved gracefully, to the place he had indicated, as if he were leading her in an intricate minuet.

Regina knew that Søren was standing too close to her, that he didn't need to stand so close, and that he was doing it on purpose. She knew she wouldn't have liked it had it lasted any longer than a few seconds, so that someone else might notice. But he stepped back the moment that the throng of people around her moved on.

Fritz Schlegel, she reminded herself. *Remember Fritz. You have an understanding with him. He loves you. Go into the other room. Immediately.*

"Regina," the Councilor called to her from the piano. "Olga has finished. Come and play for us."

"Of course, Father," Regina said, walking over. She swooshed her long silk skirts to one side to sit on the velvet-covered piano bench. She turned the built-in brass candle-holders so that the candlelight illuminated the notes on the sheet music. Hot wax fell on one of the ivory keys, and she swiped the drop away with her finger.

She chose Mozart. She could tell she had caught her father's interest by the way he tapped his foot while he talked in the doorway. Her mother passed a platter of herring, flitting in and out of conversations without seeming to listen to any of them. From where Regina sat, she could not see Søren. She wondered if he was listening.

Nearing the end of the page, Regina held her breath as she planned which hand would play and which would turn. She felt a dark figure approach. Beside her now, Søren's hand poised to turn the page. As a smile tried to force its way onto her lips, she turned her attention to her playing, feeling the notes blend and deepen as she pushed the foot pedals. The candles flickered in their holders, causing shifting patterns to fall across the music. Every time Søren's hand came near a page, the candlelight shot thin, knife-like shadows along his fingers.

But the moment she finished playing, he turned away from her. She was forced to engage with someone in whom she had no interest. By the time most of the people had progressed into the dining room to collect their supper, it had become awkward for her to linger any longer in the green room. This put her at a disadvantage. The confidence engendered by Søren's first glance had begun to fade when he finally turned to her again.

Had he waited so long only to torment her? Had he timed the intervals between first looking at her, brushing against her, touching her back, turning her sheet music, and finally greeting her, just to reduce her to a flurry of confusing and embarrassing feelings?

He smiled. His face creased into a promise that he would now focus only on her. And all thought of his manipulation disappeared. He stood with his back against the wall by the door. The last remaining guest went in to supper.

They were alone.

She moved toward him, thinking, *We are an ocean with opposing tides, each pressing against the other, each rolling to meet the other in the center of a half-moon bay.*

Even as she imagined this, she noticed that she was the one who crossed the distance between them while he stayed still. And yet, she felt as though he was reaching out to her. As she drew close, he held out the crook of his elbow, and they went into the hall together.

"It is a narrow hall," Søren said, "but it opens into many broad vistas. Like your conversation."

She smiled. It seemed to be a compliment. The hall was tiny. It had a low ceiling, and the crystal chandelier shining with candles made the ceiling seem even lower. But the wooden floor of the hall was painted to give it the effect of black and white tiles, and this led the eye upward to the staircase and outward to its many doors. On the right lay the tiny blue sitting room, beyond that the dining room, and beyond that still further, the kitchen. On the left stood the double doors that led to the green room, and behind the staircase was a hidden entrance to her father's study. An excited murmuring filled all the rooms as guests settled into their meal.

Regina and Søren walked into the stove-warmed, blue-and-white-tiled dining room together, but drifted apart as others spoke to them. She focused on the sideboard—the hot roast goose, the vegetables, the truffles, the whipped-cream meringue—and wondered how they would end up sitting together. But it happened naturally. She was hovering with her plate, reluctant to sit without him, but equally reluctant to look like she was waiting for him, when he approached.

"Søren," Bolette said, coming up behind them. She wore dark blue, and her blonde hair cascaded in soft, perfect curls. "I have a friend I'd like you to meet. She would be so perfect for you. Oh, I'm sorry, Regina. I didn't see you were together."

"Mrs. Kobke." Søren bent over so low that he almost appeared to be genuflecting. "It has been my experience that when a married woman says I would be perfect for her friend, what she really means is that she thinks I would be perfect for her." His eyes gleamed as he raised his head.

"Oh, for heaven's sake," Bolette said. "You're impossible."

Regina laughed, and Søren indulged in a tiny grin.

"Anyway," Bolette said, "I shan't introduce you to my friend, as I don't want to waste her time. After all, Søren, you love to brag about how you will never marry."

That was true. Suddenly Regina wondered when Fritz was coming back.

"Me?" Søren said, stabbing his chest with one thin, pale hand.

"You," Bolette said.

"I can't think what induced me to make such a rash proclamation," he said. "I love marriage. I love the idea of it. It is a wonderful institution. Marvelous." He took Regina's arm and squeezed it.

All thoughts of Fritz flew from Regina's head.

"But your friend will have to pine," Søren told Bolette, "as I have an arrangement with the youngest lady of this house." He gripped Regina firmly by the elbow and steered her like a rudderless ship toward two chairs nestled beside the lit fireplace in a corner of the tiny blue sitting room. It took all of Regina's willpower not to cast a gloating look back at Bolette.

"What a convenient seating arrangement," Søren said. He held out her chair, pulling it away from the cracked leather bellows that lay against the tiled fireplace. "As if providence itself had prearranged our meal."

"Or my mother," Regina said. Plate in hand, she lowered herself into the straight-backed, blue chair.

Jonas nodded briefly to her from the sofa. His arms were folded and his body was tense. Across from him sat the young Count Droghena. Jonas knew the young man from university, when he had been merely the eldest son of a dissolute count. The father had recently passed away, leaving his son extensive holdings in the Danish West Indies, a penchant for gambling, and his title. Jonas's body language said, "Don't disturb me, little sister. I'm busy impressing a count."

An elderly mustachioed gentleman who worked in the Finance Ministry with their father greeted Regina from the chintz armchair. The ends of his splendid mustache were waxed into sideways twists with pomade, the perfume of which wafted over to the fireplace and mixed with the smoky warm sparks.

The three men returned to their argument. Regina caught the words, *slavery*, *plantations*, *king*.

"I find almost inspirational the elegance with which young ladies seat themselves," Søren said.

"It takes many years of practice and, in my case, just as many years of reminders," Regina said. She opened up her napkin and balanced the white gilded plate on her lap.

"Don't give away your secrets, Miss Regina. I will take full advantage of them." He, too, opened his napkin and balanced his plate on his lap.

What kind of advantage?

Suddenly, the mustachioed minister rammed the tea table so hard with his fist that Regina, along with all the silverware and plates, jumped. "It's a foregone conclusion," he said. "King Frederik will listen only to the democratic urgings of his friend, Governor von Scholton. He completely ignores the desperate pleas of the plantation owners that freeing their slaves will bring economic ruin on them."

"What do *you* think of the way King Frederik toys with ending slavery in the Danish West Indies?" Jonas asked the count in the voice his sister knew he used when he was trying to sound clever.

"My only objection to ending slavery is that then I would actually have to pay people to work my plantations." The young count shrugged and gave a lazy, complacent smile.

Jonas laughed, a too-loud "yah, hah, hah" that boomed out of him.

"So your point," Søren interjected, "is that you are more enslaved by slavery than your slaves are?"

The minister stared at Søren. The count gave him a scornful look. And Jonas squared his shoulders. He looked like he wanted to pop Søren between the eyes.

"What was that?" Jonas said, wielding the words like a threat.

"The point is—" Søren repeated.

"That we are all a slave to something," Regina finished.

Søren roared with laughter, and the other three men smiled politely. The tension in the room lifted. Søren's eyes twinkled as he drew his chair closer to Regina.

"I don't think they appreciated your humor," she whispered.

"Good," he whispered back. "I prefer being disapproved of. A passerby who glares at me saves me the inconvenience of raising my hat. An admirer, on the other hand, becomes a liability; before I know it, they have imposed taxes and duties on me for life."

"Then why are you smiling at me," she asked.

"I can't help it," he said.

Quickly, she looked down. She cut a small piece of goose and placed it in her mouth. The meat was dark and dry on the inside, slick and greasy on the outside. She chewed it with difficulty. Søren watched her every move. When she swallowed, the noise in her throat sounded as loud as a handheld water pump. Frowning, she replaced her silver fork and knife on the plate. "Something seems off with Anna's cooking tonight," she said.

"Perhaps it is you that is off, rather than the food, Miss Olsen."

She raised her eyebrows and asked what he meant.

"Sometimes our moods alter the experience of our senses."

She pursed her lips, inviting him to continue. He hadn't yet touched his own food.

"For instance," he said, "if a young woman were displeased with the young man who had foisted himself upon her as a dinner companion at her parents' house, Anna's goose might taste dry and bitter."

"What if she were pleased?"

"The goose would still taste dry and bitter because food proves ultimately unsatisfying in comparison with our deeper longings."

She had never met a more arrogant young man. How dare he imply that she had deeper longings for him. She decided not to answer him. She began to count the china plates hanging from ribbons on the wall. Two, four, six, eight. Then she counted the still lifes suspended in gilded frames. Strips of white molding set off rectangles of blue paint, like paintings within paintings. She listened to the three men discuss whether Denmark was heading for bankruptcy.

Søren attacked his own dinner with relish. He seemed to be enjoying himself, as if they had just battled and he had won.

Don't smile, she told herself. *Don't smile.*

She couldn't help it. She grinned.

He reached out and took her hand gently in his own. "Miss Regina Olsen, with you, I feel more . . ." She could almost hear inside his head as he searched for the word. *Happy. Funny. Enticing. Clever. Witty. Amusing. Attractive. Alive.* She knew these were the words running through his head because they were the ones running through hers, and she could tell that they felt the same way about each other.

"At ease," he said. "I feel more at ease with you than I have ever felt with anyone."

She thrust away her disappointment. She knew exactly what he meant. With other people, he felt the need to put on the sardonic shell, the antagonizing, teasing self. She pictured him as she had first seen him, fork in hand, trying to shock

Bolette and Mrs. Rordam. With Regina he could relax. He could say what he felt. He could expose the softer, more vulnerable side of himself. *Perhaps*, she thought, *this is what true love is—the ability to relax so much that in the presence of the other person you become more yourself than you ever knew existed.* And she felt that in that ability to be yourself—yourself standing alone before another person—you were also more happy, funny, enticing, clever, witty, amusing, attractive, and alive than you had ever been before. She felt that the compliment he had given her encompassed all of the other compliments she had hoped for.

Regina's eyes began to sparkle and her cheeks to glow. She wondered why the men on the sofa and the guests milling in the hall beyond did not notice the change that Søren had wrought in her. Her joy must be transparent, liquid, displayed for all to see. She leaned toward him, and she became aware of Søren's smell—his distinctive, warm, overpowering, delicious scent. The smell of him was intoxicating, like opium. She wanted to draw herself closer and closer to him. It struck her that someone else she loved smelled the same way. That was it. He smelled just like her father. *How very annoying*, she thought. *To be so manipulated by one's senses.*

When the Councilor interrupted them and stole Søren away a few minutes later, Regina felt almost glad that their conversation had ended. She didn't know why this would be, except that she wanted to remain here on the pinnacle she had reached when Søren Kierkegaard had told her he felt more at ease with her than with anyone else.

She rose to help her mother, but she listened only to her father and Søren roaring together with laughter at their shared, secret joke.

10

The Calling Card

"By then I was already recommending certain passages of books to her."

Søren Kierkegaard

"Oh, that Fritz could forgive me for being a little scoundrel."

Regine Olsen

"What is this horrible skull doing here?" Cornelia asked, walking in the front door ahead of Regina and their mother the next morning. A white skull grinned from the silver tray on the hall table. The mirror on the wall above reflected the back of the skull's head.

"It must be your father's," Mrs. Olsen said, shutting the front door behind them. She dabbed at her round face with her handkerchief. "Probably something to do with that self-portrait he keeps threatening to paint. But I don't know why he has to keep it on the hall table."

"Maybe he hopes it will inspire us to find husbands sooner," Regina said. "It's lucky Marie is married; it takes some of the pressure off the rest of us."

"Regina," Mrs. Olsen said, making the three syllables ring with gentle reproach.

"It's not my fault I'm not married," Regina said. "I don't know why Father should hint so often. I'm not even confirmed yet. Not for three more days, anyway."

"If you'd been brought up in the Lutheran church like *I* wanted," Mrs. Olsen said, "you would have been confirmed years ago. I was confirmed when I was thirteen. I don't know why the Moravians wait so long."

"Someone needs to propose first anyway," Regina said.

"Oh, I think Fritz Schlegel will pounce the moment you are confirmed," Mrs. Olsen said.

Oh no, Regina thought. *What if she's right?*

"Look," Cornelia said. "Someone has been here while we were out." She picked up a white calling card half hidden beneath the skull. "S. Kierkegaard," Cornelia read out. "How unusual for Mr. Kierkegaard to pay a morning call."

The air in the front hall shimmered. The engraved, scripted letters of the calling card seemed to Regina to leap off the white paper. She felt like grabbing the card and pressing it to her lips.

Olga shot round from behind the staircase. "Thank God you're back. He's going to return any minute, and I, for one, do not want to have to see him again."

"Olga," Mrs. Olsen said while Regina whirled her shawl off her shoulders.

"If you'd seen him this morning, you'd have retired to bed with a headache. You're lucky I'm still standing. I met him on the front steps just as he was leaving. Apparently he missed all of us. He thrust this book at me." Olga held out a green book. "He literally thrust it. He didn't even notice that I was laden with packages, very heavy packages. And on a day when the weather seems to think it's July, not September. He insisted that I read the book, that we all read it. He said it was imperative, that we had not a minute to spare, that it was the most important book of the year, if not the century."

"So what did you do?" Regina asked, trying not to laugh.

"What could I do?" Olga shrugged. "He jammed the book on top of my packages. I told him I might look at it later, after I had unwrapped my heavy load. Of course he didn't get the hint."

"Just like your father," Mrs. Olsen said as she wandered away down the hall.

"And then?" Regina asked.

"Well," Olga said, "that wasn't good enough for him. He said there was nothing I could be doing, nothing, that was as important as this book. Then he ripped off a sheet of paper from heaven knows where, grabbed the book back from me—literally grabbed it mind you—and earmarked the passage that we all had to read."

Cornelia rolled her eyes. Olga's whole face lit up.

Regina tried to suppress the grin lashing its way out the corners of her mouth. Søren had intended the passage for her. Of course he had. He was probably smirking to himself right now about his cleverness. Cornelia might have kept the book to herself, devouring it for weeks; Marie might have lost it; Jonas would probably have tossed it in the trash; but to give it to Olga in this intrusive way absolutely ensured that everyone in the household would hear about it.

Regina's hands itched to grab the book out of Olga's arms. She put her hands behind her back. "Did you read the passage?" she asked.

"How could I resist, when my very *life* depended on it?"

"And?"

"It was something flowery about summer and winter, blooming and withering flowers. You know the sort of thing. Of course, not a matter of life and death at all."

Regina was tempted to point out that blooming and withering flowers were in fact a matter of life and death, but she knew that Olga did not appreciate puns. "May I?" she asked, trying desperately to conceal her eagerness.

Olga handed it over as if delighted to be rid of it. "Read it quickly," she said, "because he warned me he couldn't *bear* to let the book out of his hands for long and would be back any minute to collect it." Olga threw her hands in the air. "I've never met such an exasperating man."

Regina nodded, already halfway to the sitting room. She darted into a chair and rifled through the pages. The book was bound in dark green leather, with four soft knobs in its spine. The title read *Woodland Poetry*, in gilded letters. As Olga had said, the marked passage had to do with winter and summer, age and youth. She read a few lines.

But the skirt of her yellow organza gown kept wrinkling. Why wouldn't it behave? She smoothed it out. She smoothed it out again. She felt her curls with her fingers—only a few strays. She tucked them behind her ears and read a few more words. *Tick*, *tock*, *tick*, boomed the grandfather clock. She looked up. No, it wasn't the doorknocker. She tried to find her place in the book again.

Doom, *doom*, *doom*, cried the doorknocker.

Regina jumped. Why should she jump when she'd been waiting for that very sound? She stood up and then sat down again. She closed the book. She placed her hands on her lap. Then she opened the book and held it higher. Over the top of the book, she watched Anna walk across the hall to answer the door. *How could anybody walk so slowly?* she wondered. Anna said something in her broad, Jutland accent about Miss Regine being alone in the sitting room. Regina turned a page.

"Ah, Anna. Just the news I wanted to hear," Fritz's voice said.

Regina slammed the book shut. It made a noise as loud as the sound of the parishioners closing their hymnals just before the last "Amen." She thrust Søren's book down on her grandmother's oak-paneled blanket chest and grabbed her sewing.

Oh. She should have removed Søren's calling card from the tray.

No. It wasn't her fault that Søren had called.

"Søren's beat me to it, I see," Fritz said, his voice muffled by the distance between them.

"Olga saw him," Regina called back. *Tick, tock, tick,* insisted the clock.

"Lovely skull," Fritz said to Regina, handing Anna his top hat and walking straight into the little blue sitting room. "A relative of yours?"

"Hello, Fritz," Regina said, smiling. But her eyes looked past him, as if expecting Søren to be lurking in his shadow. Despite the heat, Fritz looked as healthy and fresh as an autumn breeze in his white trousers and shirt and his knee-length, blue-gray coat. Though his cheeks glowed from the brisk walk, his brown eyes held the look of an injured schoolboy.

He wants me to apologize for not siding with him at the open house, Regina thought. *He wants me to reassure him, to tell him I missed him.* She picked up her sewing.

"I'm sorry I haven't visited in the past week," he said, taking her mother's soft armchair. "I . . . had some arrangements to make." He paused. "Perhaps you hadn't noticed." He pursed his lips and looked at her.

He looked ridiculous. She should tell him he was right, she hadn't noticed. But what if he never called again? And what if Søren disappeared as unexpectedly as he had come?

"Of course I noticed," she said.

Fritz's face transformed. His eyes lit up. He looked as if he were going to start panting and bound over to her at any second.

Cornelia peered into the sitting room, but when she saw Fritz and her sister, she made some excuse and left them alone.

"Fritz," Mrs. Olsen said, her skirts and petticoats rustling as she swept into the sitting room. The white lace of her bonnet stuck out like a fan above her large round face. "Welcome. I'll be back with you in a minute. Look after him, Regina dear." Then she bustled out, her stiff shoes creaking with her weight.

Fritz stretched his legs out in front of him as if he were in his own sitting room, as if he were already married to Regina, as if he had been married to her for years. A knot formed in her stomach, a hard and unyielding knot. *Father wouldn't like Fritz making himself so comfortable in Mother's chair*, she told herself.

Regina opened the lid of the mother-of-pearl and mahogany sewing chest and pulled out a new thread. How could she thread a needle in front of a gentleman without licking it? She jammed the thread at the tiny hole, but the ends had already begun to unravel. She licked it quickly, furtively, and then threaded the needle.

When she glanced up, Fritz was still leaning back, his hands locked behind his head, his eyes fixed on the white stucco ceiling. He hadn't noticed her dilemma at all. But if Søren had been sitting there, he would not only have watched her struggle to thread the yarn and finally lick it, but he would have made some observation about the difficulty of restraining errant threads. And the lift of his eyebrows and twist of his lips would have implied some deeper meaning, transforming the banality of her everyday existence into an allegorical tale of good overcoming evil. If only Fritz had some of the qualities that drew her to Søren. It would make everything so much easier.

Fritz bent forward. His face took on an eager, significant look.

She stiffened.

"You look as fresh and innocent as a rose today, my little Regina."

Her needle froze mid-stitch. "Thank you," she said.

"So when are you finally going to get confirmed?"

"Soon." She twisted the ends of another thread into a knot. It wasn't exactly a lie.

"All sorts of exciting things can happen in Copenhagen to a young lady who gets confirmed, you know. How soon?"

"Soon," she said. *Too soon,* she thought. *What if Fritz proposes first?*

Regina dropped her sewing, leapt up, and walked over to the open window. Outside, several large ships rested by the pier, their sails furled. No breeze blew in. "I wonder where Mother went?" she said. She faced Fritz.

"Nervous, Regina?" He grinned.

"Of course not. Why would I be nervous?"

She knew that she would marry Fritz because she loved him and he loved her, but first she had to get over her obsession with Søren Kierkegaard. If only she could talk to Fritz about it. But he was the last person she could tell.

"Maybe I need to have a chat with your priest," Fritz said. "What's going on in that Brethren church of yours? I think you should join the Lutheran church, like the rest of us." He raised his eyebrows. "Not confirmed at eighteen? Do they know how many young men they are holding at bay? How many are lining up, waiting for the moment of Miss Regina Olsen's confirmation? How many young men are—"

"Perhaps I shall get married to the church," she interrupted. "How do you know I won't become a nun?"

She hadn't thought of this before, but as she said the words, she pictured herself spending her days inside the stone walls of a nunnery. The image was not unpleasant. In fact, an abbey suddenly seemed a peaceful place, a place where she would not have to make choices because everything would be decided for her.

"I know you will not become a nun," he said.

The look in his eyes made her need to change the subject. "I'm glad you're here, Fritz," she said. She noticed, with a feeling almost of guilt, how handsome he was looking.

"Where else would I be?" He looked content, as if there was nowhere else he'd rather be.

The heat pressed in upon her. He seemed to have no idea that her thoughts lingered with another.

Suddenly, the doorknocker sang out *rat*, *rat*, *rat*, and Regina's heart lifted and sank at the same time. Anna answered the door, and Mrs. Olsen greeted Søren and said she would be right in. Fritz stood up with such a look of pleasure at the sound of his friend that Regina felt her heart might burst with guilt. She wished Fritz would leave. Then she wished Søren would leave.

Mostly she felt like leaving herself.

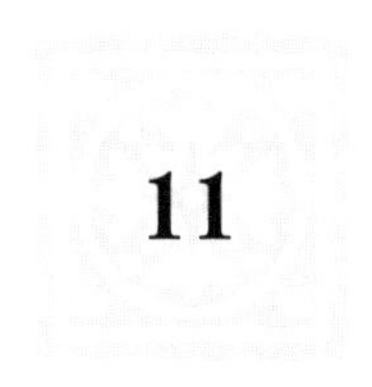

11

The Skull

"During this time I let her existence twine itself about mine."

Søren Kierkegaard

"Vis-à-vis Søren, I was the listener, the receiver."

Regine Olsen

Søren Kierkegaard entered the room holding the skull in front of his face. A ghastly, grinning set of bones cast its glittering eyes around the sitting room from above Søren's frail, crooked, black-clad body. "How do I look?"

"Like death," Regina said.

"At last! My exterior matches my interior." Søren lifted the skull to the side of his head and grinned.

"Frankly, it was an improvement from yesterday," Fritz told him, and Regina laughed. Fritz's face lit with pleasure at the sound.

Søren glanced toward Regina's lap. "Don't forget to knot the first thread, Miss Regina Olsen. Otherwise, you will miss the first stitch."

"I knew you'd transform my sewing into allegory," she said. "But don't you even say hello?"

Søren waved one hand. "Greetings are for people in the thrall of mediocrity."

"How very convenient," Fritz said. "I assume you're looking for me. Do you have one of those books you were telling me about?"

"How could I forget!" Søren popped his forehead with the skull so hard that Regina feared the bones of at least one of the two faces would crack. He bolted out of the room and returned without the skull, lugging five leather-bound green books identical to the one in front of Regina. He thrust one toward Fritz, threw himself onto the same straight-backed chair on which he'd sat the night before, and dumped the rest of the books on the floor beside him. Fritz looked tall and strong, while Søren looked like the next gust of wind would knock him off the chair. So why did she feel so drawn to Søren? Why?

"I am as nervous as a cat from spending the entire morning in the coffee shop," Søren said. "I had far too many cups of coffee. I don't know why. The second cup never tastes as good as the first. Nevertheless, I start longing for the second even before I have finished the first."

"Perhaps," Fritz said, "you should give up coffee."

"Of course you're right, Fritz," Søren said, "but all I have to do is walk by my favorite coffee shop, and the sight of the large blue cup painted on its front door makes me begin to crave coffee, just as a lover spying the glove of his beloved longs to hold the hand that wears it." His gaze fell on Regina's hand.

She looked away, flustered. How could he be so obvious in front of Fritz? Did he have no conscience at all?

"I enter the shop," Søren continued, a small smile playing about the corners of his lips, "just as I did this morning, and I tell myself that today I will only have one cup. But the moment I lift the cup to my lips, all I can think about is having another."

Was he dreaming of her? Is that what he meant? Or of other women?

"The Don Juan of coffee," Fritz said. "Bored in the moment of possession."

Regina's cheeks turned as red as the painted face and pointed shoes of a woman she had once seen leaving a house of ill repute.

Søren laughed, his blond hair standing on end as if he'd spent the entire morning rifling his fingers through it. "Yes, yes. The Don Juan of coffee. Precisely. You are a good friend to understand me so well, Fritz. But knowing the illusory nature of the temptation doesn't seem to help at all. I order the second cup even before I have finished the first, and I anticipate it throughout its preparation. Then, of course, just as I knew would happen, not only does it not taste as good as the first, but it has the unpleasant effect of turning my induced energy into a sort of nervous freneticism that is counterproductive to any kind of worthwhile activity."

Was it obvious to the two men that it was easy, so seductively easy, for Regina to look at Søren, but that she had to force herself to give Fritz the same attention? The effort began to exhaust her. It was so hot in the sitting room. She wished that a breeze would blow in through the window. The church bells tolled the half hour. The hall clock picked up the last note of the bells, like a disjointed echo. When would Søren explain the hidden message of the book?

"You do look pale, Søren," Fritz said. "I was only half joking about the skull."

"It's all this work. My thesis."

"Beware of that," Fritz said. He made a face. "Listen. You're the theology student. Make Regina tell us why she's waiting so long for her confirmation. I've been telling her that she's far too old already."

"Too old? She's too young. We should give gray wigs to the girls, false mustaches and beards to the boys, so they look old enough to understand the sacrifices involved in Christianity."

Regina burst out laughing. Then she covered her mouth with her hand. Had she laughed that hard at Fritz's joke?

Olga peered into the room to see what was so funny, spotted Søren, and looked as if she wanted to walk out again. Fritz sprang to his feet to welcome her. Søren rose so slowly that he looked like he was in pain. The family greyhound trotted in after Olga and eased his long, skinny legs down beside Fritz. Olga sat beside her sister on the blue sofa. The sofa was so soft, so cozy, it seemed ready to swallow both sisters.

"Herald," Olga called. The greyhound stared at her with impassive, regal eyes and did not move.

"Herald seems to recognize the man of the house," Søren said.

Fritz smiled.

"Søren was just telling us about the sacrifices involved in Christianity," Fritz told Olga.

"Everyone's but his own, I'm sure," Olga said.

Søren seemed not to hear her. "We are all called to follow Christ," he said. "But perhaps some of us are not up to the job."

Regina couldn't help it. She became convulsed with silent laughter. Olga cast her a quick, disapproving glare.

"Søren," Fritz said. "I hope you only talk that sarcastically to us. Because not everyone will understand you, you know. You could get yourself into a lot of trouble one day."

"Søren Kierkegaard, sarcastic?" Regina said. "Never."

Would he laugh? Had she gone too far?

Søren's eyes glittered. He seemed to be calculating how to respond. Then he laughed so hard Regina feared he would crack in two. "Employing my own methods against me? I like that."

Regina exhaled, and only then did she realize she'd been holding her breath.

"Have you come back for your book, Søren?" Olga asked.

Søren knocked his head again, violently, with one hand. Regina winced.

"The book!" he cried. "You must read it, all of you. It's the most important thing I've ever read. I have been to three booksellers already. I've bought every copy in Copenhagen. I see you have discovered it, too, Regina," Søren said, motioning to the book beside her.

"What a coincidence," Olga said, "when you dropped it off yourself this morning. Regina grabbed it out of my hand the moment she got back." Fritz turned his head round to look straight at Regina.

She gazed out the open window. The bare masts by the pier outside were listing, creaking like her guilty conscience.

"You seem to have a lot of free time on your hands, Søren," Olga said.

"Yes," Søren said. "I am thoroughly bored."

"You don't bore us," Regina said.

"Those who bore themselves amuse others," Søren said in a resigned voice. "Those who interest themselves usually bore others." He looked straight at Olga.

"I read the lines you recommended," Regina said hoping to distract Olga before she worked out what Søren meant. "In the book." Fritz glanced over at her again.

"I have noticed," Søren said, his eyes impenetrable, "that although there is a time when winter and summer almost meet, somewhere in May perhaps, they do not tarry long together."

"They cannot," Regina said. She spoke quickly, longing to show him that her mind could keep up with his. "They cancel each other out. They are opposites."

Olga squeezed her eyes shut. She looked like she was in pain.

"Sorry?" Fritz said, his ready smile leaping politely to his face as he strained to understand what they were talking about. "I don't . . ."

"Don't even bother trying to understand those two," Olga told him.

"You are right," Søren said to Regina alone. He jumped to his feet again and bolted from the room.

"You forgot your books . . . ," Regina called. But the front door slammed behind him.

"What was that about?" Fritz asked in a strange voice.

"I don't know," Regina said. If only Fritz would leave so she could sort it all out. Was Søren referring to himself as winter, and her as summer? Was he warning that they couldn't tarry together? She suddenly wondered if Søren's propensity to see symbolism in every detail was such a good thing.

The heavy tread of Mrs. Olsen's feet echoed on the hall floor. She appeared in the open doorway, her large, round face expectant, then disappointed. "Where did Søren go?"

"Regina scared him off," Olga said.

"You have to excuse Søren, Mrs. Olsen," Fritz said. "One of his moods strikes him, and he's off in an instant."

The three women in the room stiffened in unison.

"What kind of moods?" Mrs. Olsen asked. Regina saw two dark pink spots stain her mother's soft cheeks.

"Moods of . . ." Fritz paused. His honest, open face stiffened too as he seemed to sense their anxiety.

"Don't stop," Mrs. Olsen said. "I don't want to pry, but he interests me very much, this young man. My husband likes him. And I won't hide it from you; you're here too often for that. You know that Mr. Olsen suffers from . . . moods."

Regina clamped her arms across her chest. Beside her, Olga's frozen posture seemed to mirror her own.

"I understand," Fritz said. He spoke in a calm, kind voice that made Regina think, *Oh, he really is a treasure.* "Søren's moods are different than your husband's. Søren suffers from depression, yes—depression so crippling that sometimes he can barely get out of bed."

No, Regina thought. *That can't be right. Søren's not really depressed. He's not as bad as Father.*

Mrs. Olsen nodded.

"But Søren has other moods," Fritz said. "It's as if the melancholy has a twin, a sort of mania, and the twins take turns with his moods."

Why was Fritz saying this? Was he jealous?

Fritz leaned forward in his chair, staring at Olga, then at Mrs. Olsen, but not at Regina. "Søren can go for days without sleeping, without eating. I've never seen anything like it. He scribbles page after page of ideas. He speaks for hours on end. And, to be quite frank, I don't always understand what he's talking about when these maniacal moods hit. Just as I don't always agree with what he says when the depression strikes."

"What do you mean?" Mrs. Olsen said quietly. She turned toward Fritz, listening as intently as if he were talking to her about herself.

"Well," Fritz said, "the depression makes Søren exaggerate the bad. And then the other mood, the exuberant, maniacal mood, makes him exaggerate the . . . what's the word I want? The grandiose. The big."

"So what you're saying is, he's a lunatic and we should ignore everything he says," Olga said. Regina looked quickly at Fritz. For once, Olga had asked the question in her own heart.

"No," Fritz said slowly, shaking his head. "No. Sometimes I think Søren Kierkegaard makes more sense than the rest of us put together."

"Phooey," Olga said. "The man thinks only of himself. Have you ever heard him speak about anything else?"

Just like Olga, Regina thought. *We always dislike in others our own worst habits.*

Fritz laughed. "Well, yes, Søren speaks mostly of himself. But he uses himself as the particular, the example, in order to open his listeners' minds to the universal."

"What a wonderful excuse to talk about himself," Olga said. "I'll have to try that one." Everybody laughed, Regina most of all.

Mrs. Olsen spoke quietly again. "Fritz, I value your opinion very much. And I like to make sure that my husband is around people who are a good influence. You're saying you trust Søren Kierkegaard?"

"It's so hot in here," Regina said, crossly.

Fritz paused a long time before answering Mrs. Olsen. "Yes, I do. There's something about the man that I really like. Behind all the bravado, I think he's sincere. And I trust him to do the right thing in the end."

"I'm so glad," Mrs. Olsen said.

"I should go," Fritz said, without moving.

Regina looked down.

Fritz rose.

"Won't you stay for dinner, Fritz dear?" Mrs. Olsen asked. "Anna has been poaching salmon all morning."

Fritz paused. He looked at Regina.

Regina stabbed her needle into the canvas.

"Thank you," Fritz said to Mrs. Olsen, "but not today."

"I'm sorry to hear that," Mrs. Olsen told him. "Do come again. I so enjoy your visits. Regina, dear, accompany Mr. Schlegel to the door."

Regina took the arm Fritz offered her. She let him lead her into the narrow hall. Fritz opened the front door. The sky outside was a sheet of peacock blue, so bright and clear it made Regina's heart ache.

"Good-bye," Fritz said in a strange voice. He looked down at Regina as they stood together on the threshold.

She should tell Fritz right now. She should just say it. The clarity of the sky urged her on. "Fritz, I'm falling in love with Søren Kierkegaard," she should say.

She opened her mouth to speak the truth, but a tight, suffocating darkness wound its way around her stomach, her heart, her throat. Church bells pealed. The masts of the boats hit each other with a repetitive, insistent clanging. A wisp of white cloud scudded across the sky.

You might marry Fritz, she told herself. *It is possible. After all, you loved him once. You love him now. Don't you?*

Just beneath the surface of her thoughts lay a deep thicket of fears in tangled, thorny heaps. For the moment, the fears lay jumbled just the way their author—Satan, the author of all lies—wanted them. Regina could hear the fears humming now, skimming low, buzzing out their deadly refrain: *You must keep Fritz around, just in case. You're not really cheating him. He likes being with you. You're doing him a favor. And what if no one else wants to marry you? Who would want to marry you anyway? Do you really want to be alone for the rest of your life? "That's Regina Olsen," people will say. "She's the one who never married. Poor dear. She looks after her sister Olga's children now."*

"Actually," Regina said, grasping Fritz's wrist, "won't you stay for lunch? Anna has been poaching salmon all morning."

"I'd love to." The sharp angles of Fritz's face softened in that quick, sweet way of his as he heard the words he wanted to hear, as Regina fed him sumptuously with her lies.

12

The Confirmation

"She was not religiously inclined."

Søren Kierkegaard

"I was by nature religiously inclined."

Regine Olsen

For her confirmation, Regina wore white. Her body trembled with the sweetness of the essence of lily of the valley her father had given her that morning as a present. But as Regina gave herself to God, as the flames flickered on the tall white candles lining the pews, as the scent of incense cascaded through her, Regina searched for Søren Kierkegaard's pale face in every dark corner of the simple wooden church.

"I see many beautiful young souls before me," the priest said. His long, white beard reached his collar, and his large bony hands hung at his sides. The row of ten girls in white stood up taller, each hoping to be thought the most beautiful soul. Parents and friends nodded, smiling from the pews.

"I see many beautiful young girls, each pining for love, each wishing for marriage."

The girls shifted. *"Not I,"* their faces seemed to say. Each girl looked askance at her neighbor. Perhaps *she* was the desperate one.

"Young ladies, beware. There is a pale horse, whose rider is death," the priest said. "Do not open the door to him. There is only one who can satisfy you in the way you want."

Peering out over the tops of the bonneted heads of the women and the uncovered heads of the men, Regina sought the one she wanted. He was not there.

"Jesus is the brave warrior for whom your heart clamors. Jesus is the rider on the white horse, the one whose name is Faithful and True. He alone knows you in the way you long to be known, and yet loves you still. He is the one who finds you altogether lovely, who is ravished by your beauty."

No one would be ravished by my beauty if they really knew me, Regina thought. *It's lucky I don't let them in.*

"Jesus is the bridegroom, the one who has given up everything for you. He died so that you might live. Girls, on this day when you marry the church, I urge you to seek one thing and one thing only. Satisfy yourself with the Lord, and He will give you all the desires of your heart."

Yes, Regina thought. *Yes. I will satisfy myself with God so He will give me Søren. God, I seek You.*

She filled her mind with the rectangles of the pews, the tiny squares of blue sky visible through the windows, the intersection of the simple wooden cross on the altar. *There. I've done it. I've sought God. I wonder when I'll get Søren.*

The priest paused, his eyes scanning each girl.

"But do not think . . . ," he said, so quietly that Regina felt as if he were talking directly to her. "Do not think that if you satisfy yourself with God, your desires will remain as they are now. No. Your desires will be for the Lord, for intimacy with

Him, for His will. Only when God is at the center of your heart will your other relationships be healthy. And who else could you trust? God is the only one who will never leave you, never forsake you."

The priest chanted the blessings over the line of girls. The organ struck up a refrain. *Lord, forgive me*, Regina prayed. *Help me love You and You alone. Make me pure.*

But she found it hard to listen to anything but the beating of her heart. *Sø-ren-Kier-ke-gaard.* It beat louder and louder, drowning out the service, causing her to stumble over her prayers and muting whatever answer God was trying to give her.

A small, single-hearted prayer crept out of the heartbeat. *Lord, make Søren Kierkegaard propose before Fritz does.* As the prayer wound its way up the candle smoke, Regina Olsen ceased to be. In her place, stood only a girl in white who loved a man named Søren.

That afternoon, Regina had just sat down at the piano to sing for her family when the doorknocker called. *Let it be him*, Regina thought. *It couldn't be him.*

"Søren Kierkegaard," Anna announced. She stood in the hallway, her soft, downy face unsure whether to usher him in to the family gathering.

"I am interrupting," Søren said, holding his hat poised above his head.

The Councilor dragged him in by the elbow. "You must hear Regina," he said. "She sings like an angel."

"He's heard me before," Regina said.

"I will stay for only one song," Søren said.

Regina felt her stomach quake as she sang. "Do oh na. No oh bis. Pa ah chem. Pa chem." Regina wasn't really watching Søren, of course, but she did notice that he closed his eyes while she sang, as if drinking in the sound of her voice.

She finished and swung round on the piano bench. As Søren stood up and approached her, something strange happened to her vision. Her parents, Olga, Jonas, Cornelia, Marie, and Marie's husband Johan all faded into the background; only Søren stood out in sharp relief. A narrow beam of sun poured down on him through the tall windows of the drawing room.

Regina's heart throbbed in her chest.

"You looked beautiful in white this morning," Søren said.

"That's impossible. I didn't see you anywhere." She halted abruptly. Had she given away the fact that she'd been looking for him?

"I lurk only in the darkest corners," he said. He leaned closer. "Is that enticing scent lily of the valley?"

"My father gave it to me," she said, picking at the edges of her dark gown with her fingers, "for my confirmation."

"It is my favorite," he said. Then he bowed to leave.

Don't go, she thought.

"I will call on you tomorrow," he said, "because I always have your permission."

13

The Compromising Situation

"We met on the street just outside her house. She said there was no one home. I was audacious enough to understand this as an invitation."

SØREN KIERKEGAARD

"When he met me on the street one day and wanted to accompany me home, I hardly noticed that he ignored my reply that no one was home and followed along with me."

REGINE OLSEN

The next morning, Regina returned from the patisserie feeling as lifeless as the September day. A chill had woven its way into the air overnight. The sea and sky were a dull gray. Regina drew her white lace shawl more tightly around her shoulders.

Lord, she prayed. *Let the gentlemen callers come soon.*

The rubbish collector strode toward her, swinging his rattle in front of the Six Sisters. Aproned maids carting rubbish popped out the front doors of the houses like cuckoo birds from a row of clocks. But the door to the second house remained closed.

Instead, a lone figure clad in black stood in front of the Olsen's steps. Regina's heart leapt up in pinpricking, agonizing sweetness.

Don't get your hopes up, she warned herself.

As Regina drew closer, she saw the thin man stamp his black umbrella up and down, the metal tip ringing against the cobblestones. When she was almost close enough to embrace him, the man turned.

"Søren?" She was shocked at his appearance. His cheeks seemed hollow, his skin was yellow, and his eyes were blood-shot. He tipped his tall black hat. She touched the sleeve of his coat with her free hand. "Are you all right?"

"Take me inside," he said. He stared at her as if seeing and not seeing her at the same time.

She withdrew her hand. "I don't think anyone's home."

A quick burst of anger crossed his face. "I must go in with you," he said. "You don't understand."

"I'm sorry," she said. Her stomach squirmed. "No one is home."

He clasped her wrist. "Please."

The wind rose, howling across the open sea. Her hair swept up from beneath her gray bonnet, lashing at her face. She shivered and clutched her bundle of pastries more tightly. "All right."

She rapped the doorknocker twice, longing for the welcome clang and rattle of the door being opened from within. Silence. She withdrew her brass key from her tiny chain purse, sensing Søren's nervous body hovering behind her.

Hurry, hurry. Before anyone sees, she thought.

"This wretched key won't . . ." *Click. Snap.* She pushed the door open. Inside, a suggestive darkness lingered in the front hall.

"Which room?" she asked, walking quickly, talking quickly. The skirts of her dark gray gown whispered, and the floor spread out beneath her. She swept her bonnet off her head, hoping it didn't look like she was undressing. "The blue room or the green?"

Søren stood as still and tense as a coiled spring.

"The blue room is cozier," she said, feeling herself babble, "but the green room has a certain—"

"Play for me," he demanded. "The same song you played yesterday."

That would be the green room. Her feet seemed to skim over the surface of the floor. She sat down at the instrument, lifted the cover, and gazed at the music that still lay on the stand. The notes were obscured in the half light from the half-drawn curtains.

She lifted her hands to play, when Søren seized the music and threw it across the room. The pages snapped as they soared and landed with a ripping sound against the far wall. Regina swung round and gripped the sides of the bench, poised to leap away from him if necessary.

"What do I care for music?" Søren cried, coming closer. She leaned back. "It is you I want. It is you I've been seeking for years."

Her eyes widened. *Is he going to ravish me?*

He fell to his knees.

She exhaled. He could hardly ravish her from there.

Søren leaned closer, his face inches from hers. His eyes seemed so large, his cheeks so gaunt.

I must be in shock, she thought.

"Will you be my bride, my darling, sweet Regina?"

The proposal shimmered in the air before her. *Yes! No! Oh, . . . Fritz.*

The grandfather clock ticked in the hall. Three dying flies buzzed loudly in the windowsill. The black and white keys of the piano grew larger. The gold letters spelling the piano's manufacturer, "Hornung," receded.

"Please," Søren begged. "Without you, Regina, I will die."

That was easy to believe. He looked almost dead already. His face was so haggard and desperate.

"Before you answer, I must warn you. It is only right to tell you. I suffer terribly from depression. Terribly." He paused. "There. I have done it. I have warned you against myself."

He wouldn't be depressed with me around. The moment she thought this, the image of Fritz's reproachful gaze opened in her mind's eye and she couldn't speak.

"I love you," Søren said.

Her mouth felt frozen. Only his word, *love*, echoed in her head.

"I love you." He said the words again, as if she owed him something.

The silence expanded. Søren rose to his feet. "May I at least approach your father?" he asked.

She couldn't say yes. She couldn't say no.

Tension seemed to emanate from his frail body in visible waves. He came closer. His lips curled. His blue eyes vibrated with passion and aggression. He was going to kiss her, take advantage. Her lips puckered.

"I must leave," he said. "I do not want to compromise you. But I'll be back." He retreated from the room and the house, leaving her stunned on the velvet piano bench.

A few moments later, the doorknocker rapped. Regina froze. Had he come back already? A pit formed in her stomach. She couldn't move. What did he expect from her? To reply so soon? Impossible.

The knocker sounded again. Regina pictured Søren pounding holes in the door with the tip of his umbrella. She pictured him slamming his fist against its wooden panels. She imagined him ripping the door off its hinges. The muscles of her stomach clenched.

She sprang to her feet and threw open the door. Fritz, his eyes curious, stood in the dim gray light. "Regina?" He looked worried.

Her heart scattered. Søren's proposal lay in Regina's palm like a sealed letter. An offer had been made. If she accepted it, Søren Kierkegaard would be hers forever.

"Regina? Is everything all right?"

She cocked her head to one side, opened her mouth, then closed it.

Fritz grasped her arm. "I saw him leaving. He has upset you. Did he harm you?"

She pulled away from him. "No one is home," she said, not yet seeing what this would make him see. "I'm sorry."

Fritz stared at her. He stood there like something discarded. If he kept standing there looking like that, she would make her choice out of pity, she would choose just to please someone else.

"I'm sorry." She hardened the weak pounding thing in her chest and shut the front door in his face.

She stood stock still, frozen with terror, shock, and shame. She could sense Fritz on the other side of the door. Only a few feet separated them. He was thinking it through. She stared at the brass doorknob. She longed to throw open the door, to ask him for help, to tell him everything. Instead, she flattened her body against the wall between them and began to sob quietly.

After awhile, she heard Fritz's footsteps echo on the cobblestones and die away.

14

Permission

"Regina, sovereign queen of my heart; . . . hidden in the deepest privacy of my bosom."

SØREN KIERKEGAARD

"When Søren proposed, I was quite overwhelmed."

REGINE OLSEN

Regina stayed indoors for the rest of the day, trembling, waiting for her father to come home. She avoided Olga's eyes, not wanting her sister to pick up on her agitation.

At five o'clock, Regina heard the front door open and slam shut. She heard her father's heavy steps, heard her mother's greeting, heard him take off his coat. When he entered the drawing room where she sat sewing with Cornelia, she couldn't meet his gaze. She kept seeing Søren on his knees before her in this very room, and the image impeded her.

Her father walked over to the sofa. She could sense his presence towering over her. "Hello, young ladies," he said.

Cornelia greeted him, but Regina kept her eyes on his black boots, her mouth sewed shut. He sat on a chair across from them and kept looking in her direction. She couldn't bring herself to speak. She was afraid that if he began to probe, he would discover the wellspring of her heart, and she didn't want to divulge that to anyone, especially not her father.

By the time the family had finished supper and gathered in the drawing room, she could tell that her siblings knew about her afternoon because everyone became very quiet. They kept looking at her and then away. She felt sure that someone, probably Olga, would mention Fritz. Every time anyone spoke, she jumped, expecting an attack.

But no one said a thing. She was surprised that here, in the most important moment of her life, no one offered advice. It was as if they expected her to make her own decision.

When Olga suggested a game of cards, Regina bolted from the room carrying a lit candle. She walked upstairs, put the candle on her bedside table, and shut her bedroom door.

She threw herself, fully clothed, on her bed. Her body was still trembling. A husband, babies, happiness—all of it was within her grasp. She could hardly stand herself. Would her children look like Søren? Would they have wild blond hair? Piercing blue eyes? Would they be sharp as tacks? Gadflies? Her sons might be, but not her daughters. They would be kind and thoughtful, brown-haired and brown-eyed.

Think it through. Slowly, now.

She leapt off her bed and peered out her window. Søren's face loomed in front of her, pinched and yearning. Through the glimmer of his face in the glass, she saw a man far below, tottering on a ladder as he lit the street lamps. People in cloaks and shawls thronged the streets. A night watchman swung his spiked mace and lantern. The sea, dark and empty, rocked beside the pier as a full moon cast a thin, white trail along the water.

She forced herself to conjure Fritz's face in the window. Her muscles tensed as she pictured his brown, trusting eyes gazing at her in confusion. The bones of his face jutted out at sharper and sharper angles every second that she pictured him.

Stop it! It wasn't her fault. Who would choose someone out of pity?

She bolted across the room and threw herself onto the chair of her vanity. She stared at herself in the mirror. *Does he think this face is pretty?* She touched her cheek. *Does he really?* The crescent ache in her stomach curved sharper.

She closed her eyes and fell into fervent prayer. *Tell me if I can say yes, Lord. Give me a sign.* Opening her eyes, she looked about the room. She saw only the yellow curtains, opaque in the light of the single candle. She prayed faster, harder. *I hear no answer. What's wrong? What have I done? Why won't You speak to me? Tell me, Lord. I'm waiting. I'm here. I'm listening. I'm really listening.*

The flurry of words fell from her like so many paper snowflakes, each saying the same thing, over and over: *I want this, Lord. I deserve this. I'm going to grasp it now, quickly, before it spills through my fingers.*

And she bowed her head in submission to herself.

The next morning, Regina awoke to harsh sunlight streaming through her curtains. She felt as if she'd missed something. Her eyes flew open.

Did I imagine it? Was it real? She felt a rush of anticipation in the hollow of her stomach, followed swiftly by the sharp punch of panic. *Why didn't I talk to Father last night? I must speak to him now, before it's too late.*

Resentfully, she remembered she was supposed to read her Bible before breakfast. Then a thought came to her, loud and insistent. *What if Father leaves before I can speak to him?* Another thought trembled beneath the wings of the first. *And what if the Bible tells me something I don't want to hear?*

Regina threw off her quilts and raced over to her wardrobe. She slipped on her white stockings, buttoned the garters, and eyed the silk stays of her corset with disdain. *Forget about lacing up that thing. You'll be here all day.* She pulled on the horsehair crinoline, squeezed into a buttercup-yellow dress, and called out for Olga, who was trudging up the stairs. Olga came in and began to fumble at the line of silk-covered buttons on Regina's back.

"Please hurry," Regina said. *Oh, why do dressmakers have to sew on so many buttons?*

"Stop fidgeting," Olga said. "Why aren't you wearing a corset? It makes my job much harder. Father's waiting for you. Of course he told us. We're all in shock. Who would have guessed? We're all dying to talk to—"

"Are you done yet?" Regina interrupted.

"I'm doing my best," Olga said in a snippy voice. She finished the last button and left Regina's room without another word.

Regina sat at her vanity, ran her fingers through her side curls, slipped on her butter-yellow silk shoes, wrapped the ribbons of the slippers around her ankles, and tied them tight. Then she bolted to the stairs, smoothing the high-waisted dress down around her stomach. *Calm down. Don't look so nervous.* She forced herself to walk more slowly. She could picture her father sitting at the breakfast table, waiting for her. To steady herself as she turned the corner of the staircase, she placed her hand in its usual place against the wall, comforted by the knowledge that she was leaving her imprint in the very place she had left so many imprints before.

The Councilor sat alone in the dining room in front of a boiled egg. He looked up at her and nodded. She felt his eyes upon her as she went to the sideboard and took an egg from a covered porcelain dish. The shell of the egg felt hot and vulnerable. She set it in a blue and white china eggcup and crossed over to the table, the egg rattling against the sides of the cup as she walked. When she sat down across from her father, his eyes darkened then brightened. His prominent nose, high cheekbones, and curling sideburns looked soft in the clear morning light. In fact, he seemed younger, uncertain—more like a suitor than a father.

The silver bell sat beside Regina, ready to summon Anna. Fine, yellow farm butter lay in a dish. The blue and white tiles lining the walls, the crisp white tablecloth, the sparkling crystal, and the yellow flowers of the dining room hummed to her a familiar, cheerful tune that began to chase the anxiety from her thoughts.

"I assume you know what I want to talk to you about," the Councilor said.

Regina nodded. A bright winter-like light filtered in through the tall windows. A candle flickered on the table, black smoke rising from its pale flame. The candlelight seemed out of place, theatrical almost, in the morning sun.

"Søren visited me yesterday," the Councilor said. Regina stiffened, then tried to lower her shoulders. "I wasn't surprised, the way he's been hanging around here so much. The man is clearly in love with you."

He's in love with me? They were words that Regina had not dared let herself believe. But as her father said them, and made them true by saying them, Regina felt herself become lighter and more solid, all at the same time.

She looked at her father—fascinated, curious. Had permission been asked and granted, the transaction sealed?

"I haven't answered him yet," the Councilor said. "I told him I needed to talk to you first." The Councilor watched Regina. She looked down at her empty teacup, and the

Councilor resumed. "He would make a good husband, in some ways. He has inherited his father's wealth, so supporting you is not an issue." The Councilor paused. "There is another who also loves you. He would make a very different sort of husband."

The ordinary sort. The echo of her father's words about the Schlegels in the snowbound garden reverberated in Regina's head.

"The choice is yours," her father said. "In my opinion neither of these men is good enough for you. But that is because I am your father." The Councilor looked at Regina more tenderly than ever before. And in the moment in which she had the power to leave him forever, Regina loved him more than she ever had.

The Councilor cleared his throat, as if dislodging a flock of birds that had nested there. Regina looked down and tapped on the egg with the back of her spoon until tiny cracks formed.

"I told him he could call on you tomorrow," the Councilor continued, his voice thick. "He will come in the morning."

Regina almost knocked her egg out of the cup. She put two fingers around it, leveled the back of her spoon on the eggshell, and whacked it. Then she pulled the shell off its glutinous seal and picked at the egg with a tiny teaspoon. But when she put it in her mouth, she felt like retching. She put down the spoon. Who could eat at a time like this anyway?

"Only one thing matters, Regina," the Councilor said, his voice retreating.

She looked up.

"Is Søren Kierkegaard a Christian?"

Regina reached for the teapot. It was so full she had to grip the handle with one hand to keep the flow steady while she poured. "A Christian?"

"You know what I mean, Regina. God's Word is very clear.

Believers may not marry unbelievers. There are always consequences for disobedience. One of those consequences is being miserable. And I don't want to see you miserable."

Regina lifted the blue and white china teacup to her lips. The handle was so delicate, she felt it might snap. The scented steam rose into her face. She blew on the surface of the liquid, stirring up fissures.

"He must be a Christian," she said, wrinkling her brow to show her sincerity. "He thinks of nothing else."

"Even the demons knew Jesus was God's Son. That didn't mean they obeyed Him."

The image came to her of Søren's father—of the hard, unyielding look in his eyes, of his anger, his unassuaged guilt. Perpetual punishment. Graceless.

"Is Søren a believer?" she repeated softly, looking out the window. The pale September light glowed with a wan beauty that spoke of something deep and eternal that she knew she had found in Søren Kierkegaard. *How could he make me feel so beautiful if he were not tapped into the divine?*

"Oh yes," she said. "I feel sure of it." She took a tiny sip of scented tea.

"Then why did he say two weeks ago that he should have told Fritz he wasn't a Christian?"

"He didn't want to sound smug. You know what he's like, Father." She put down the cup.

"I do. And there's something off, there. I just can't put my finger on what it is."

Regina stared straight into her father's face, hardened her heart, and delivered the truth. "It's melancholy, Father. He has a melancholy way of looking at things."

The Councilor's face registered guilt and fear at the same time, and Regina's stomach squirmed in agony. *Take it back*, she told herself. *He might say no, now.*

"Do you want to be married to a depressive, Regina? They can be very difficult." The Councilor's eyes focused inward.

"I wouldn't call him—he's not that—he means—" She began to play with pieces of her eggshell. "Do you think he's very depressed?"

Her father nodded. "I think you're right. At heart, I think he's very lonely."

"That's why he needs me."

Her father's eyes flickered toward her and then away. "I don't agree with everything Søren says about Christianity. Several things I find offensive. I want you to assure me that before you actually accept him, you will make sure he really believes in God. With all his heart. That he's saved. That the Holy Spirit resides in him."

Regina nodded. "I will Father, I will," she said, trying not to make the words tumble out. "I'll find out before I answer him. I promise." She rolled her tiny teaspoon around and around in her fingers.

The Councilor smiled. The bloom in his cheeks, the sparkle in his eyes, whispered the message she wanted to hear: "I like Søren, I approve. He is suitable, he is wealthy, it is a good match. I'm going to believe whatever you tell me."

Regina picked up her cup again and smiled into her scented tea. She began to count the seconds until she could leave the table. *Be polite*, she told herself. *Sit with him until he finishes. Wait calmly. Don't let him know that you're dying to leave.*

The Councilor glanced over at her. "Go ahead," he said with a smile.

She grinned back. "Thank you," she said, bolting from the table. She swung open the door to the hall and knocked into Olga, who was leaning against the crack in the dining room door.

"Were you eavesdropping?" Regina asked, narrowing her eyes.

"Of course! But I could hardly hear a thing. What did Father say?"

"He said Søren is coming back tomorrow." Regina shut the door behind her and tried to lead Olga further down the hall.

"So tell me. Did Søren actually propose?" Olga's tiny brown eyes gleamed.

"Of course. Did you think I made it up?"

"No, I mean, did Søren really ask you? Outright? Or did he tell you how he'd thought of asking you, but wasn't sure, then reconsidered, but couldn't help himself, but then—"

"He asked."

"How long did it take him? An hour? Two?" Olga raised her sharp eyebrows.

"Five seconds," Regina said, picturing the flying sheet music.

"It must have been the only straightforward thing he's ever done in his entire life," Olga said.

"You may be right about that," Regina said. And the two sisters grinned, enjoying a brief, uncustomary moment of complicity.

"So what are you going to tell him?" Olga asked.

Regina tilted her chin in the air and said in her most priggish voice. "I have to find out if he's a Christian first."

Olga snorted with laughter. "I'd like to hear that conversation. Søren Kierkegaard likes to be pinned down as much as a butterfly. How are you going to find out?"

"I'll ask him."

"Regina. You know he'll say no."

"Shhhh!" Regina flapped her hand in angry waves toward the dining room.

Olga rolled her eyes and lowered her voice. "He'll say no. He'll say that considering the cavalier way people claim to be Christians these days, even the cats and dogs in Copenhagen are saved."

The sisters stared at each other, and then they burst out laughing.

"You're right," Regina said. "But I don't have a choice." She tapped her finger against her chin. "I just hope he can be straightforward with me."

15

The Question

"When Søren renewed his proposal two days later, I frankly and honestly responded that there was a teacher from my school days to whom I was very much attached."

REGINE OLSEN

The next day, Regina waited for Søren in the blue room with Olga, her heart thudding in her chest. Mrs. Olsen fluttered about in the front hall. Regina could picture her father in his study, pacing back and forth, the floorboards creaking beneath him. Regina clicked her knitting needles together, twisting her neck right and left as she peered at Olga, at the sofa, the window, the china plates, their mother. "I should have worn the ivory dress," she said. "I feel so ugly in pink. Maybe I should change."

"Don't worry," Olga said, dryly. "Søren won't notice."

"Thanks a lot," Regina said. Olga grinned.

Three sharp raps sounded on the front door. Regina grabbed Olga's arm. "Don't leave."

"I hardly think Søren wants to propose to me, Regina," Olga said, rising to go.

Anna opened the door, and Søren strode into the hall. Regina caught sight of his thin frame bent forward in determination. His black suit looked pressed, his white frilled shirt starched for perhaps the first time since she had known him. A burst of excitement shot through her. Mrs. Olsen flapped her arms at her sides, making conversation that Regina heard without comprehending. The Councilor joined them and said a few words. Then Søren advanced into the blue room, his lips drawn, his eyes asking.

On the threshold, her mother, father, and sister stared at Regina, and then faded away. Someone pushed the door shut.

Søren seated himself in her mother's soft armchair and stared at her.

She had to find the truth out now. Quickly. *Before her resolve weakened.* "Søren, are you a Christian?"

"Does this question have a point?" He leaned forward.

"No, no. I just thought . . . maybe we should . . . you know . . . discuss some things. Before we . . . discuss some things."

The man is an intellectual giant. Is that the best you can do?

"Can we discuss those other things first?"

She shook her head, dark ringlets flying around her cheeks.

He drew his lips together, and in a flash, she knew she wasn't going to get the truth. "I like to think of myself as *becoming* a Christian." He emphasized the word *becoming* like a challenge.

Father would have a fit. She narrowed her eyes. "You mean becoming a *better* Christian?"

"I choose my words carefully, Regina," he said, leaning further forward. "You know that. Like when I tell a woman I love her—"

She sprang off the sofa. If she sat in that sofa any longer, it would swallow her up, leaving only her knitting behind. "I mean, of course, you must have been saved, felt the joy and peace of the Holy Spirit flood your heart, and all that."

"Joy," he said, staring at her.

She rocked on her enslippered toes in front of the window. Sunlight traced a warm trail across the back of her hair. "Tell me, Søren," she said. "Tell me the truth. At least tell me."

"Joy," he repeated. "Yes. I have felt indescribable joy. Just before my father died." The church bell across the pier pealed at that very moment, and their eyes caught each other's and held.

"So you believe," Regina said, thinking, *yes, yes, yes, this is so easy, the pathway is clear; I'm free to say yes.*

"You mean, objectively?" Søren said, tilting his head to one side.

Regina's stomach knotted. She recognized that tilt. He was about to cause trouble. "I think so," she said. What was he up to? Why couldn't he behave?

"No," he said, tapping one finger against the side of his cheek. "I don't believe Christianity is objectively true."

Father need never know.

He raised one eyebrow. "Is that what you wanted to know?"

"I—it wasn't—of course—" She shut her mouth and squeezed her face up as if shielding herself from a glare. "You don't?"

"No, not objectively. I don't care about objective truth. You can't prove Christianity objectively, and it doesn't matter. Truth is subjective."

Subjective? Subject? Whose subject? What subject? What is he talking about?

He rose to his feet.

She took a step backward, the crinoline padding beneath her pink skirt knocking into the delicate china objects on the windowsill.

"Do you mean truth is different for each person?" she asked. "That it's different for you than it is for me?"

"What I believe," he said, "shouldn't matter to you, since truth is subjective."

Oh, but it does matter.

"Now can we talk about those other things?" he asked with a lift of his eyebrows. He took a step toward her. She edged sideways, her fingers running along the rim of the windowsill.

"Actually," she said, "I really do want to know what you believe."

He took another step closer. "Really?"

"Really," she said. She took another step away from him. Her leg hit the sofa, and she collapsed into its soft embrace. She picked up the pink silk edges of her gown and shook them out as if she'd intended to land there.

"My faith," he said, "has everything to do with passion." He advanced on her. "And decision."

"I—" She had a thousand questions, a thousand complaints. Before she could voice any of them, he was at her side, pinning her to the softness of the sofa, kissing her.

Warmth on her lips, then slowness, then more warmth. A heavy languor in her eyelids, her eyelashes, spreading, then speeding up, then a sinking into her self.

Oh, it was true. He loved her. Loved only her. Passionately. Decisively.

He drew away. The weighty scent of cigar smoke in the wool of his coat made her want to draw him back. She had to tell him now. She had to give him the same gift he had just given her. The words burst out of her. "I love you, Søren."

He shut his eyes. "Say it again, Regina. Please. I need to hear it."

"I love you," she repeated.

His lips parted. "Again," he said.

"I love you."

"My tiny bride," he said, opening his eyes.

"I haven't said yes—yet," she said. "I mean . . ." She let her eyes dance. "There's always Fritz to consider."

Søren's face billowed with anger. He leapt off the sofa. "Schlegel? What of him? What of him?" Søren's intensity almost scared her. He remained standing while she shrank into the blue sofa like a cornered animal.

"He has made . . ." Her voice trailed off.

"Do you have an understanding with him?" Søren demanded, stepping closer.

"I—"

"Has he made a declaration?" Søren's face looked so angry and tense that Regina felt guilty although she had done nothing.

"No," she said with relief. Fritz hadn't proposed. *Not exactly.* It was more of an understanding.

"Then let that relationship be a parenthesis in your life, Regina."

"A parenthesis," repeated Regina, bending the air with her fingers.

Søren slipped down onto his knees. He took one hand from her lap and pressed it to his soft cheek. "Please marry me, Regina. Please."

Who could resist a man begging? Maybe Fritz would move somewhere far away.

She nodded.

Søren's arms were around her even before she was aware he had risen from his knees. His face hovered close to hers. For a moment he looked like a stranger, the nose too big, the eyes too sharp. The next moment she was surrounded by his distinctive, seductive father smell. His lips curved into the shape of delight, and she felt her own lips curve into a matching shape. Then they pressed their mouths together, seeking each other out, searching to share the joy they felt and transform it by the joining of their lips into something far more glorious than either of them could have accomplished alone.

16

A Walk in the Forest

"My love for Søren Kierkegaard was a spiritual love."

REGINE OLSEN

"I cannot quite understand the purely erotic impact she made on me."

SØREN KIERKEGAARD

Every morning Regina woke up and felt like her heart was being torn in two. Part of her longed to leap out of bed, dress quickly and find Søren, and the other half wanted to stay holed up at home to avoid Fritz. She knew that he'd heard the news by now. Olga had seen him the day after the engagement and reported that he'd barely greeted her.

Regina had no idea how to behave. The easy way would be to pretend that there had never been anything between her and Fritz, that they were just good friends, and he was consequently delighted for her. The truth was that with every breath he had spoken of his life as it would be lived at her side.

One week after the engagement, Marie and Johan took Søren and Regina on a picnic. The two couples faced each other in an open surrey driven by Johan's coachman. They headed to the forest, passing meadows studded with gracious oaks. Sunlight liquified the greens and browns into a medley of stippled, speckled colors.

The surrey swayed, the horses snorted, and Søren's black-trousered leg was so close to Regina's that she could feel the heat emanating from him. She shifted her legs beneath her dark blue, high-waisted, sprigged muslin gown. A gentle breeze rippled the fringe of her blue brocade shawl and the ostrich feathers on her bonnet, and a thousand kisses rippled on the edges of her imagination.

Beside her, Søren stared blankly at the scenery.

"Our uncle wants to give you two an engagement party," Marie said. Søren bowed his chin over steeple fingers. The thick white points of his stocks pierced his cheeks.

"Don't make such a face, Søren," Regina said.

"Poor Søren," Johan said, tugging on the velvet trim of his greatcoat. "It's all over for you now. Your life is no longer your own." He laughed.

"What color dress will you have made up for the party, Regina?" Marie asked quickly.

"Green, I think," Regina said, leaning forward, her eyes gleaming. "With a new green cape."

"What about you Søren?" Johan said. "Organizing new outfits? Consulting your tailor?"

"I shall wear black to both my engagement party and my wedding. As will my bride."

"Not this bride," Regina said.

Johan's chins wobbled. He slapped his knee. "No white wedding for you, eh, Kierkegaard?"

"White should be worn only to funerals," Søren said. His eyes gleamed.

"Stop trying to impress Johan," Regina said. Søren grinned as if delighted at being caught. "Will your brother come to our party?" she asked him.

"Parties are too frivolous for Peter Christian," Søren said, pursing his lips.

Regina laughed. "Oh! And you'll never guess who Mother's already asked to do my engagement portrait."

"I give up," Søren said.

"Mr. Baerentzen!"

"Lucky you," Marie said. "He was too busy to do mine even though next door."

"He's coming round in a week or two," Regina said, "once the dress is ready. Now, Søren, you can't escape me by cracking jokes. Who do you want to invite to our party?"

"You," Søren said. "Only you."

Johan laughed again, and Regina caught a glimpse of another quick grin creasing Søren's face. Marie gave Regina a sympathetic smile.

"Please, Søren," Regina said. "What about your other relatives?"

"Most of my relatives are too depressed to get out of bed." Søren smiled as he watched the alarmed expression on her face. "But fear not. A few will rally round. You'd better do the lion's share of the inviting. Is this what it is to be engaged? To make laundry lists?"

"Oh, no! Not at all! Not. At. All. Are you bored? You are! You're bored to tears. I'm sorry. I so love my ring." She stripped off her glove and held her hand out for Marie and Johan to admire. "We exchanged rings yesterday," she said. She glanced toward Søren, but he sat on his ringed hand and did not seem to get the hint.

"Argh! All those diamonds are blinding me," Johan said, shutting his eyes in mock pain.

"Look," Marie said, as adept in the art of distraction as Regina herself. "We're here." She pointed to the tall, stately beech and spruce trees growing alongside the road. A pathway led into the forest. Johan called out to his coachman, and the surrey turned off the road and then shuddered to a halt.

All through lunch, the forest trails kept beckoning to Regina, whispering to her of possibilities. The moment they cleared the dishes and placed the food back into the huge wicker basket, Regina sprang to her feet. "Who wants to go for a walk?"

"I don't need to take walks in the forest anymore since I'm married," Johan said, smirking.

The nerve of him.

"I suppose it would be dangerous for you to go alone," Søren said, rising slowly to his feet. "All those ravenous squirrels and predatory chipmunks."

"Don't go too far," Marie said.

Regina and Søren strolled along a narrow trail. She hesitated, then took his arm. Ferns carpeted the spaces between the trees. The rich scent of damp leaves thickened the air. The forest became denser; sunlight shot through only in glimmering patches. The colors receded into one.

Søren leaned closer to her. "You are beautiful, Regina," he said. "I have been dreaming of you for years. And here you are, so close to me, so present, that I am transfigured."

Inside her boots, she pointed her toes, stretching her body longer. She felt warmer, softer, prettier than she ever had before. The green of the leaves looked more vibrant, the trunks of the birch trees seemed whiter, the bark of the oak trees held more texture than she had ever noticed. And every fifty yards or so her eyes lit on a tree whose leaves had turned a fiery gold. The color seemed to match the burning feeling in her heart, as her heart hammered so wantonly beneath her loosely tied stays.

They reached a clearing, and the sky above shimmered with a hue of blue that seemed more intense a color than she had ever seen, let alone imagined.

Søren's quick eyes darted here and there among the trees. His lips curved, as if he'd thought of something amusing, but he did not speak. He walked faster. Birds sang from trees all over the forest. The wind rustled leaves. Twigs crunched underfoot. And a strange noise came out of Søren's mouth.

She glanced over at him.

"Listen to this," he said with surprise. "I am humming."

"Is that new?"

"I've never hummed before—oh!"

"What's the matter?"

"Will it last? How can it? I am too melancholy to become a hummer."

"Shhh," she said, laying one finger to her lips. "Don't think so much."

"Hmm. Hmm. Hmm."

"Stop! You're not humming. You're thinking."

He grinned. "So are you, my dear. You can't help it either."

She glanced about the forest, looking for something to distract him. All around her, amid the trees and the sky, her love lay quivering before her like a pale, vulnerable thing.

"Tell me," she said, "I must know. When did you first start to love me?"

"The moment I saw you sitting between those two overdone monkeys at the Rordams. I made up my mind then and there that I would have you."

A smile coursed across her lips, her cheeks, her eyes. A chorus of winged angels seemed to cry out from the forest, singing joyful praises to the Lord God Almighty.

"And I was the first, Søren? The very first one you ever loved?"

He seemed to pause.

She wished she could suck the question back inside her.

He shrugged. "I once cared for Bolette Rordam, but only in a purely innocent, purely intellectual sense, of course."

"Of course," she said.

The angels seemed to sing less loudly.

Søren picked up his pace. She peeked sideways at him from beneath the brim of her bonnet. His nose looked sharp beneath his tall black hat. His right shoulder jutted forward; his right hand clenched in a fist; his right elbow stuck out at a sharp angle. She longed to relax him, to draw him to her. She rehearsed in her head her questions about her dress, her portrait, her ring, her party, but each sounded like a parody of a newly engaged woman.

"Tell me about your thesis," she finally said, frowning intently. "What did you say it was on? Irony?"

"Yes. Socratic irony." He seemed to slow his pace, and she tried not to gloat.

"I wanted to write my thesis on suicide," he added, "but for some reason the topic wasn't well received."

She laughed. "Why Socrates? What does he have to do with theology?"

"Socrates had one advantage over the rest of us."

"Which was?"

"Socrates knew that he knew nothing."

"I see," she said. She watched with pleasure the way his hunched shoulders lowered slightly at her sarcasm. "And the rest of us foolishly believe we know something. No wonder you like the Greeks. Are they all such skeptics?"

He laughed. "Mostly." His right elbow relaxed. "The thesis is on the underlying irony of life."

"I see. But what underlies the irony?" she asked, wondering what underlay the clenching of his fingers, the jutting out of his jaw.

He shrugged.

"You can't go on poking holes forever," she said, keeping a careful eye on the claw-like cast of his fingers. "That's like saying everything is a metaphor. Eventually you have to say there's something behind it all."

"Why?"

"Well, because there is." *Because the Holy Spirit testifies in my heart*, she thought, *telling me the truth of the Bible every time I open it up. But I can't prove it. I can't even speak it out loud without sounding sanctimonious.*

"Prove it," he said.

"You know I can't. But if you don't acknowledge it, your professors might burn you at the stake," she said. *And my father will get out his pistols and drive you off.*

"Let them," Søren said, his voice becoming grandiose, his elbow jutting out even further as her spirit sank. "Let them smear me with honey so insects will eat me. I'm not afraid of martyrdom."

No, she thought, her heart pinging about in her chest. *You're just looking for an excuse to do away with yourself.* She grasped a stalk of foxglove and waved the flowers upside down while they walked. He had taken her to the end of her logic. He had taken her to the end of her rope.

She pursed her lips and spoke in her sweetest voice. "If you say everything's ironic, aren't you worried your professors will fail you on the grounds you haven't said anything at all?"

"My dear Regina. If I were to elicit that much understanding from my readers, I would rejoice in my failing grade."

"Of course. For a whole second."

He laughed. "How you see through me." The fingers of his right hand uncurled.

The thrill of victory shot through her face. She had untwisted him. She bit her lower lip, trying to hide the way her mouth twisted upward into a victorious smile. She was so pleased with herself, she felt like humming.

"Your thesis is really that all truth is ironic except Søren Kierkegaard's, isn't it?" She let herself smile now, playfully, triumphantly.

"No, no, of course not. Absolutely not." He clenched his right hand into a fist again, and shook it in front of him.

Her stomach thudded. Anxiety coursed along the same pathway that pride had only moments before. *Quick, make him happy again.* "Are you leading me down the garden path of philosophy, Mr. Søren Kierkegaard?" She opened her eyes wide and fluttered her lashes.

"I like leading you down garden paths," he said, running his finger along the side of her cheek so softly she shivered. "You are so charming. So sweet. So perfectly ignorant. I talk of only the most simple things with you."

She withdrew her hand from his arm. "I'm not ignorant. I know perfectly well that there's something wrong with your saying everything's ironic."

Unleashed, he walked a few paces without her. Then he stopped and turned. In that moment of transition, a hardness came into his face, followed swiftly by softness, and she suddenly saw it all. He was afraid. He was afraid to be vulnerable, afraid of intimacy. All this blustering about irony and subjectivity was to cover over his doubt.

Søren must doubt that God was really strong enough to heal him of his depression. He must doubt that God could bind up the wounds left by the loss of all but one of his beloved family. He must doubt that God could forgive his doubt.

Yet God is at work healing him this very moment. If only he knew. The depth and certainty of her perception gave Regina a feeling of superiority—the kind of superiority that every woman likes to feel over the man she loves. She took his arm and motioned with her chin. They resumed walking in silence. How could she convey God's power and goodness to him? How?

The wind rose. The leaves rustled. Branches cracked. She lifted her free hand to her eyes to shield them from the unsettled dust. She looked around at the stippled bark of the beech trees, the wildflowers, the broken twigs. It was all so real, so palpable, so God-made. God's love—His gentle care and concern, His artistry, His intimate, individual attention—spoke to her from every graceful curve of every sunlit tree.

"Don't you ever look at the ocean," she said, "especially during a storm, and think how sad it would be if the ocean were just an ocean, the waves were just waves, and the power of it didn't make you admire and wonder and fear its creator?"

"The ocean scares you, too?" He turned his head and stared at her.

She dropped his arm. They stood still. She had been speaking of faith, but he had heard her doubt.

"Sometimes," she whispered. An image of the ocean's powerful, depthless waves beating on the shore loomed in front of her. The shriek and power of the storm, the dark, opaque swells, seemed so random and menacing.

Søren's eyes blackened. She encircled his pale hand in her gloved one. "But even when I doubt," she said, "I know that it's just a moment of doubt. I know that deep down, I love God. I believe in Him. Ultimately, the power I see in the waves points me to the source of that power."

"How?" he asked. "How?"

The forest faded and the image of her salvation rose before her. It had happened a few months before she'd met Søren. She sat on her bed, dusk falling, tears falling, mourning her sin and convinced of God's love. Conviction, repentance, and unconditional love rolled through her in a succession of waves. After that, peace. A peace that made every detail of the moment—of her room, the skin of her hand, the printed words on the thin page of her open Bible—stand out in sharper detail than ever before. One moment of perfect clarity. One moment leaping out amidst all the dimmer memories of her life.

"Did you take a leap?" Søren asked, turning over her hand. "Of faith?"

She nodded. She had been so restless, so unhappy, that she had begged God for faith, begged Him, and He had given it.

"You, in your short life? Already?" He turned to her, looking more interested than he had all day.

"Yes."

"You grasped Christianity inwardly, passionately, with both of your tiny hands, and held on, not letting go?"

She cocked her head to one side. It had only been a moment, after all. "I did once. I can't say that I've held on so tight ever since."

"No, of course not," he said. "You couldn't have. You haven't suffered enough. You haven't reached bottom yet."

"There have been moments," she said, picturing the vein throbbing on her father's neck, his mouth an angry gash.

Søren waved his hand dismissively. "No, no. You can't have real faith until you recognize that at bottom your life is a dark pit, a deep abyss, an emptiness."

"Mine isn't."

"Maybe that's because you're not really a Christian."

She was furious. Her chest heaved. Her breath came in quick bursts.

He grinned. "Not yet anyway," he said.

"Let's go back," she said, turning away. How dare he? Didn't he know that ever since she had repented and believed, the Holy Spirit had entered her heart, that she was sealed as Christ's own, forever?

"I may not be a very mature Christian," she said. "But I am a Christian. Unlike some other people I know."

He raised one eyebrow high above the other. "Don't be angry with me. I can help you with your problem." He took a step closer.

She frowned. "What problem?"

"I can help you suffer. I can help you suffer so much that you will sing."

"That is the sweetest offer," she said. "But—no."

He laughed. His face became pensive. "I learned about that from Peter Christian's first wife. I lived in the same house with her and Peter Christian the summer she died. She lay in bed, going from weak to weaker. But the more she suffered, the more sweetly she sang. I used to joke with her: 'Please suffer some more so that I can hear you sing.'"

Søren spoke so tenderly of this woman that Regina wanted, then and there, to be a memory in Søren's head. "I hope she understood your irony," she said.

He nodded. "She was lovely, like you. You always understand me. Better than anyone else I have ever met in my life."

Probably not, Regina thought. *I'm just nicer to you, that's all, because I enjoy making you happy.*

Søren reached inside her cape and slipped his pale hands around her waist—the waist now trembling with anticipation. "You have the tiniest waist. My hands can almost meet each other."

Two more inches and he could encircle her. She sucked in her stomach. Why hadn't she tightened her corset properly this morning?

Søren closed his eyes and shifted his head from side to side as if smelling the sweetest of flowers.

Something unloosened inside of her. He seemed to sense her moving toward him even before she did, and he swept her in close. He kissed her face and her neck. He pulled off her gloves, one by one, and kissed the tips of her fingers, the palms of her hands, and the softest part of her wrists. He kissed her until her toes curled and her knees buckled and such powerful, depthless waves beat upon the shore of her heart that she wanted to lie upon a bed of fiery gold leaves and succumb to him.

"That was what you wanted all along, wasn't it," he said when he pulled away.

"Of course not!"

How did he know?

"We'd better hurry," he said, grinning. "Your sister will think I've ravished you by now."

"She trusts me," Regina said, crinkling up her nose. But anxiety beat a frenetic pattern in her stomach, and she picked up her pace. She didn't have a peaceful moment until she returned to the security of the clearing, her clothes neat, her forty muslin-covered buttons untouched.

17

The Family Portrait

"Fritz Schlegel bore his sorrow over my engagement in a quiet and fine manner."

REGINE OLSEN

"Anxiety is the psychological state that precedes sin."

SØREN KIERKEGAARD

The next morning, a love letter arrived from Søren. Regina read it, smiling, alone in the green room. He said that he would write to her every Wednesday for the rest of his life in honor of that first Wednesday when he approached her at the parsonage. He wrote that his love was like that of the merchant who sold everything to buy the field in which the precious pearl was buried. He wrote that neither death, nor life, nor angels, nor principalities, nor powers, nor the present, nor that which is to come, nor any other creature could tear him away from her. Regina closed her eyes and let the sacred words wash over her in warm, welcome waves.

The front door flew open. Olga clattered into the hall, breathless. "I just saw Fritz again," she announced, stripping off her gray bonnet.

"How did he look?"

"Awful," Olga said, stalking into the living room to unleash her news. "Pale. Angry. He's grown a terrible scrabble of a beard. Most unattractive. He glared at me as if it were my fault."

"Fritz grew a beard?"

"If you could call it that. It was a messy, scratchy, horrible thing."

"A beard," Regina repeated.

"Yes, Regina, a beard. Any callers?"

Maybe she should write Fritz a letter explaining. Explaining what?

"Hello, wake up, Regine Olsen. Any callers?"

Regina shook herself. "No."

"No? Not even your lovesick swain?"

"He wrote me a letter," Regina said, waving the paper around.

"A letter," Olga repeated.

"Yes, a letter. You know. Quill. Ink. Paper. Hot wax."

"A letter," Olga repeated.

"It's a nice letter," Regina said.

Olga eyed her. How was it that her sister could make her so furious with a single look?

Regina glanced down at the letter, but instead of seeing Søren's words, the art exhibition rooms of Charlottenborg Palace began to sing to her their siren song. Fritz's face—kind, handsome, dependable—loomed in front of her. He was certain to be at the opening of the new exhibition.

Don't go looking for Fritz, she told herself. *It's not fair to him. And what would Søren say?* But she felt so restless, so hemmed in.

"I'm going out," Regina said. She sidled past Olga and withdrew her new black velvet coat and scuttle bonnet from the closet beneath the stairs. She whistled tunelessly under her breath.

Olga followed her. "Me too."

"Don't you have anything better to do?" Regina strode to the hall mirror and yanked the ribbons tight under her chin.

Olga slid her gray bonnet back on her head for an answer.

Maybe I can ditch her in the flower market.

Regina scribbled a note for their mother and pushed open the front door. Olga followed close behind.

"I'd really prefer to be alone," Regina said.

"Of course you wouldn't," Olga said. "You can't go looking for Fritz all by yourself. You're engaged to somebody else now."

Regina gave her a sideways glance. "How did you know?"

"You're an open book, Regina."

Regina pursed her lips. Maybe she'd underestimated Olga.

They walked down the front steps in silence. Enticing smells from the pastry shop next door wafted over them. A stout nurse passed by, her legs moving in stiff, jerky stamps as she tried to keep up with a pair of boys in short pants who were enticing a puppy by holding sticks just out of its reach.

"I really do want to go to the opening anyway," Regina said, starting out in that direction. "The art is supposed to be spectacular."

"Of course it is," Olga said, her voice thick with sarcasm. "So spectacular that Fritz Schlegel is certain to be there."

Regina grinned sheepishly. She screwed up her face. "Did Fritz look really bad?" Men wearing tall hats, gray coats, and close-fitting trousers nodded to them as they walked past. The two sisters nodded back. The air held a mid-September crispness.

"Like death," Olga said.

Regina winced.

"You deserve it," Olga said.

"I know," Regina said.

"Why did you do it, Regina?"

Regina shook her head. How could you explain to your sister those trembling sparks in the pit of your stomach every single time you think of a man? The way you imagine him encircling you when you wake up in the middle of the night? The way you turn over the palm of your hand and see in your lifelines only his fingers trailing in their depths?

"It's complicated," she said.

When they reached the square outside the palace, Regina glanced at the line of palace arches. Although they were the same size, the perspective made the second one look smaller, suggesting an infinite row of arches growing steadily smaller and smaller until there were none.

Regina and Olga picked their way over the uneven cobblestones and entered the door on the right. They purchased tickets, checked their cloaks, and Olga led the way up the Italian staircase to the second floor.

Regina followed, her heart thudding. The soft leather of her shoes picked out a refrain on the marble staircase.

Calm down, she told herself. *It's perfectly plausible for you to be here.*

The cupola room was crowded, full of people winding around one another as they analyzed and examined and compared themselves to the people in the portraits. There was no sign of Fritz. "I'll leave you alone now that I've escorted you here," Olga said, walking off into another room.

"Thank you," Regina said. She was surprised. She had expected Olga to linger at her side, her eyes turned on Regina like magnifying lenses. Was Olga actually becoming considerate?

Regina stared up at the portrait of Mr. Wagerpetersen, a prominent merchant shown with his wife and a chorus of dancing children. She shot quick glances around the room, wishing her hands weren't trembling.

He probably wouldn't even come.

Then she heard Fritz approaching from behind. Her stomach lurched. She would have recognized his footsteps anywhere. She wondered if that would change and fifty years from now she would be walking through an art exhibition as Mrs. Søren Kierkegaard and be surprised when Mr. Fritz Schlegel walked up behind her.

"Hello, Regina," he said, coming abreast of her.

"Fritz."

Like two magnets, drawn together. Her words echoed in the air, in the floorboards, in their collective memory.

She glanced over at him, at his humble, proud profile and the way he bit his lower lip, at the unruly stubble he'd grown on his chin. Everything about him accused her.

"I'm sorry," she whispered.

"Really?" He spoke with an irony she'd never heard in his voice before.

"Please, don't be like that."

"This is very difficult for me, Regina."

Her heart was pounding, lashing at her chest. She had to get away. What a mistake it had been to come. She spun around, but he said very quietly, "Stay."

She turned to face him. He looked straight at her, his soft, brown eyes probing into with such a hurt, bewildered look that she felt pain behind her own eyes. It was a pain she had to fight back. *Don't cry,* she told herself. *Don't make a scene.*

"Regina," he said. Her ache grew deeper, harder. A few heads turned her way. "It's not too late," he said. "You can break it off."

"Please, Fritz," she whispered. *Don't beg. I can't bear it.*

"Regina, if there's anything I've done that's offended you, anything at all, I'm sorry. I will change. I'll change anything—" He broke off. "Regina," he said in a low, urgent voice. "I *beg* you to reconsider."

Something in her snapped. "I love you, Fritz," she said. His face lit up, transformed by unexpected grace, and she held up her hand to finish. "But I'm not in love with you."

He crumpled visibly, and she felt herself sink with him. Within seconds, he transformed himself again. He straightened up so proudly that she winced. "Then my only hope, Regina, is that he does not betray you as he has betrayed me. You should know that he befriended me only to get at you. There is nothing more for us to say on this subject. I wish you all the happiness you deserve—"

"No, Fritz, not deserve."

"I will never mention our understanding again, and I want you to know that if you ever need help of any kind, you must come to me."

"Thank you."

His eyes registered shock, then hardened again. He turned on his heels with almost military precision and strode out.

Regina had to restrain herself from running after him. The fact that she could no longer have him made her want him more than she ever had before.

How could this be? True love was black and white. It wasn't possible to love two men at the same time. Not for her. She was a Christian.

Regina jerked her eyes up to the painting of the Wagerpetersens. She tried to imagine herself as the round woman in the white-frilled cap, surrounded by daughters. But she couldn't turn the self-satisfied husband into either Fritz or Søren. The thought occurred to her that if she could not be in love with two men at the same time, perhaps she loved neither of them.

She decided it would be better if she didn't see Fritz Schlegel for awhile.

18

The Palace Riding Ring

"I met Søren in the arched passageway of the palace riding ring shortly after the engagement, and it was as if he was completely changed—absent and cold. My youthful pride felt wounded by this."

REGINE OLSEN

"I was debating whether I could become engaged to her—and there she was, my fiancée beside me."

SØREN KIERKEGAARD

The following morning, it rained. While Olga and Cornelia played a duet, Regina stood at the green room window, the rain drilling against the glass, against the windowsill, against her heart. Regina looked left and right, searching the wet streets for a thin but ardent form. Didn't Søren know how much she needed to see him?

He hadn't come yesterday at all, and her guilt etched a refrain in her brain. *He knows I saw Fritz. Someone must have told him.*

She spotted Søren's ancient servant, Anders, approaching their house beneath a large black umbrella. Regina's back twinged. Søren wasn't coming.

Anna scurried into the living room holding a letter. Her round, innocent face looked so pleased to be delivering good news. "A note for Miss Regina."

Regina grabbed the envelope and escaped to the solitude of the sitting room. Trembling, she threw herself into her mother's soft armchair. She thrust her finger beneath the seal of the envelope, slicing the paper into her skin. She pulled out a letter. "To Our own little Regine," he had written and underlined at the top of the letter. He then went on about pulling the letters of her name farther and farther apart. R–e–g–i–n–e.

She pulled in her stomach, tighter and tighter, as she read. It was his veiled way of apologizing for not showing up. It had to be.

"I take it he's not coming again," Olga said, trying to read over Regina's shoulder.

Regina clutched the letter to her breast. "It's private, Olga," she said.

"So I'm right."

"He's busy," Regina said. "He sent a love letter instead."

"How nice."

Regina felt as if claws had seized her chest. "As if you'd know anything about love letters," she said.

Olga turned and walked away.

"I'm sorry, Olga," Regina called after her. She sprang to her feet. "I'm sorry!" But Olga walked upstairs, the staircase creaking.

What is my problem? Regina thought. *Just when we were finally getting along.*

By early afternoon, the rain had stopped, but the day remained gray and ominous. Another note arrived from Søren, this one accompanied by a scarf wrapped in brown paper. The scarf was blue muslin laced with pink flowers. The letter was long, elaborate, and pedantic. It didn't say when he was coming next.

She'd gone two whole days without seeing him, just when she needed to see him most. Regina tucked the letter under her embroidery, then threw on her bonnet, shawl, and white gloves.

"Going out?" Mrs. Olsen asked. Cornelia looked up from the piano bench. Regina nodded and left before anyone could ask where she was going.

She ran down the front steps toward the Stock Exchange. She walked the streets. *Exercise,* she told herself. *There's nothing wrong with a lady getting a little exercise.*

But she couldn't find him.

She began to walk faster. Her fingers stiffened with cold beneath her thin gloves. Paupers swept the city streets. Soldiers in red coats and tall hats paraded by. It was moving day, and wagons piled high with chairs and mirrors and people creaked past. A songstress sang the news, trying to thrust a broadsheet into Regina's hand. Regina shook her off. She imagined Søren holed up in his apartment. *Is it his melancholy, Lord? Is he depressed again?* Leaves had begun to fall, cluttering the drains. She lifted her skirts and crossed the rough wooden planks set over the swollen drains. She walked past every library in Copenhagen, but saw no sign of him.

She walked past butchers, past confectioneries, past coppersmiths and vendors in the streets selling birds, plaster figures, and other sundries. A group of blue-uniformed boys from the orphanage clattered past her. "Number thirty-three, get back in line," a matron scolded. A little boy no higher than Regina's waist scurried away from the window of a pastry shop.

A stitch formed in Regina's stomach. But still she walked. Where was he? She couldn't go home. She had to get control over herself first. Round and round she walked until she thought she couldn't last a second longer. In the back of her head crouched an image of Fritz. A few minutes more, and she knew she would start to look for Fritz instead of Søren.

When Regina reached the rose garden in the park, she stopped. Her heart pounding, she sat on an empty bench shrouded on both sides by thick hedges. The skeleton of the rose garden lay stretched out before her. The boxwood hedges grew in neat, manicured crosses. Beyond the garden, past a moat to her left, Rosenborg Palace rose up in all its pinkness. A single swan swam along the moat, leaving two thin ripples fanning out in its wake. A guard stood as motionless as a statue beside his red sentry box across the moat. Was his heart pounding in his chest, too? Two soldiers exchanged duty on the castle grounds. They saluted each other and then spun in opposite directions. Bells from all across the city began to toll the hour. Although each bell struck only three times, the accumulated effect, emanating from all the churches in the city, sounded like an ecstatic, disjointed rejoicing of some mystical event.

Regina leapt to her feet. She raced out of the park, turned corners, sped down alleyways, and reached into open places. At Christianborg Palace, she turned into a little pedestrian arch. Riders exercised the king's horses in the ring at the center of the courtyard. Regina leaned up against the fence and watched the horses' powerful legs, their pounding hooves. She was out of breath, panting.

Out of the corner of her eye, she spotted a familiar figure, far away. Søren was walking in her direction under the arched passageway of the buildings beside the riding ring. His head was down, his back bent forward, his umbrella sagging low in his hand.

She lit up inside. She could feel her body's chemistry

changing, the energy levels shifting. She let go of the wooden rail, splinters sticking into her white gloves, and darted over to the passageway.

Søren didn't look up. He kept walking, hugging the palace wall.

She walked directly toward him. The space between them narrowed. Twenty feet. Fifteen feet. Ten. He kept his head down.

When he was so close she could have embraced him, she said, "Søren?"

He kept his head down.

"Søren," she repeated, louder.

At the last possible second, he looked up.

She was shocked at his appearance. His eyes were blood-shot, his face unshaven. He looked as if he hadn't slept in the two days since she had seen him.

"What's the matter?" She reached out to touch him, then stopped herself.

"Nothing." He turned heavy-lidded eyes her way.

"You don't look well."

"No one has ever called me handsome, Regina."

She winced. He had purposely misunderstood her. "I don't want to detain you," she said.

"Thank you." He walked on.

She turned, confused, after he had passed her. "Søren?"

Her voice trailed off. He did not answer.

Fear etched a violent circle in her stomach. How could he treat her like this? She stood still under the passageway, her insides swirling.

White pillars framed her view of the riding ring. The horses were being ridden in tighter and tighter circles. Dirt flew up around their bodies in large clumps whenever their hooves touched the ground. She slapped her gloved hand against her thigh, startling herself by the violence of the slap.

She would never treat anybody she loved this way. Never.

What's more, she would marry Fritz. She knew he would take her back if she begged his forgiveness. Her nerves began to shiver inside her skin. She imagined herself and Fritz, sitting side by side in front of a crackling fire. Both of them had gray hair; hers was knotted into a tight bun. She sat in a rocking chair, knitting, while Fritz read the paper, sprawled in a well-worn armchair covered in a faded rose chintz. They did not speak.

She exhaled bursts of panicked breath. No, she wouldn't marry Fritz. The peacefulness of this fireside scene appealed to only a small part of her. The younger, vibrant, part of her needed much more. She had so much to give, and if she gave herself to Søren, he would appreciate it for the very reason that he was disabled. Fritz didn't need her, not in the same way.

Besides, after what she'd said yesterday, Fritz probably wouldn't take her back.

Søren must be sick. His depression must have taken over. He doesn't know what he's doing. The prayer moaned inside of her. *Lord, all I want to do is help him.* She longed to go to his house, to comfort him. But she knew she would have to restrain herself and wait until he came to her.

On her way home, she stopped at a shop that displayed a painting of a thin, beautiful woman. There, she bought a new corset.

19

The Silent Waltz

"She surrendered and was
transfigured into the most lovable being. . . .
This was more than I could bear."

Søren Kierkegaard

"Søren suffered frightfully from melancholia;
many a time he sat by me and wept."

Regine Olsen

The next morning, light stole into Regina's bedroom. It was a cold, thin light, without gradation or shadow, signaling only that the day had begun, that it was morning. Regina shivered under her goose-down quilt and felt herself longing for color and warmth. She winced as sharp pain cut into her stomach. Her armpits were sore from where the whalebone edging of her new corset had risen during the night. She leapt out of bed and measured her waist. Fifteen and a half inches. "Cornelia!"

Sleepy-eyed, Cornelia appeared in the doorway in her long, white nightgown. Her brown hair, curled up in paper, fell about her shoulders. Her face, sweet and gentle, looked in awe at her sister.

"Come and tighten me," Regina said, pointing to her silk stays.

"When did you start sleeping in your corset?"

"Just tighten me, please," Regina said. She crouched down onto her knees and lay on the floor.

"Regina! Get up!"

"You can get it tighter this way," Regina said. "Put your foot on my back."

"No!"

"I'll wake Olga. She'll have no problem torturing me."

"Oh, all right." Cornelia put one bare foot on Regina's back and yanked.

Regina's whole body jolted, as the pain cut into her stomach, armpits, and shoulder blades.

"Regina, I'm so sorry," Cornelia cried. "I hate hurting you. Let me loosen them."

"Just tie them up," Regina gasped. "I'm fine." She rolled onto her side, but winced again as the corset pinched below her ribs.

"Please, Regina," Cornelia said, tying the stays.

"I like lacing tightly," Regina said. "It feels good." She tried to get up without tipping sideways so that the corset didn't cut into the new sores.

After breakfast, she jiggled her slippered foot before the large oval windows of her father's study. The day had brightened, and a blinding light now streamed in through the windows. Regina watched a leaf curl its way down from the linden tree, cushioned on the wind until it landed gently on the ground. Her head tilted to one side as she traced the pathway of the leaf.

Inside, the light coming through the window transformed everything. It fell upon the new cape that Regina had draped over a chair, transforming the cape from the green of silk into the emerald of a jewel, making its threads appear translucent.

Regina turned away from the window. She paced her father's office, trying to control her rage at Søren. Journals, both conservative and liberal, lay on his large desk, held in place by his heavy brass compass. She spun his globe round and round, her fingers pushing off on the ridges of the mountains. She slid her hand along the soft leather spines of the books on his shelves.

Regina plucked a book out at random. *Carnival Magic.* She threw herself down in a curved leather armchair just in case someone should walk through the door and find her idling in a room not her own. But instead of seeing the words on the pages, she was distracted by the frenzied beating of her heart.

Why couldn't she even read? Why did he have such power over her?

Regina pictured Søren grinning at her, and a harsh feeling coursed through her—the kind of feeling that usually overtook her only when Olga was her most cruel or Jonas his most condemning. She realized with a stab of fear that she hated Søren.

How could that be? She was engaged to him. Besides that, hate was evil. The Bible said that anyone who hates, doesn't love God.

She wanted to slam the book, shutting Søren up inside the pages, but she resisted. *He's sick,* she told herself. *He didn't know what he was doing yesterday. He didn't mean it.*

She put the book down gently and rose, feeling the urge to kick something. Instead, she forced her limbs to move in the graceful, easy way in which she'd been trained. She stood at the window again. Perhaps the transforming light could restore her peace.

For a moment Regina thought she could feel God in the light. She closed her eyes to try and absorb the warmth of His love.

But then Fritz, tall, eager Fritz, stood behind her in her imagination. He spun her round and took away the anxious pounding of her heart. She forced her eyes open with a shock. What she'd felt frightened her.

She jammed back her shoulders, shifting herself inside the pads of her corset. She snapped her back upright and transferred her weight: left foot, right foot, left. She pressed both palms against the window, lifting them slightly as the coldness of the pane made her skin stick to the glass. Then she blew a cloud of condensation on the pane and drew a squeaky circle in the cloud.

A strain of music crowded her head. She tapped her fingernails against the cold windowpane as if playing the tune on the piano. It was a waltz, a beautiful Viennese waltz, and as she bathed in the sunlight and filled her mind with strains of Shubert, Regina willed herself to be happy. For she knew what could happen if you let yourself be overcome by melancholy.

A man put his hands around her waist and buried his lips in the curve of her neck.

She cried out and sprang away. "Who let you in?"

Søren grinned at her. "Your mother's marvelous Anna. She told me with a wink that Miss Regina could be found at the back of the house."

"Anna winked at you?" Regina felt outraged, betrayed.

"Anna likes me, I think." He moved closer in an easy fluid motion. "It was from you that I was unsure of my reception today."

She edged further away. "As you should be."

"The Knippelsbro drawbridge detained me. But while the businessmen stalked about in suppressed fury, I found it a convenient opportunity to meditate."

"Is that all you have to say?" She sat down in the chair,

crushing the green cape behind her back. "What were you doing on the other side of the drawbridge, anyway? You should have been pacing outside my house since before dawn, ready to beg my pardon."

"I didn't have to. I knew you'd wait for me."

She looked out the window, struggling not to show her fury and shame.

"You look anxious," he said. She narrowed her eyes.

"Of course I'm anxious. Who wouldn't be anxious after what you did yesterday?"

"Did you know," he asked, creeping closer, "that anxiety is the psychological state that precedes sin?"

"Are you implying that I'm anxious because I'm tempted to bean you in the head with Father's compass? What a genius you are."

He laughed.

She suppressed a tiny, betraying grin.

"Did you know," he asked again, "that anxiety is the dizziness of freedom?"

She stepped back. The thought of how close his hand crept to her waist, of how alone they were in this room, made her feel light-headed.

"You look dizzy," he said with a wicked grin.

"I am dizzy," she said. "With the freedom of knowing you deserve to be discarded right now."

"But you can't, can you?" he said. He touched her cheek, and she allowed it. "So you feel guilty. And the guilt makes you anxious."

She summoned forth an eye roll. "Oh, please," she said. "I'm anxious that you won't apologize."

"I was waiting for this moment," he said, "when the sun would be streaming in the windows."

"That's manipulative."

"Yes," he smiled, "I know. But one must orchestrate these things properly, especially when one is in the wrong."

She held out one hand as if to grasp the olive twig. "If you had arrived a few minutes later," she said, "you would have caught me waltzing with myself."

"Then I'm sorry I couldn't wait any longer. For I delight in discovering people in their unguarded moments." The light wreathed his hair in brightness and lent a glow to his skin. "But what is to stop us from waltzing now?" He held out his arms.

"Søren," she reproached him, trying not to smile. Of course he couldn't explain what had happened yesterday. It would be too embarrassing for him to discuss his depression. Just like her father.

Regina relented and held out her hand. Søren leaned in, but at the last second he sped past her hand, yanked the green cape off the chair, and began to waltz with it. She dropped her arm.

"Almost as good as the real thing," he said. He dipped and turned with his imaginary green woman, then looked up and grinned at Regina. "Perhaps more compliant."

"She's too thin," Regina said. She lifted up her right hand to be held in his left. He dropped the cape to the floor and kicked it away violently. She put her left hand on his shoulder.

He led her straight into a waltz. He stared at her, counting "*one* two three, *one* two three" in a low voice. *Step*, turn, turn. *Step*, turn, turn. The closer his face came to hers, the faster he turned her and the more she reproached herself.

Why did you give in so easily? Why?

"*One* two three, *one* two three, *one* two—"

"Was it your—" she said out loud, then breaking off. She felt frozen in her conciliatory pose.

You can do it. You're not your mother. He's not your father.

"Was it your depression, Søren? Was that why you were so rude to me?"

He gripped her shoulders. They stopped moving. Had he stopped breathing?

"I thought so," she said. "You suffer terribly from it, I know. You warned me. Is there no cure?"

"Not for me," he said, releasing her.

"What about horseback riding? That's supposed to help."

"Not even a hobbyhorse helps."

"Doesn't anything help?"

"A radical treatment? A spa in the Swiss Alps perhaps?" He shrugged. "Walking helps. Carriage rides help. Writing helps enormously. When I am writing, I feel fine. Then I forget all the disagreeable things in life."

"But forgetting isn't the solution. Writing isn't real life."

I am.

He shrugged. The cape on the floor cast a green glow on his trouser legs. "Soon my melancholy will be all I have left," he said. "Because if I keep going like this, I'll drive you away, I know I will."

"No," she said. "Never. I would die first."

"So you say," he said. Something outside in the withering garden seemed to attract him.

Regina reached down and picked up the green cape. As she withdrew her eyes from Søren's face, she recalled the source of all truth. *Lord, give me the words. Please. I have to help him.* She let her prayers soar along with her imagination to the only place where all wounds could be healed, all sorrows cured.

"Søren," she said, balling up the cape in her arms. "Nothing is impossible with God. He can heal your depression, if you ask Him."

He swirled round. "But what if depression is the thorn in my flesh—the thing God refuses to take away so I can learn that His power is made perfect in weakness?"

She froze. She knew exactly what he meant. If it was *his* thorn, it had become hers, too. She forced herself to speak calmly. "No, Søren. You can do all things through Christ. He can heal you."

"I know—but oh, Regina—I'm *afraid* to have hope."

"Don't be afraid." She moved closer so that her shoulder touched his arm. He turned and put one hand on each side of her waist.

"Even if He doesn't heal you of depression, Søren, He'll bring good out of it. Somehow."

"How?"

"I don't know," she said. "Maybe you can write about it—help other depressed people."

"That doesn't make me feel better."

"I know. I'm sorry. I don't know what else to say."

"What's the thorn in your side, Regina?"

"You."

He threw back his head and laughed. "Oh, Regina. Why don't I just tell you the truth? God knows, at home I delight like a child in planning something that will please you." She opened her mouth, but he released her waist and put a finger to her lips. "Shh. Let me speak before prudence steals it away. There is a cure to my melancholy. Her name is Regina. When I am with her, I'm not depressed. I am free of it entirely." He hopped on one leg. "See? I am free."

Her mouth swept into a smile.

"Regina," he said. "You look so happy. I want you always to look that happy. I am tortured with guilt about the way I treated you in the riding ring. It is inexcusable. Will you forgive me?"

At that moment, she would have forgiven him anything. In the space of ten seconds, he had lifted her so completely that she could have walked on water.

"Of course," she said. "You had no idea what you were doing, did you? You were just having a bad day, that's all."

He seemed to crumple in on himself. "No. It is my fault. Entirely mine. You were right. My depression is a cardinal sin."

"What? No! It's just something you were born with—a sickness. Your father had it, too, didn't he?"

He shook his head. "My depression occurs when my spirit wants to become eternal, and I halt it and press it back. You're right. If I had more faith, I wouldn't be depressed."

"What are you talking about?"

"I trust only in the finite," he said, scowling in disgust, "but this life is despair."

Regina frowned. His scowl seemed to include her. "*Everything* in this life is despair?" She asked. "And *should* be?"

"Of course."

She stiffened as she saw the logical conclusion to his thinking. If she accepted his theology, she was accepting that he should renounce her, that she was part of his despair. She set her mouth in an angry straight line. She couldn't agree with him. She had to find the gaping hole in his logic.

If only she could think straight. What was missing? She frowned again, her brow creasing, her hands fretting. Something illogical and extreme wove through the warp and woof of his words. There was a leap involved, a fanatical leap, a leap too far. He had leapt from longing for the eternal to completely rejecting everything else. Why couldn't the things God created be good? Why did they have to be renounced, scowled at? All you had to do was recognize that created things—created people—weren't God. All you had to do was make sure you didn't make a false idol out of another person.

It was easy.

"I don't believe you," she said. "You're just saying that because you're scared of me—of the power I have over you—of losing control."

He came close and kissed her.

She pulled away. "Stop! Someone will come in."

He shrugged, pulled the crumpled cape from her arms, shook it out, and began to waltz with it again. He whistled as he turned. This time she didn't try to stop him even though she ached for him to abandon the green cape and waltz with her again, even though she longed to be the cure for his soul, even though she felt the sharp deep pain of no longer hating him.

20

The Engagement Party

"A party [was] held some time after the engagement for a group of young people, mostly Kierkegaard's nieces and nephews."

HENRIETTE ("JETTA") LUND

"Do you ever get bored at parties, Regina?" Søren whispered to her. His voice was, as it had been for the last six weeks, intimate and mocking at the same time. Regina's new green dress made a soft rustling whisper as the two of them stole into the room where the Jorgensens were soon to hold their party. The room had a subterranean feeling to it. It had a low ceiling and one leaded-glass window, but the earth had been tunneled through to reach up to the November sky. Frost crept along the edges of the window pane. Heavy, carved oak furniture crowded the room, making it seem even smaller and darker than it was. The light of three lit candles danced from a wall sconce, creating an intimacy that drew Søren and Regina closer together in the darkness.

"No, I don't plan on being bored at my own engagement party," she whispered back. "You will be nice to everybody, including my elderly grandparents."

"I am especially adept at handling elderly grandparents."

"Good. Why do you ask if I'll be bored?"

"Because I always feel restless at parties," he said.

"Why?"

"It comes from ignoring the infinite inside of me."

Not that again.

"Maybe you're just shy," she said. "Or bored because not every conversation centers on you."

He laughed. "Do you really think me so very selfish?"

She nodded. "Yes. I know you, because I'm the same. Everyone is."

Søren seemed not to hear her. He wandered over to inspect the wooden carvings on the doors of a tall oak chest. The upper panel held the initials and coat of arms of her uncle's ancestors. Each of the lower panels depicted a different biblical scene in bas relief: Jacob wrestling with the angel; Jesus healing a sick woman; Boaz embracing Ruth, who leaned away but looked happy.

Søren was riveted on the panel that showed Abraham tying Isaac to the altar. Isaac's mouth was twisted in anguish; Abraham's eyes were lifted to heaven. There was no sign of the ram caught in the thicket. Søren traced his fingers along the wooden carving of Abraham.

Regina wished he would trace the curves of her face instead.

"I can't stop thinking about Abraham," Søren said, now caressing the thick ropes around Isaac.

"I can't stop thinking about our party." Regina twisted her mouth into the shape of Isaac's. "What if no one comes?"

"I long for that sort of order from God," Søren said. "To kill my most beloved thing. It would strengthen my faith."

"You would *want* God to tell you to kill the person you most loved in all the world? That's ridiculous," Regina said. She placed her hand along the triangular panel on the front of her green dress. The narrow band of lace etched a line across her chest.

"Yes, precisely! It is faith in the ridiculous. Faith in the absurd. Faith in the unethical. A leap into the unknown. It is believing that even if you renounced the thing you most loved, you'd get it back, just as Abraham got Isaac back from the dead, as it were."

"Really? Then what are you going to renounce?"

"Prunes."

She laughed. "Do you think Peter Christian will change his mind tonight and come anyway?" She spoke in her most distracting, most beguiling voice.

"I long to become so absorbed in the service of the spirit that it would never even occur to me to obtain food or drink," Søren said, pointing to the long tables laden with goose liver, smoked mackerel, and herring with onion.

"You wouldn't last very long," Regina said. "About three days maximum, I think. The thirst would do you in first."

"If I had been Abraham," Søren went on, "I would never have told Isaac that God had commanded me to sacrifice him. I'd rather Isaac think me a monster than that he hate God."

"Of course you would have told him," Regina said. "I know you. You couldn't have helped yourself. Even if you didn't tell him up front, you'd have dropped hints for the rest of your life."

Søren finally turned to her and grinned. "Aren't you supposed to be agreeing with everything I say? Or did all that fly out the window when I asked to have you?"

"It flew out the window," Regina said.

He laughed. He looked so handsome when he laughed like that. She wished her grandparents would arrive now, so they'd see him at his best.

Søren touched her cheek. His fingers felt so soft against her skin that she wondered if his fingers had been made for that very thing, if they'd been carved by God for the express purpose of caressing her cheek.

Regina's gangly uncle walked into the room and then stopped, making all three of them conscious that he had interrupted something. The apology in his smile seemed to say, "Ah, I remember what it was like to be in love."

"Your first guests have arrived," he said as a maid bustled in to light the rest of the candles.

Excitement shot through Regina. The widow Rordam floated in, swaddled in a huge black brocade dress. She was followed by her four daughters and her son-in-law. Regina watched the ironic smile twisting Søren's face when he greeted Bolette and her husband. Then Mrs. Olsen wandered in with her parents. The sight of her tall, handsome grandfather and her petite, beautiful grandmother always made Regina smile. Nothing could go wrong when they were around. The Councilor strode in next. He took one look at the crowd and headed for the schnapps. Søren's cousins arrived. Emil Boesen, one of Søren's few friends, inched into the room, his spectacles gleaming. Everyone greeted Regina, congratulated her, and then cornered Søren. Søren shot helpless looks at Regina every few minutes, and she had to cover her mouth to hide her laughter.

As the party progressed, Regina watched to make sure everyone was happy. She spotted Søren's young nephew and niece, Henrik and Jetta Lund, cowering in a corner and she dispatched herself to their rescue. Despite her short skirts and the two braids that hung down her back, Jetta spoke with the seriousness of an adult. She could not talk enough about her uncle Søren—his fine expressive eyes, his kindness, his playfulness and sense of humor. Jetta had a thin, sharp face, but it softened when she discussed her uncle. She'd even adopted many of Søren's speech patterns. "I suffer from melancholy, too, just as he does," she suddenly confessed.

"Surely not, Jetta," Regina said, turning her back on the girl. "Henrik," she said, "tell me about yourself." She asked him gentle questions. Was he a student? How often did he see his uncle Søren? What were his favorite memories of his uncle? Henrik blossomed under her attention. He, too, seemed to idolize his uncle and told her stories of Søren's kindness to him and his sisters when they were younger. Basking in a rosy glow of mutual appreciation, Regina surveyed the scene with pride. This was her very own engagement party, and everything was going better than she could have imagined.

"What a lovely group of friends," her grandmother was saying to Søren. "And everyone looks so happy!"

"Yes," Søren said, "man is always happiest in a herd." Her grandmother laughed.

Søren began to cough. He became convulsed by coughing. Regina stopped talking, mid-sentence, and stared. Her grandmother pulled out an embroidered handkerchief. Søren rammed it to his lips. The handkerchief turned dark red, a black red. Regina screamed. Everyone stopped talking. Henrik rushed to Søren's side. The Councilor stormed over. Søren coughed some more. He doubled over, giving himself up to the coughs, and reached for his own handkerchief. As he removed the embroidered one from his mouth, blood spilled on the dark wooden floor, black on black.

"Father," Regina cried.

"I'm fine," Søren muttered. He coughed up more blood.

"I'll take him," Henrik said. The Councilor put a hand on Søren's arm, but Søren shook him off.

"Let Henrik," Søren started to say, then he sputtered. Bent over, without looking at Regina, Søren crept out gripping Henrik's arm. The Councilor followed at a distance, then returned.

Hushed silence gripped the room. "We should call the doctor for him," Regina said. "We must call the surgeon." She said it so many times that her father left and sought out the surgeon himself. The guests drifted away one by one, whispering solicitude, pressing their hands to hers and assuring her that her fiancé would recover. Her father returned an hour later to say that the surgeon's services had not been required. Søren already had his own doctor.

21

The Music Stand

"While the party was at its liveliest, however,
Søren was taken ill, to the point of spitting up blood.
His fiancée, who had become very frightened, went to his
house several days later to hear how he was."

HENRIETTE ("JETTA") LUND

"I am so listless and dismal that I not only have nothing which fills my soul, but I cannot conceive of anything that could possibly satisfy it—alas, not even the bliss of heaven."

SØREN KIERKEGAARD

On the day after the party, Regina received no word from Søren. She didn't go out, afraid that she might run into someone who would ask after her fiancé. It would be mortifying to admit that she had no idea.

The next morning, her mother called up the stairs. "Hurry, darling! Mr. Baerentzen is here to do your portrait."

Regina jumped. She was sitting at her wooden vanity, fingering the few precious things she kept in a jewelry box while she stared at her face unraveling in the mirror.

"Regina! You're not even dressed?"

Regina flinched. Her mother stood in the doorway, surprise lifting the soft lines of her face.

"Sorry," Regina said. She turned back to the table as if trying to decide which earrings to wear. The china ballerina that stood inside her jewelry box tilted sideways. Inside lay her gold cross, three pairs of earrings, and a silver brush that had once belonged to her great-grandmother Regine. It had an *R* punched out in small holes in its silver back. Regina held an earring up to her face.

"For heavens sake, Regina, what's wrong with you?" Mrs. Olsen stepped into the room. "Stop looking at yourself in the mirror. Where's your dress?"

Without waiting for an answer, Mrs. Olsen opened the armoire, took out the engagement dress, and laid it on the bed. The emerald green of the dress made a lovely contrast to the pale yellow of the coverlet.

"It's beautiful," Regina said, without moving.

"What's wrong, Regina?"

"Nothing." As she said it, however, Regina felt something soft inside descend from her throat down into her stomach.

"Good." Her mother's eyes sparkled with intrigue. "Then I will go downstairs and ply the very famous Mr. Baerentzen with hot tea, and, with any luck, he'll not even notice that his young subject has not arrived." She turned to walk out. "Are you sure I can't help? At least your hair is done. Can I lace you?"

Regina shook her head. "I'm already laced," she said. It had been a long time since she'd been unlaced.

Regina held the cross up to her neck but put it down again. No necklace, she decided. She frowned at her reflection in the mirror. The skin on her chest looked too pale. She pinched her cheeks to pink them. She looked so young, like a baby. She stood up, then sat down again and stared at the dress. What could she have done while wearing this dress that had so offended Søren? She could hardly stand to touch it, let alone put it on.

Regina felt as if she had two selves—one made of skin stretched tight across bone and muscle, the other, inside, as ephemeral as silk. She could imagine the bone and flesh self putting on this dress, marching downstairs, and posing as the intended of Søren Kierkegaard. But even as she pictured this, she could feel the other self crumple inside of her and fall with a soft floating motion down to her toes.

The muscle-bone self put on the dress, greeted Mr. Baerentzen, smiled graciously, apologized for detaining him, sat on a chair, and kept a smile hovering about her lips for an hour while the soft, silken self remained lying upstairs on her bedroom floor.

"I like to see a woman well draped," Mr. Baerentzen said, nodding at the black, satin-lined velvet stole draped around Regina's shoulders.

"Regina," her mother cried, clapping her soft hands together. "Where's your new green cape?"

"Søren prefers black," she said.

"Yes, yes!" Mr. Baerentzen proclaimed, holding up one hand, the white sleeve of his painter's smock billowing and his blue eyes blazing. "Not green on green. Boring, boring. Like a late summer forest. Black over green is superb, like joy at a funeral."

Regina's mother raised an eyebrow but said nothing.

Regina coughed into her hand.

The moment Mr. Baerentzen left, Regina lifted her new tilting casquet high over her head. It was a black velvet hat built along the lines of a classic helmet—appropriate, Regina thought, for doing battle with a difficult man. She fastened the buttons of her pelisse, marched out the front door, and set out alone for Søren's apartment on Norregade. The waves across the street slapped at the wharf. Green slime coated the base of the boats. The tang of salt water sharpened the frown on her face. She walked quickly, head down against the wind, head down against her doubts. But the soles of her black boots tapped out the rebukes on the cobbled streets: *you shouldn't go there alone, it isn't right, everyone is watching.*

Regina sped up. It was so cold, she felt as if the wind had wound its way inside her bones. Falling leaves swirled from the trees lining the streets. The trees rocked in the wind with dignity, their limbs elegant and stately despite their reduced palette of brown, rust, and burnt sienna. Carriages rolled past, and gentlemen walked toward her. She stopped on the street outside Søren's apartment and gazed up at the second floor. There were so many windows.

Regina guessed that there were about four rooms in the front and as many in the back. Lamps shone from behind a few of the curtained windows, but the others looked dark. Was anyone standing behind the curtains, looking down at her? She clutched her arms around her and shivered. She felt exposed standing outside Søren's windows wondering what lay concealed behind the glass.

The wind picked up, and the wizened leaves swirled in an updance, like migrating birds. "You should go home," the leaves seemed to rustle.

She lunged forward and throttled the doorbell. It gave a high-pitched, ratchety wail and then died out.

No answer. Regina hesitated, her hand hovering over the bell's lever. Should she ring again?

The silence taunted her. *He doesn't love you. He never loved you. He couldn't treat you like this if he did.*

She jammed her finger on the lever a second time. It made another tinny, ratchety noise. After several seconds, she swung round. She would go home where she belonged.

The door creaked open. She turned back. "Sør—"

It was his houseman, Anders. Anders's creased face creased further. He looked around.

"Is Mr. Kierkegaard at home?" Regina asked.

Anders frowned and looked past her again.

Regina stepped forward.

Anders didn't move. She was so close to him, she could have pushed him over.

"I am here to inquire if my fiancé is all right," she said in her stateliest voice.

"Mr. Kierkegaard is recovering well," Anders said, not budging.

"I'd like to see that for myself."

Anders moved aside just enough to let her pass, but not enough to make her feel welcome. She marched into the darkness. He walked past her and led the way up one warped, wooden flight of stairs. The stairs cracked and groaned as if they might give way at any second.

Anders opened a door onto a hall lit by a single candle on the wall. Except for the grandfather clock ticking nearby, the house was quiet. The stillness contrasted markedly with the busy street noises she had left outside.

Anders looked at the wall.

"Is there a room where I might wait?" she asked.

He straightened his back like a soldier coming to attention, and seized upon her words. "A room to wait in," he repeated. He shuffled through the gloomy hall and pushed open a heavy door to the right. An unearthly glow beckoned from the open door.

She entered the room alone, passing Anders with a smile as if to reassure him that it was all right, that he had put her in the right place. He closed the door behind her.

She stared around the room. It seemed to be a sort of library. The thick, velvet curtains were drawn shut, yet she counted ten oil lamps lit. It was an extraordinary number for such a small room. They hung in the enforced darkness like multiple moons, flooding the room with an overbright glow. The air was heavy with the pungent scent of burning oil and something that smelled vaguely of *eau de cologne.*

She remained standing in the center of the room, her confidence fading away as she realized she was indeed alone. Leather-bound books filled the dark walnut shelves. A leather wing-backed chair, a large rosewood desk, and a thick, walnut desk chair with round brass studs sat in a nook. On the desk lay a room thermometer. She checked it; it read 60 degrees.

She shivered. The curtains bulged in the middle and a freezing cold draft blasted in. Were all the windows open? And why were the curtains shut in the middle of the morning? Just wait until this was her house. The curtains would be opened, the windows closed, the stove lit, the open surfaces covered with fresh flowers.

As Regina tried to reassure herself, she sensed something intruding upon her. Something large and worrisome bore down on her. She turned to face it. It was a huge mahogany stand to the right of the desk—the sort of stand a conductor uses to hold sheet music. It stood alone, erect as a fir tree. An inkstand lay open beside it, and a pen lay on the base of the stand, as if Søren had stopped writing mid-sentence. The stand was covered with quarto sheets of paper, each square filled to the margins with Søren's scrawled black handwriting. Papers littered the floor as if Søren had stood there for days writing so fast that the pages had poured off the stand as quickly as the words from his pen. The papers looked so forlorn they reminded her of tear drops fallen to the floor, now abandoned.

She averted her eyes from the stand. Søren would not like for her to be here; he would not like for her to see this testimony to his mania.

She planted herself on the edge of a small love seat. If Søren was going to walk in on her, he should find her as far as possible from that music stand. She ran her hand along the scratchy surface of the beige and maroon sofa. It was the ugliest she'd ever seen. Who on earth had purchased it?

It must have been Søren's mother. After all, she'd been a servant in the household while Mr. Kierkegaard's first wife lay dying. Søren's mother, with her peasant background, probably wouldn't have had the good taste exhibited by the other furnishings in this room.

Regina gave a mental snap of her fingers. No, Søren had once told her that his father had taken care of all purchases himself, right down to the Christmas goose. The poor mother hadn't been allowed to buy anything. What accounted for this tasteless piece, this aberration in an otherwise attractive room?

In contrast to the sofa, a leather, maroon chair in the corner looked invitingly shiny and smooth. She exhaled, imagining Søren spending his days perusing a book, sprawled in this sedate chair, one ankle crossed over the other knee. She didn't like to think of him standing at that music stand, frenetic activity forced from aching fingers.

She jiggled up and down on the sofa and clutched her black stole around her shoulders. She wished she weren't here. It was Anders's fault for choosing this room. It was her mother's fault for making her do that ridiculous portrait.

It was her own fault.

She rose to go, and it was then that her feet wandered over to the music stand. Her eyes took in the words before she could admit to herself that she was spying.

> *"Once in his early youth a man allowed himself to be so far carried away in an overwrought irresponsible state as to visit a prostitute. It is all forgotten. Now he wants to get married. Then anxiety stirs. He is tortured day and*

night with the thought that he might possibly be a father, that somewhere in the world there could be a created being who owes his life to him."

The entry broke off there.

Regina's hand flew to her mouth. She stumbled backward, away from the music stand. A prostitute? Søren?

Was that what Mrs. Rordam and Mrs. Schlegel had meant when they referred to Søren's profligate ways? Regina's stomach twisted. She pictured the rouged, red-shoed woman she had seen walking out of that brothel so long ago. She pictured the woman's complacent smile. She imagined Søren's pale hands reaching, his expressive lips . . .

No! She held out one hand. It wasn't possible. This was just fiction. Søren liked to imagine things. He wasn't writing about himself—just making up a story. Perhaps it was to be a novel. Yes, it had to be that. It was her fault—this trembling in her stomach, this aching in her chest—for spying. She felt as if the weight of her body were dragging her groundward.

But reason intruded on her fantasy. It would be exactly like Søren to think that visiting a prostitute created an impediment to marriage. He was the sort of person who would consider himself virtually married to this prostitute. It was ridiculous, pitiable. And yet . . . It all had to do with forgiveness, with not feeling forgiven, with . . .

Regina's frenzied thoughts were interrupted by a knock on the door. Søren walked in, looking paler than she'd ever seen him. "What are you doing here?" His voice was cold.

She took a step backward. "I know, I know. I shouldn't have come. But I had to know how you are." She fought to control her limbs, to prevent him from seeing how violently she was trembling. She took a few steps closer to the ugly sofa.

Søren's eyes darted from her to the music stand. He strode into the room and stopped in the middle, blocking her path to it. "Are you spying on me?"

"I'm—I—Anders—" She broke off and regathered herself. "What do you mean, am I spying on you? You leave our party, coughing up blood, then you send no word? What am I to think? Everyone has asked after you. I had no answer. I was mortified. And of course worried about you. I'm worried sick." She stopped and stared at him, defiant, panting.

Could he guess she'd read about the prostitute?

"You shouldn't have come here without a chaperone," he said.

She cringed. Of course she knew that. Did he think her a fool?

"Fine," she said. "I'm leaving." She swung round so sharply that the bottom of her corset dug into the soft part of her stomach.

"Good," he said. "Anders will see you out."

She glared at him, but he'd already turned away from her and was heading over to the stand. Just as she walked out the door, she heard herself speak, as if from a distance. "I will write to you."

Anders waited in the hall. Was that a triumphant look in his narrow eyes? She whirled away from him.

From the study came Søren's voice. "See Miss Olsen out, Anders. And when you come back, adjust this room. It is two degrees too warm."

Back in the street, Regina came to herself again. *There's no way I'm writing to him.* But then the image loomed in front of her of the alarm on Søren's face when he had begun to spit up blood. And she remembered the awful redness of his blood in contrast to the paleness of his face. And that redness blended with the redness of the prostitute's shoes, of her cheeks, of her petticoat.

I'm writing to him the moment I get home.

She walked slowly past the Church of Our Lady, trying to calm down. She had to walk herself into a reasonable explanation for the prostitute story, but the slower she walked, the lower her imagination dove. It took every muscle in her body to prevent herself from turning back, confessing her spying, and confronting him.

Regina crossed the bridge and headed to the Six Sisters. The wind, swarming over the open water beside her, seemed even colder than before. Her feet felt the coldest. She wondered what frostbite felt like. Then she remembered that frostbite set in after the numbness, after one ceased to feel anything.

She sped down Borsgade, wishing she didn't have to expose herself to the cold, and pushed open her front door. A letter and bulky package lay on the claw-footed silver tray. She knew it was from Søren even before she raced over to read her name on the envelope.

He must have written the letter the moment she'd left. He probably ordered poor Anders to run. Why, if his heart had been so full, couldn't he have told her what he had to say in person? She ripped open the package, letting the brown paper fall around her onto the black and white floor.

It was a leather-bound copy of the New Testament. Why was Søren sending her the New Testament? The hypocrite. He was the one who needed it—him and his prostitute.

She tore open the letter:

"*My Regina!*

Whom most they love they most chastise:
'Tis folly in the whole world's eyes.
Both walk as one to death and grave:
The world thinks 'madly' they behave.

When I have spoken with you as I did today, not coldly and severely (I would never be able to do that) but seriously albeit mildly and tenderly, I should not like you to think for a moment that I feel myself superior at such times; and to show you that I chastise myself in the same way, I send you as a remembrance of this morning a copy of the New Testament and thank God that I became the person charged with providing you with that which we all need. You know that the angels in heaven rejoice in your every victory, but surely their joy is not diminished by the presence of one person on earth, an insignificant being to be sure, who humbly shares their joy.

Your S.K."

She scowled. The letter was so patronizing. She grew angrier the more she read. She wanted to heave her chest, to huff and puff, but her corset was too tight. She could only exhale quick, short, angry breaths. Did he think he was her spiritual mentor?

Lord, she prayed, *take away my anger. Let me not resent someone giving me the Bible.*

She waited, but her anger refused to subside.

"What is it, Regina?" Cornelia, her voice gentle, stood an arm's length away. "What did he give you?"

"A book," Regina said, flipping over the cover. "Just a book."

❖ ❖ ❖

Søren visited the next day. She waited in the sitting room. She did not look up when he entered. This time she was determined to maintain her air of wounded pride.

He took his usual seat across from her and said all of the things he hadn't said in the letter. He was touched by her concern. He thanked her for it. He told her that the coughing attack was probably connected to back pains from which he often suffered as a result of a fall from a tree when he was a boy. He spoke in a low, alluring voice. She looked up, once, and saw that some color had returned to his cheeks.

"It was wrong of me," she said, "to visit you without a chaperone. But it was worse for you not to have sent me any word after you were ill."

"True," he said.

"At least you admit it," she said. She felt herself beginning to soften again, and she spurred herself on. "I was humiliated when you sent me a copy of the New Testament."

"Humility is the goal of the New Testament," he said, raising one eyebrow.

"Something you know little of."

"I thought we were discussing you, Regina."

"If the shoe fits," she said, "wear it." The red shoe.

"Is there something else bothering you, Regina? Because you look very agitated."

"Something besides your rudeness?"

A still, small voice told her not to lie. It whispered to her of another way—a way of truth, of confessing your faults, of asking the man you wanted to marry about a pair of red shoes that lay sprawled on the floor between you, sprawled and poised to trip whoever tried to walk that way.

"No," she said, allowing the darkness to overtake the truth the way a darkened doorway might swallow up a lady of the night.

"Good, because I've come to tell you I've changed my mind. You won't be a country pastor's wife."

"No? Out with the geese, cows, and ducks? In with the cathedrals and palaces?"

"No, no. I don't mean I'll be a city pastor. I mean, I won't be a pastor at all. Not for awhile, anyway."

"Oh, what will you be?"

"What will I become? I don't know. There is so much glory, beauty, love overflowing in my soul. I feel I must empty myself of it first—a sort of poetic emptying."

"Yes. You might scare your parishioners to death if you talk like that."

"Ha! Ha! But do you mind . . . will you mind?"

"Watching you empty yourself poetically? Not if some of the poems are for me."

"Everything I write will be for you. Always. No matter what." He rose to go.

Already? She jammed her lips together. *Don't beg. Don't ask him to stay.*

The moment the front door closed behind him, Regina darted over to the window and hid behind the curtains. The last thing she wanted was for him to see her spying on him.

Out on the street, Søren turned and looked right up at her as if he'd known she would be there. Furious with herself, she wanted to turn away. But she couldn't help smiling at him instead.

22

The Deer Park

"I had never really thought of being married."

Søren Kierkegaard

"That I one day should marry Søren was actually quite foreign to my thoughts."

Regine Olsen

"You look thin, Regina." Her grandmother reached across the coach with a concerned expression in her lovely eyes.

"It's the shock of being engaged to me for an entire winter," Søren said.

The Councilor laughed. Regina tried to smile to hide her distress from her parents. But it seemed as if Søren had been in an irritable mood for months, and she didn't know how to fix it. She was seated between her father and Søren in a tall Holstein coach with wicker sides and wide seats. Her grandparents sat with her mother on the opposite seat. To Regina's dismay, Jonas and Peter Christian sat together up on the driver's seat. Peter Christian had dismissed the driver and insisted on driving them all himself. His hooked nose, heavy jowls, and the severely straight, thin hair hanging beneath his hat seemed to announce his disapproval of his younger brother.

Regina hoped that the day would be peaceful, and that Søren would behave himself. It seemed ominous, however, that two of his favorite targets were sitting together. She feared the challenge would spur Søren on to new heights of sarcasm.

She hugged her green cape around her high-waisted yellow brocade dress. She looked around at the scenery in order to calm herself. The willow trees dipped their branches to the edge of the water, leaning close as if to whisper in each other's ears. Daffodils and red tulips grew in profusion, lending to the idyllic pastoral feeling of this entrance to the Deer Park. Maybe the scenery would cast a spell over Søren, lulling him into contentment.

"The birds are so loud," Søren said. "Squawking like women at the dressmakers."

Regina laughed. "They're so happy it's spring."

She was happy it was spring. It had been a long winter. On many an evening, Søren had sat beside her reading Mynster's sermons, weeping. She knew how strongly the light affected depressive people. Sixteen blizzards that season hadn't exactly helped Søren's spirits.

Thank You, Lord, she whispered, *for sending the sunshine*, *for sending the spring. Everything will be all right now.*

"How damp it smells," Søren said.

Regina breathed in. He was right. Why hadn't she noticed the murky smell of the lake before?

"It always smells damp in the Deer Park," the Councilor agreed. Peter Christian turned around and glanced at Søren.

"The movement of the carriage wheels gives me the illusion I can feel the earth moving," Søren said. "Do you think a person would go insane if he were constantly aware the earth was going around?"

"Definitely," Regina said, putting one hand on his knee to steady him.

Further along down the forest road past the lake, the sun played among the new leaves of the beech trees. Beneath the trees, a carpet of grass lay interspersed with patches of white and yellow flowers. Male deer rubbed their newly sprouting antlers against the bases of the trees, gnawing at the bark and stripping the trees bare.

The wheels of the carriage creaked as they turned. They passed a group of white deer who eyed the carriage without moving. The musky deer odor became stronger even than the smell of the horses.

"We're lucky it's not yet mating season," Regina's grandfather said. "I was once in an open coach that passed between the two wives of a male deer. The young buck charged straight at me." Her grandfather goggled his large eyes as if in alarm, and all the women in the carriage laughed at his self-deprecating, good-natured manner. He had a way of making everyone feel better about themselves. *Like Fritz,* Regina thought.

"We had cut that young buck off from the wife he preferred," Regina's grandmother added, "and I can tell you he did not like it."

"Perhaps it wasn't even his favorite," Søren said. "Perhaps he just didn't like the idea of being separated from any of his possessions."

"Yes," Regina's father replied, reaching across the open space in the center of the carriage to pat his wife's knee. "We animals are possessive of our possessions."

Søren and Regina's father guffawed together at the implied parallels between the animal kingdom and humans. Regina cringed at their suggested bawdiness, especially in relation to her mother. As they drew close to the older bucks, Regina could see the muscles of their necks straining in order to hold up their huge antlers. It seemed unfair to her, even ridiculous, that they should be so burdened by their masculinity.

Jonas turned in the driver's seat to look down at Søren. "Regina says you've almost finished writing your thesis."

Søren nodded.

"What's it about, anyway?" Jonas asked.

Regina looked up at Jonas to see if he was mocking. But the sculpted lines of Jonas's face looked handsome and relaxed. Regina felt flattered that her brother was making an effort with her fiancé.

"Irony," Søren said. He began whistling an aria from *Don Giovanni.*

"Ironing?" Jonas cupped one hand to his ear.

Søren stopped whistling.

"Irony," Regina said quickly.

"Have you read it, Regina?" Mrs. Olsen asked.

"I tried," she said, "but I fell asleep. Its irony was too absolute for me."

Søren did not laugh.

"Oh, Søren," Regina said. "Don't you get it? It's funny! In the middle of reading about how irony leads you to nothing, it led me into a deep dreamless nothing."

"I see," Søren said. He turned away and picked a small feather out of his cape.

"Irony is all Søren can write about," Peter Christian said without turning around.

Søren stiffened.

"What do you mean?" the Councilor called up. Regina gave a warning frown to her father, but he ignored her.

"I mean, now that Søren has given up seminary, he has nothing left but irony," Peter Christian said.

Søren's lips curled.

The Councilor laughed. Regina tried to shush him again, but her father just grinned. "I take it you disapprove?" the Councilor said.

"My brother has been so busy searching for himself," Peter Christian said, "that he's got nothing else left."

"Except me," Regina said, gripping Søren's arm and feeling the tension coursing through his still limbs. She watched him out of the corner of her eye. Slowly, he lit a cigar. Tiny muscles rippled in his face.

He was trying to think of a clever retort.

"My brother is right," Søren said. Slowly, he exhaled. Thick black smoke hit Regina's eyes, making them sting. "My search for a profession has ended nowhere. I considered being a detective, then a doctor. But I barely read or think about an illness before I have it. The anxiety of studying all those maladies would completely undo me."

Even Peter Christian laughed at this.

"Then I landed on being a country priest. But, unlike my brother, I realized that my whole life devoted to the service of God would scarcely be enough to atone for the dissipation of my youth."

Regina looked out at the pools of water collecting in low-lying indentations in the ground. Moss coated the base of the trees that grew out of these pools. A duck with a translucent green head rested beside the rainwater. The red tulips seemed to transform before her eyes into a field of red shoes.

Why can't he learn about forgiveness, Lord?

"Then I realized that none of these choices are significant," Søren said in a loud voice. "They are aesthetic, irrelevant."

"True," Peter Christian said. "Your consolation is the next world, not this one."

"No," Regina said so sharply that everyone stared at her. "I mean . . . God promises joy in this world, too."

"Not for the Kierkegaards, I think," the Councilor said.

"Holy Scripture teaches that those whom God has loved are always unhappy," Søren said.

"That's wrong," Regina said.

"Regina," her grandmother said, putting a restraining hand on Regina's knee from across the seat.

"God is love," Regina said. "He can't have put us here just to suffer."

"Your daughter," Søren said to the Councilor, "is in the thrall of mediocrity." Søren sighed and shook his head. "Like the rest of her country, she doesn't understand that to be a Christian is to suffer."

The Councilor laughed. "I've been telling her her whole life that Christianity is renunciation. She just refuses to believe me."

"I've never heard such piffle," Regina's grandmother said.

Regina laughed, thrilled that her grandmother had switched sides. "You two just want to make everyone else as depressed as you are," Regina said.

"The problem with women," Søren said to the Councilor, "is that they have all those tears and sighs to defend themselves against suffering. Only we men have the strength to accept and bear suffering straight up."

"Is he always like this?" Regina's grandmother asked her.

Regina nodded.

"Good heavens," her grandmother said. "I wouldn't stand for it."

"Of course, I don't blame poor Regina," Søren went on. "Everyone wants to get hold of the truth without suffering. Unfortunately, God has arranged this existence such that it is impossible to be related in truth to truth without suffering. But it takes an originality—"

"A genius, really," the Councilor added.

"To understand," Søren finished.

"Why do I need to suffer?" Regina raised her eyebrows. "I can just watch you two truth seekers enjoy it."

"Cannibal," Søren said.

"I thought we came here to enjoy the balmy spring weather," Regina's grandfather complained.

"Pardon me," Søren said, a glint in his eyes.

"Finish your story of your search for a profession, Søren," the Councilor said. "We'll talk of existence later."

"So," Søren continued, his eyes still gleaming, "on a recent Sunday afternoon, I sat smoking my cigar as usual in the café in Frederiksberg Gardens, and I got the notion to try my hand at being an author. In other words, I decided to be nothing at all, as my brother says."

"It's not too late to change your mind," Peter Christian said.

"I don't want to. Everyone else stays so busy pursuing the moment. They don't have time to consider life. They need me to sit around doing nothing so I can point out their weaknesses."

"Don't!" Regina said. "No one will ask us to any parties at all. Why do you have to point out everyone else's faults?"

"It's my only talent," Søren said.

"That's true," Peter Christian said.

"Look!" cried Regina's mother. "There's the King's Tree."

Now that she was an adult, Regina recognized her mother's tactics. However, there was something so compelling in her mother's voice that she, along with everyone else, turned to stare at the huge oak tree that stood by itself in a small, grassy clearing. It looked like such a peaceful spot, Regina found it hard to believe that the king who had built the nearby hunting lodge had sat down to die beneath that tree after being attacked by a stag he had wounded.

"How tragic," her grandmother remarked, "that the king should have died so soon after finishing his lodge."

"Perhaps," Søren said, "he would have done better not to have hunted a wily hunter like a stag if enjoying a ripe old age had been his goal."

"Yes, yes," Regina's father laughed. "He who lives by the sword dies by the sword."

Regina admired the stateliness of the grand tree. "It doesn't look like a place of danger," she said. "Especially on such a warm, clear day."

"This whole park is a bog," Søren said in a loud voice. "Its beauty is a temptation enticing the mind to dream and wander and imagine that all is well, while beneath us lies a quaking bog. Do you see the billowing grass on the open plain beyond us? It is really a bog, quaking and quaking, and beneath it lies eternity. Indeed, I find it hard to believe my brother would want to be coachman on such treacherous ground."

Jonas looked all around with alarm.

Regina suppressed a smile. Jonas was probably imagining their carriage wheels sinking into thick, wet mud.

Peter Christian swung round, holding on to the reins with one hand. "Søren, there is something other than the green of springtime that should cover over your anxiety about eternity."

"Your excellent driving?" Søren opened his eyes wide as the carriage swerved to the left.

Regina could tell that Søren had successfully annoyed his brother by the way Peter Christian immediately returned both hands to the reins. "No, no. The Word of God."

Søren touched his forehead. "Of course," he said. "How could I have forgotten?"

"Yes, how could you?" Peter Christian said.

"Oh, look," Regina cried. "What are those three grassy mounds over there?"

"They're ancient burial grounds," Peter Christian said, "for pagans who don't believe the Word of God." He gave Søren a significant look.

Søren patted Regina's knee. He said in an undertone, "I see your mother is not the only one adept at changing the subject." He left his hand on her knee for a moment longer than was necessary. Regina smiled and looked down.

A flock of small black birds landed in the carriage's path. Seconds later, the birds flew off in disarray. Regina wondered why they hadn't noticed the horses before, why they'd wasted all the energy it had taken to land in front of the horses, only to have to scatter moments later.

After picnicking by the Hermitage on sandwiches, champagne, and a marzipan cake covered with pink and green flowers, the party left the Deer Park in order to visit the amusement fair at Dyrehavsbakken. As they strolled into the fair, Regina found herself again between Søren and her father. She took one arm of each. They both wore long blue coats, gray trousers, black shoes and tall black hats. Jonas slipped away to catch up with a young lady. Peter Christian walked ahead with Regina's mother and grandparents.

"I find these amusement parks anything but amusing," Regina heard Peter Christian say as they walked past a dwarf doing battle with a one-armed man.

"My brother finds it difficult to take off his ecclesiastical hat," Søren said.

"He seems annoyed that you took off yours," Regina said.

"Of course. We geniuses are always misunderstood—especially by our closest relatives."

The Councilor laughed, and Regina rolled her eyes on cue.

They walked slowly through the park, passing the elephant tent, a clown, a ventriloquist, and a small puppet theater.

The air was rank with the smell of animals. Children ran in and out amid the crowd. Søren stared at the children, and Regina's heart lurched.

Is he looking for his daughter?

"Let us see what attracts the bare-necks," Søren said, tearing his eyes from the children and pointing at a large, tight crowd in which the men had no cravats wrapped around their necks. "We are sure not to like it, but it is inestimably interesting to have one's knowledge of human nature enriched."

They found a gap in the ring. An organ grinder played a squeaky, slow rendering of an old folk tune. In a dirt clearing danced a ballerina with a muscled body and the ugliest face that Regina had ever seen. The woman's teeth stuck out of her mouth almost at right angles. Her eyes were round rather than oval. Her blonde hair was wet with sweat and matted to her forehead.

"Well, Søren," the Councilor remarked. "I think that is one woman who would like to hear you say that the exterior is irrelevant."

Søren and her father laughed together.

Regina stepped forward and dumped every rixdollar she had into the woman's upturned hat. "She's a beautiful dancer," Regina said. The ballerina lifted one leg behind her ear and then lowered into a second position plié. "So flexible."

"Leave it to Regina to point out the good in everything," her father said.

"Thank God for that," Søren said. "How else could she stand being with me?"

Regina couldn't resist being amused by Søren's uncustomary modesty. She turned away to avoid watching the woman being subjected to their scrutiny. A couple walked past her, arm in arm. They were walking slowly, barely six feet away from her. The man was tall and thin, with long sideburns and brown hair curling beneath his gray hat. The woman had white-blonde hair, a turquoise bonnet, and wore a matching turquoise gown. The young woman gazed up at the man with adoration, and when he smiled back, Regina realized that she was watching Fritz Schlegel walk arm in arm with Thrine Dahl.

Regina's cheeks burned hot. She felt an aching, wrenching feeling in her stomach. Had Fritz been courting Thrine for a long time? Was she the last to know? *Look away,* she told herself. *Don't torture yourself.* But she couldn't.

Fritz nodded his head at Thrine in a sweet way that made Regina's stomach lurch. Then he saw Regina. He stared at Regina for a moment over Thrine's head. Regina saw the color rise in his cheeks. She felt the color rise in her own.

When Thrine turned her head, Regina was mortified. She told herself to pretend that she was looking at something else. Instead, she smiled at Thrine. She hated herself for smiling. She wished she could have been as aloof as Thrine was. Thrine did not smile back. She looked in the other direction.

Then they walked away. From behind, it looked to Regina like Thrine tightened her grasp on Fritz's arm. But Regina knew that Thrine could have nothing to fear.

Regina watched Fritz's retreating back. It looked so foreign, like something she'd never seen before. He bent to Thrine's ear, probably telling her that Regina meant nothing to him. Thrine laughed, and the sound cut at Regina's heart.

Regina turned back to the performance in time to see the ballerina toss four flaming torches into the air. She bit her lip. Had Søren noticed her watching Fritz? He was gazing at something in the distance. Regina twisted her engagement ring round and round her finger. The April sunlight reflected the cut surfaces of the diamonds.

"Søren," her father said, "would you like to move on to that monkey over there?" He pointed at a mangy monkey perched on a man's shoulder, scratching itself.

Søren grimaced. "There's something unseemly about monkeys."

"What is that?" Regina's father asked.

"They remind me too much of myself," Søren said. "Like God is holding a mirror up to me."

Regina laughed. Søren's humor released something inside of her. She took his arm and squeezed it. She needed his humor because when she had seen Fritz holding Thrine's arm, she'd been consumed with something that felt very much like regret.

23

The Music Lesson

"Mondays and Thursdays from 4 to 5 p.m., her music lessons."

SØREN KIERKEGAARD

The next day, Søren arrived at the Olsens' early. "Come," he cried, pulling Regina outside into her mother's garden. "It is spring. Sit with me. Talk to me. Tell me everything. I'm going to spend the entire day with you—every minute. I'm going to drown myself in you."

She laughed. Tulips were blooming all over the garden—pink and red, yellow and orange. "You can't," she said, sitting on the bench and swinging her legs beneath the long narrow skirt of her gown. "Not all day. I have my music lesson in the afternoon."

"What could be more important than me?"

"Nothing—but I must go to my music lesson."

A small twist of anger creased his face. "But I'm only happy when I'm with you."

"You're with me now," she said, "and you don't seem very happy."

He laughed, and she felt a surge of pride.

"How is it that you are able to agree and disagree with everything I say, without upsetting me in the least?"

"There are certain people to whom you have to communicate the truth indirectly."

"How ironic. I have already learned that—it has become my guiding principle. And yet you think I am one of those people?"

She nodded.

He grinned. "You may be right."

At quarter to four, Regina stomped out of the house. She hated her stupid lesson. She hated anything that took her away from being with Søren, or writing to him, or at the very least thinking about him.

Mrs. Regina Kierkegaard. Mrs. Regine Kierkegaard. She kept rehearsing the name in her head. She walked in a constant state of expectation that might find Søren around every street corner.

"Breathe," Miss Wad told her during the singing part of the lesson. "You must never forget to breathe."

But the word *breathe* brought Regina back to the garden that morning. She saw Søren at her side, heard the sound of the water rushing in the canal, and felt again how even the sensation of breathing could change when she was in love.

She sat down at the piano and began to play. Miss Wad tilted one shoulder higher than the other. "You are not paying attention, Miss Olsen."

Miss Wad's lips were too thick, her forehead too broad. Would all people now seem unattractive to Regina unless they looked like Søren Kierkegaard?

Regina's fingernails clicked against the keys. The music room smelled of oranges—the smell of spring, of blossoms. Of love. Where was Søren right now?

Miss Wad frowned at her.

Regina smiled back at her, innocently, and tried to focus on her playing. It was difficult because Miss Wad was humming along with her now, out of tune.

"Miss Olsen," Miss Wad said, "you have not been practicing." She wagged a stubby finger as she spoke.

It was true. Regina had not been practicing. She grew frustrated with her own playing. There was a glorious new song in her heart, but she couldn't find the music to express it. She became more and more annoyed with herself. It was useless.

"No, no," Miss Wad exclaimed, disgust etched in the thick creases of her aging face. She looked at Regina as if she had just stolen a purse. "Not fortissimo, Miss Olsen. Piano. Piano."

Regina tried piano. But fortissimo kept creeping in as she banged her anger at herself out on the keys.

When the hour was up, Regina scrambled to her feet. She whipped over to her shawl and bonnet, and began to lace the thick green satin ribbons under her chin.

"Miss Olsen," Miss Wad said. "I will not be able to continue teaching you unless you practice."

"What a shame," Regina said. "But I don't have time for these lessons anyway. Now that I'm engaged."

Miss Wad, a gaunt spinster, sniffed, and Regina instantly repented. "But thank you so much for all your help. You've been the kindest teacher," she lied.

Miss Wad did not respond.

Regina closed the door behind her, feeling deflated. *At last*, she told herself, *you are free to dream only of Søren*. She skittered down the stairs and threw open the door onto the narrow street.

In the window of the small, run-down coffee shop across the street, something caught her eye. It was a man staring at her—Søren sitting at the front table.

Delight skimmed a trail through her heart. A smile sprang to her lips. She ran across the street, cast her fingers up against the glass, and pressed her nose against the pane. Her breath coated the window with an ephemeral white cloud. Søren beckoned to her, and she shot in.

"Imagine finding you here," she said as she slid into the chair next to him. "And alone. What luck."

"Not luck," Søren said, watching her carefully. "I wait here almost every Monday and Thursday afternoon from four to five o'clock. I have waited here for years."

Regina felt a strange sort of dread curl inside her stomach, as if a cat had just pricked its claws into her before turning around to sleep. She had taken a music lesson on this street every Monday and Thursday afternoon from four to five o'clock for as long as she could remember. He must be teasing her again.

"No, really," she said, "what are you doing here?"

"As I said, I am waiting to see you walk to and fro, as I have done for years. My friends are mystified as to why I come to such a second-rate coffee shop." Søren scraped his chair along the floorboards, leaning closer, lowering his voice. Regina expanded and recoiled simultaneously. "I tell them how extraordinary the coffee is here, and they join me, but only once. Then they leave me alone in disgust, marveling at my poor taste. They don't know that being alone is the very thing I crave, because I want to be able to enjoy in privacy the pleasure of seeing you walk past me not once but twice. And in the hour of waiting, I used to imagine you hard at work, perfecting your craft. I imagined beautiful music pouring from your delicate fingers, your youthful passion—inflamed by me—transformed into melodious ballads."

An image flashed in her mind of Søren lurking in darkened doorways, obscuring his face in a cloak. What had he seen?

What she had done? She felt violated. Disgust ruffled her mouth. Objections crowded her thoughts. *How dare he? I would never spy on anyone like that.*

"You must be joking," she said.

"I'm serious," Søren said, watching her the way a scientist watches a chemical reaction in a beaker. "You can ask my good friend Peder."

Søren called out to a short, surly looking man who came out from a curtain behind the counter. The man had such an unpleasant expression that Regina's insides twisted. She wished Søren hadn't disturbed him. The smell of alcohol wafted over from his direction. The man didn't look as if he'd washed himself or his clothes in a long time. The corners of his mouth drooped and quivered.

Regina's eyes roved to the wooden door. Part of her longed to bolt out of the coffee shop and run along the ramparts. The other part of her, the stronger, weaker, captivated self, felt frozen in the chair, locked in by her desires.

"My dear Peder," Søren called out without taking his eyes off Regina. "How long have I been coming to your fine establishment?"

A generous title for this filthy dump.

"A long time," the man replied in a way that suggested it had been too long. "Years."

"When," Søren persisted. "What days?"

"Mondays and Thursdays. From four to five."

The man stumbled away. He did not seem pleased to have had Søren as a customer for all those years, nor did he ask Regina if she wanted anything.

"The service," Søren whispered, "is not as good as the view. I think they make the coffee with acorns."

"Why do you come then?" she managed to ask, struggling to keep her voice level.

"How vain young girls are these days, fishing for compliments. Tsk. Tsk. Do you really want me to tell you again? How I've been lovesick, pining for you, following you everywhere since the day I met you at the Rordams?"

To Regina's disgust, a smile forced itself upon her mouth, a smile so vain and foolish she was ashamed of herself.

Something shifted on Søren's face. He picked up the chipped china cup on the greasy table in front of him. His fingers gripped the handle of the cup as if it were something he cherished. He inhaled the scent of the coffee. When he tipped the cup to his lips, a look of satisfaction creased the corners of his eyes.

"It doesn't look like you are drinking a second-rate cup of coffee," she said. He hadn't even ordered a cup for her.

"The cultivation of the mood is everything," he said, swirling the cup and sniffing as if testing a fine wine.

"Your mood may be good," she said, "but mine is not."

"No?" he said mildly. "I didn't think it would be."

"Why tell me then?"

Søren's blue eyes clouded over. He looked past her out the grimy window, a dreamy expression on his lips. "It didn't work today."

"What didn't?"

"Thinking about you. It just wasn't the same. So I moved to the front table so you would see me."

"I don't understand. Why did you want me to see you today?"

"I'm afraid," he said, twisting and turning his wrist, twisting and turning the cup, sloshing and spilling the coffee, "that I may have confused the ideal with the reality."

"What?" Shameful tremors of fear hammered at her stomach, her chest, her heart. Why should she care so much? Now, after he'd confessed this violation?

He released the cup onto the saucer. Its murky, gray contents trembled and quivered for a few moments before stilling. One drip traced a slow course down the concave edges. He smiled at her. "Oh, my own dear little Regina. You know I'm joking. Don't pay me any attention. I like to put people on a wild horse and then scare the horse. You know that."

"It's working," she said. "I'm scared. Did you mean it?"

"Of course not." He placed his hand on hers. One thick blue vein protruded from the back of his thin hand.

"Are you saying you only love some imagined me?"

"No. No. No. Of. Course. Not."

"That's it, isn't it?" She stared at him. "Now that you have a real person to deal with, you can't stand it." She shot to her feet, knocking over the chair. "I'm leaving."

The twist of anger she'd occasionally seen lurking behind Søren's eyes sprang forward. He leapt to his feet and grabbed her around the waist. "No," he said. "You can't!" His face quivered. "I'm sorry," he whispered. "It's just that I love you so much. I need you so badly. I didn't know how happy a human being could be until I met you."

She let him pull her to him even though the thought of Peder's leering eyes made her stiffen with loathing. Søren's head fell on her neck. Was he crying?

She softened immediately, cradling him tenderly. So long as she could still penetrate his hateful mocking, perhaps everything would be all right.

The next day, during breakfast, a note came. Regina grabbed the envelope from Anna's hand and sought the solitude of the sitting room. Trembling, she dropped into her mother's soft armchair. The room lay in darkness, shrouded by the drawn velvet curtains. Last night's chess game lay toppled in victory and defeat. She thrust her finger into the envelope and pulled out a letter with elaborate expressions of love and a stick-figure cartoon of Søren standing on Knippelsbro bridge holding a large telescope aimed at her house. She smiled and read the note over and over again.

It was his way of apologizing for spying on her. Definitely.

She twitched again as her corset cut into her armpits. She felt faint.

"Regina! Come and finish your breakfast," her mother called.

"No, thanks," she called back. "I'm not hungry." She mounted the stairs, pausing at the entrance to the hall on the second floor. As she did so, she remembered a little girl who'd paused in the very same place a long time ago.

24

The Father's Dressing Room

"Really she doesn't understand him at all . . . . But while he thus builds up her faith, at the same time he undermines it, for in the end he becomes an object of faith, a god and not a man."

SØREN KIERKEGAARD

She had been playing hide and seek. Olga was *It.* The others had already taken the nursery, the sewing room, and the closet under the stairs. *No, no, no, yes,* the little girl thought, as she examined the remaining rooms in her head. Her father's dressing room beckoned her.

While Olga counted out loud downstairs, the little girl shut the door behind her and stopped in the middle of her father's quiet sanctuary. A cool winter light infused the room. It smelled of her father, but not of her father. The room held his presence and his absence at the same time.

She considered each piece of furniture. A small cavity lay between the cream-colored wall and her father's smooth mahogany chest of drawers. She ruled this space out as too obvious for her to hide in. Neither did the walnut chair, nor the dark desk inlaid with leaves of a lighter wood, seem safe enough.

She opened the armoire. Before her lay her father's spare but magnificent wardrobe. His velvet and tweed and wool coats and trousers in blacks and grays and dark blues hung side by side. Clothes occupied every inch of space. His black, fitted Hessian riding boots poked out beneath the clothes. A wooden mold of her father's calf and foot filled each boot. The molds seemed like carved-off parts of a soldier, ready to march out of the armoire if she left the door open too long. She couldn't imagine pushing the boots or any of the shoes aside. The armoire was arranged with such perfection that there seemed to be no room for her.

A door banged at the end of the hall. The metal handles on the dressers rattled. She fastened the armoire shut, darted across the room and wedged herself into the space between the chest of drawers and the wall. She grabbed her father's tortoiseshell brush off the top of the chest as she went. Feeling exposed, she pulled a soft slipper chair in front of the cavity, further obscuring her body from view. She crouched in the narrow space.

The door to the dressing room flung open, banging the chest of drawers with an irreverent crash. The little girl pressed her back against the wall.

Olga's rapid breaths paused in the center of the room. The armoire door opened and then banged shut. The little girl closed her eyes. She imagined the riding boots pointing the way to her hiding spot. Then Olga's footsteps crashed out of the room and faded away.

Olga had left the door ajar. The opening had changed the light in the dressing room. The little girl longed to sneak out of her hiding place and close the door again to recapture her father's presence in the room. But now that Olga lurked in the hall outside, her hiding place had trapped her. She rubbed the soft, yellowing bristles of the brush against her hand while she waited.

Her father's blue cashmere vest hung over the top of the slipper chair. The vest was old and worn and soft, the color of a robin's egg. She drank in its scent. It smelled of her father—his distinctive, strong, father smell. Crouching there, smelling his vest, its softness now against her forehead, she felt as secure as if her father had had his arms around her.

Someone entered the room and shut the door. The little girl crouched lower in her hiding place. She hugged her calves. She heard a shuffling noise. A drawer banged. After a few seconds, she peered around the side of the slipper chair and saw her father seated at his desk with his head buried in his arms.

She opened her mouth to whisper to him that she was hiding and would he please not give her away, when she saw that he was shaking with laughter. She hadn't seen him laugh in a long time. For the last month, he'd barely left his bedroom. Although she longed to know what the joke was, she restrained herself from speaking. She didn't want to interrupt his joy.

As her father's back continued to shake and shiver, the little girl thought something seemed disjointed about his silent laugh. A moan escaped him. Slowly, it dawned on her that he was sobbing. She felt his pain reverberating, echoing, whipping around inside her. She longed to be somewhere else, anywhere else, someone else. She wished Olga had found her, that she had lost the game. Her father didn't leave his desk chair. Eventually, his back stopped shaking and he went limp, his head still bowed over his arms. The little girl's limbs were aching, but she didn't dare move. She had long ago stopped sliding the soft bristles of the brush against her hand. She had long ago stopped breathing.

She heard a light step pause outside the door. Her mother came into the room and approached her father. He looked up.

Then, somehow, their places were reversed and it was her mother seated in the chair and her father on the floor beside her, his head in her lap. Her mother bent her head over her father, and her fingers caressed his hair. She crooned quiet words to him in a voice that the little girl recognized from times she'd had pains of her own. "It's all right," her mother said softly. "It will be all right."

The little girl watching from behind the chair urged her mother on, hoping, wishing that her father would respond. And as she watched, she felt as if her own hand were caressing her father's dark hair, her own voice whispering in his ear.

Her parents stayed still for a long time. Just as the little girl thought that her knees would explode if she didn't stand up, that she must confess her secret participation in this moment of intimacy, her father whispered, "Regina."

The little girl froze. She'd been discovered.

Then Regina realized that her father was speaking to her mother, for mother and daughter bore the same name.

Her father sprang to his feet and strode out of the room. Regina heard him swear loudly, and she saw her mother run after him, crying his name.

Quickly, Regina stood up. Just then, her father returned. He looked at his youngest daughter pushing her way past the slipper chair. His face changed. It became darker. His handsome features grew menacing. His large, dark eyes narrowed to small slits. "What are you doing in here?" he yelled. "What were you looking at? Why are you spying?"

Regina jumped. All she could hear was a voice inside her head saying over and over, *don't hit me, don't hit me.*

She stared at her father's face while he yelled. A vein popped out on his neck, long and bulbous as a twisted snake. His face turned red.

He looks so ugly. Does he know how ugly he looks?

She longed to escape her father's furious presence, but his large form blocked the doorway. She held her body rigid, bracing herself.

Her mother came in with a worried, almost frightened look on her face. Relief flooded Regina.

"She was spying on us," her father yelled.

Regina's mother shrank back from him. Her brown hair was out of place. Regina crept toward the door, trying to sneak around her parents on her mother's side. As she drew near them, a sharp pain seared her arm where her father's hand caught her on its descent.

She gasped. She hadn't even seen it coming.

"Terkild, no!" Her mother screamed.

Regina ran up the stairs to her room. Each step thudded beneath her weight, each step jolted the pain in her arm. She slammed the door, slamming her hatred, slamming her father, slamming herself, and picked up Henriette, a doll with curled blonde hair, a white china face, and real lace underclothes.

"Did you see him crying?" she whispered to Joan of Arc, who had come to join her.

Joan nodded. Regina didn't need her to speak. Regina just wanted to know that she hadn't been alone, that someone else had been a witness. She passed the doll to Joan, who began whispering secrets in Henriette's ear. Regina strained to hear. Joan was so wise, so close to God. If she could just manage to listen to what Joan had to say, if she could only decipher the rush of Joan's soft breath, then maybe the pain that had gripped her in her father's dressing room, the dark void of a hunger that had nothing to do with food, would disappear.

25

The Ramparts

"I can imagine him being able to bring a girl to the point where he was sure she would sacrifice all."

Søren Kierkegaard

Regina and Søren walked shoulder to shoulder along the ramparts—the planked walkway above the crumbling defenses of the old city. "And now that you have submitted your thesis, Søren, what happens next?"

The question Regina really wanted to ask was, "What happened to my Wednesday letters?" But her stomach clenched every time she imagined accusing him. She kept picturing his face creasing in anger. She imagined him blaming her for being needy, and so she shut the words inside, curled them up in a little ball, and rocked them quietly to sleep.

It was the hour before dusk. The shadows fell, long and elegant, from the trees and windmills that lined this stretch of water. The yellow light, with its almost palpable thickness, caught the leaves of the trees in the midst of their rustlings, creating a symphony of greens. An incoming breeze held a sweetness and a hint of mellow summer warmth. Birds cried out. A barely visible moon hung low in the sky.

Regina felt the long skirt of her gown shimmer and rustle as she walked. Her dangling gold earrings swung under her ear lobes. An energy cast itself around her legs and arms. She felt herself rise and fall, graceful and sure, as she kept pace with her fiancé. This was the way to meet him—with attention, not angry words. There were certain truths she couldn't communicate to him directly.

They walked so slowly that couple after couple passed them. As she waited for Søren to answer her, she noticed with a feeling of elation that their strides matched each other's. Her legs copied his legs; her feet landed heel to toe just like his feet; her weight shifted from her knees to her thighs to her hips just as his did. Did he have any idea that she was capable of this mimicry? She wondered if, after they'd been married a long time, she would begin to copy his speech and perhaps finish his sentences for him. She wondered if they would reach a place where words would be irrelevant and they'd communicate through looks and touch—the prints of his fingers passing her messages like a scrimshaw map engraved on the ivory tusk of a whale.

"Now that I have finished my thesis," Søren said, speaking slowly as if he, too, had entered a trancelike state, "I am through with irony."

"Do you expect me to believe an ironist who says he is through with irony?"

He roared with laughter. But his laugh sounded too loud, like a child copying the laugh of an adult when he hasn't really understood the joke. An elderly woman turned from the arm of her husband and stared.

"Absolutely not! Believe nothing I say or . . . ," and he hopped, missing a beat in his stride as he added, "more to the point, nothing I do."

Regina regretted that she'd given in to her own desire for

irony. She sighed. The elderly woman turned back to her husband and led him off the ramparts.

"Can't you just speak openly sometimes, Søren? Without having to be so clever? It's only me here."

"I speak to you the way I speak to everyone. What I have to say can't be communicated directly."

What an excuse, she thought. The intensity with which he spoke made her nervous. They no longer walked in unison, and as she looked at how his leg now kicked out to the right while she stumbled against her left hip bone, the image rose in her mind of his crabbed, jerky handwriting.

"But what is it you want to say, Søren?"

He put one finger to the side of his nose. "Oh! So you want me to tell you directly what every man has to learn for himself? You want to cheat? Avoid the deep dark night of the soul? Avoid swimming alone sixty thousand fathoms out at sea? Avoid the howling of wolves, the eternal power appearing, the I choosing itself?"

"Definitely."

"Too bad," he said, looking down the stretch of packed dirt on top of the ramparts.

"You should help me, Søren. We're engaged."

"But why would you want me to tell you, when I just told you that you should believe nothing I say."

Her legs suddenly felt heavy. "Could we sit down?"

"I have that effect on most people. An hour in my presence and they're exhausted." His lips turned upward.

He picked up speed. They had to veer at sharp angles to pass the other couples. She gripped his arm as he sped her along. She felt as if he was dragging her. This would never do.

She pushed past her fatigue and matched his quick stride. Now, as they hurried past the rampart strollers, they were walking in unison again—like yoked oxen whose shoulders rubbed together as they moved.

The wind lifted and ruffled the folds of his white cravat. He smiled. "I expect all my thesis readers to react like you just did. With outrage."

"So why do it?"

"The only way to be popular in this world is to tell people that God is within them, that if they stare at their navels long enough, they'll see God." He punctured the air with one fist. "But I refuse to tell the crowd what it wants to hear. I refuse to be a bellows pumper."

"If you go around telling people they're as sick as you are, you will be very unpopular."

"That's too bad. I was raised by my father to tell the truth, no matter what. And everyone *is* as sick as I am. I'm like the person who brings an emetic at the end of a banquet—giving people what they require."

"Søren! That's disgusting."

"Sorry." He ducked his head. "I forgot my audience. But I'm serious. Everyone else is all caught up in marrying and being married."

"What's wrong with that?"

He swiped the air like a swooning opera singer. "It is weakness to need to unite to another human."

"Weakness?" She raised both eyebrows. She forced a smile. *Don't let him know you're hurt. Don't let him see your weakness.*

Regina looked ahead as they neared a tall couple. Dark blue broadcloth stretched tight across the man's tall, strong shoulders. The woman had glittering blue eyes. They were not speaking to each other. Regina's stomach clenched. Why did Fritz have to look so attractive today, at this particular second? And with Thrine?

I don't care, she told herself. *It doesn't matter.*

Does Fritz think she's prettier than me?

Just as Søren and Regina came abreast of them, Fritz's back stiffened. He turned and nodded to Søren, his eyes avoiding Regina. It was an awkward, injured nod. Even now, after almost a year.

Regina's heart tugged at her.

"A handsome couple," Søren said after a few moments. He watched Regina closely.

She nodded.

"You look sad. It's true—don't shake your head. Perhaps its not too late for you. Schlegel would take you back in an instant, you know he would."

Regina felt anxiety attack her, an anxiety so strong it forced words to gush out of her mouth—uncensored words. "Fritz?" She laughed a high-pitched, mocking laugh. "I wouldn't marry him for all the rixdollars in the bank of Denmark."

"You should marry him," Søren's lips jutted out, goading her. "He's a wonderful man, a gentleman. And his star is rising fast in the colonial office. He's well-liked, perfectly respectable, perfectly dependable, perfectly—"

"Ordinary." Regina interrupted. One word. One word that made her heart stop with its betrayal.

"Tsk. Tsk. For a little miss to be so proud—it isn't good."

"Stop it. Just stop talking about it, would you? Please."

"At last, your oasis," he said, pointing to a vacant wooden bench set back at the edge of the ramparts. They settled themselves a discreet distance apart, but something in her ached at that distance, and with the tips of her finger she lifted up one of his hands from his knee so that their palms touched each other. After a few moments, Thrine and Fritz caught up to and walked past them again. Regina examined a distant windmill. She wished she hadn't taken Søren's hand, but it was too late.

"Do you think that there is room for a wife in the life of this impassioned writer?" she asked him.

He didn't remove his hand from the place in the air where she had lifted it, but he held it still. In order for their palms to keep touching, she had to do all the pushing, make all the adjustments. The effort strained the muscles in her arm. It embarrassed her. She dropped her hand into her lap. He placed his hand back on his knee.

"Ah," he said as if in response to her question, "the good wife."

She heard mockery and even condemnation in his tone. Another couple walked past them, arm in arm. The woman wore red pointed shoes beneath her red and black gown. An image rose in Regina's mind of Søren standing at the music stand in his study, writing while she knelt at his feet. He held up one foot without looking down, and she eased off his shoe and slid on a slipper. He continued to write as she repeated the same procedure with the other foot, and then she slipped out of the room as unobtrusively as possible.

"No," he said. "Now that you mention it, there may not be room for you."

She froze. This was why the Wednesday letters had stopped. This was why she'd been afraid to ask him, to speak directly. She forced herself to smile and shake her head. "That's just your depression talking, Søren."

"How do you know?" He looked away.

"I know all about it, Søren."

"You couldn't."

"I do."

He looked disdainful, almost mocking, as if depression were a special gift only a few could experience.

"Søren, you need me. You'd be so lonely without me. You'd regret it."

She pictured herself sitting at her window, looking for a cloaked figure who never came, and she felt the window begin to crack all along the seams of her heart. Words burst out of her, like a tiny child waking up crying, screaming for her father. "Søren, I'll do anything to keep you—anything!"

"Anything?" He gripped her arm so tightly it hurt.

"Anything," she said in a small voice as the last shred of her dignity, her self, slipped away from her. "I'd be happy to—to—to live in a cabinet in your house as long as I could live with you."

Where had the words come from? The idea? How could she so lower herself? She turned her head away and looked out at the water. It was a uniform dark blue, almost a gray. The sun had lowered in the sky, easing itself onto the horizon. She tightened her green cape around her shoulders with a savage yank.

"It would be very dark," he said.

"Excuse me?"

"In a cabinet. It would be very dark in a cabinet in my house."

She stared at him. He seemed to be joking. Why did she let her mouth speak before she could think? Why?

"I'd come out only when it looked safe," she said, trying to lift her shoulders and pretend she'd been joking.

"At night, I hope," he said.

"Søren!" She blushed.

"Wait," he said. His face quivered with delight. "Listen!"

She stared at him.

"There are two men behind us having a conversation. They are from the poor house. One of them has just said that he does not believe in God. And the other has responded that he would believe in God if a blue one would descend from the sky at this very minute." Søren pulled a rixdollar from his pocket. "And I happen to have a blue one right here." His eyes gleamed. "I'll be right back." He leapt from the bench and dashed behind some shrubbery.

She hadn't even noticed those men. Had Søren been listening to a word she'd said? Regina wanted to crumple, to sink down low. It took every ounce of training, every whalebone in her tightly laced corset, to keep her upright. She longed to slink away and wander along the ramparts by herself. But what if she saw Thrine and Fritz again?

She waited for her fiancé. Through the gaps in the shrubbery, she saw Søren hand the bill to one of the men and tip his hat. Then he returned to her side, grinning broadly.

"So," she said, coldly. "Have you just restored somebody's faith in God?"

"Without a doubt," he grinned. "Now what were you saying about a cabinet?"

"Nothing," she said. She pictured a huge, blue rixdollar descending from the sky, and as she pictured it, it seemed that it became reality. As the dusk fell, the dark haze of blue all around her lowered itself like a curtain.

26

The Test

"Uncle Søren's fiancée was a pretty young girl of eighteen extremely loving to us children and eager to win our love in return. . . . It was through her parents' windows that I also remember having seen the procession when Princess Marianne arrived at the bridge of the crown prince . . . . On that occasion there was a great gathering in the apartment of Regina's parents. A lot of ladies, in particular, were there, and they all asked eagerly after her sweetheart."

HENRIETTE ("JETTA") LUND

"To forsake all things as being absolutely superfluous luxuries—this is worship."

SØREN KIERKEGAARD

"How very convenient of the crown prince to have his barge proceed right past your house," Søren's niece Jetta exclaimed to Regina's mother. It was the sort of remark Søren might have made, if he had come.

The royal barge glided by the harbor outside the Olsen's living room. Prinzessin Marianne, wearing pink, stood beside the crown prince. This was the way a couple was supposed to stand—side by side.

The crowd cheered, music played, the pink-muzzled white horses pranced, and Regina's heart shuddered with every cannon shot. The sun shone as the couple glided toward the king and queen, who waited on the scarlet-clothed arcade. Sailors cheered from the many ships in the pier.

"And where is my uncle?" Jetta asked, looking around.

Regina picked at the blue ribbons on her skirt.

"Haven't you heard?" Olga turned Jetta to observe the impact of her news. "He and my father have gone on a walk together in the woods."

"Today?" Jetta's blue eyes grew rounder.

"They both declared that they would much rather talk philosophy than gawk at pomp and circumstance," Regina said.

"They said they don't care for kings," Olga added.

"How very like my uncle," Jetta said. She tittered into her hand.

"Yes," Regina said, "but I would have preferred that they were both here with us, even if only to hear them mock the entire event."

"But at least my uncle was not alone in his eccentricity."

"If you want to call it that," Olga said.

Regina returned to the window as if she found the parade captivating. Søren's face loomed in the window. The chin grew sharper, the eyes beadier.

"Do forgive him his moods, Regina," Jetta said. She put a hand tentatively on Regina's arm. "Aren't his letters wonderful?"

Regina tried to smile.

"He told me that once he was so busy thinking about you, he completely forgot to show up," Jetta said.

"That was his excuse," Regina said, "yes."

"He has such a fine sense of humor," Jetta sighed.

"Oh yes," Regina said.

"He said he writes you every Wednesday."

"He seems to confide in you quite a bit, Jetta."

A look of confusion came into Jetta's trusting eyes. "Not all that much," she said.

Regina wished the floor would open up and swallow her. "I'm sorry, Jetta," she said, touching the girl's sleeve. "I'm just upset he's not here."

Regina paced around the room. He had sat there, and there, and there. Was there any chair, any sofa, free of him? In the past, when Søren did not come to her as he had promised, he would send elaborate letters full of charming explanation: *"The moment will not favor us. All right, let us recollect instead."* But ever since her embarrassment on the ramparts, ever since she had offered to live in a cabinet in his home, the letters had grown shorter and shorter: "*My Regina! You must not expect me this afternoon, as I find myself prevented from coming. Your S.K.*" "*My Regina! You must not expect me this evening, as I find myself prevented from coming. Your S.K.*"

He had even lost his originality.

Yesterday, she had waited for him all morning because he'd promised to come. At dinnertime, Olga had come prancing in. "Søren entered the Rordams' just as I was leaving," Olga had told her, watching Regina closely. "He said he was lending a book to the daughters of the house."

"Oh, yes," Regina answered, as if she had known of it all along. But an inner knife of bone and blood carved its way through her stomach. She knew exactly what had reawakened Søren's interest in the widow's daughters. She knew all about his methods, about how he lent books to girls he wanted to seduce.

Her mouth quivering, she turned away from Olga. *Why did you say you'd live in a closet?* she asked herself. *Like some slave. Why? You've made him despise you. Familiarity breeds contempt. You must stay aloof.*

After the procession was over and Jetta and the other guests had left, Søren and the Councilor strode into the hall looking pleased with themselves. Regina looked out the window of the green room. Flags lay deserted on the street below.

"Your youngest daughter looks unhappy," Søren said to the Councilor in a loud voice. "Oh, ho, she's listening! Did you see her eyes flare up when I spoke? That look makes me as uneasy as cows that have not been milked at the proper time."

A gurgling sound came from the Councilor, as if he was stifling a laugh.

Regina joined Olga and Mrs. Olsen in stacking plates of half-eaten food.

"You should thank me for not showing up," Søren said.

Regina's eyes lashed through him and away.

"Really," he said. "The best thing a man could do for his beloved—the very best—is to lead her out of shallow water into the depths, where there are forty thousand fathoms of water beneath her, and shout, 'If you do not become happy now, it is your own fault!'" Søren cupped his hands around his mouth as he shouted.

The Councilor laughed. He looked at his youngest daughter. He stopped laughing.

"I'm having trouble being grateful," Regina said.

"Coffee, dear Søren?" Mrs. Olsen's hand was poised over the spigot of the samovar.

Søren shook his head as if he was angry. "No, no," he said, punching the air. "I gave it up." He stepped further into the room. "Regina, your father and I didn't come because we were doing our Christian duty."

"Oh, really," Regina said. She sought Olga's eyes, knowing Olga would join her in condemning him.

"Yes," Søren said. "It is our duty to seek solitude, to draw on the eternal."

Regina rounded on him. Out of the corner of her eye, she saw her father step quickly back, as if he had important business elsewhere. "Is it your duty to stand someone up?" she said. "Is that what Jesus would recommend?"

"If you must put it that way . . . ," Søren said in an injured tone.

"I must," she said. "Draw on the eternal some other time. Not when you invite guests to my house. Jetta was devastated."

"You are right, my dear." He took her hand and lifted it to his mouth. His lips were so soft, it just wasn't fair. She longed for more kisses just when she'd told herself she didn't want any.

"I will make it up to you," he said. "I will meet you at the theater tomorrow. Unless," he leaned closer and whispered, "you're in your cabinet."

"My—" Her mouth scalloped. "Quiet! Oh, how I wish I'd never said that!"

"Too late."

"Please," she said, "pretend I never said anything about it."

"I couldn't," he said. "I'll always remember. Olga!"

Olga turned around, a plate of half-eaten mackerel in her hand.

"Does your sister keep things in a . . . cabinet?"

Regina jabbed Søren in the side. He caught her hand in his own and scooted out of reach. Olga eyed him.

"A little cabinet," he repeated. "About . . . How tall are you, Regina?"

"None of your business."

"She's five-foot-two," Olga said.

"Yes," Søren said. "That will do splendidly. A little five-foot-two-inch cabinet."

Olga squinted at him. "It would be a tight squeeze, I think. For the longer dresses."

"A tight squeeze sounds perfect," Søren grinned. "Just right."

"Søren, please," Regina begged.

"All right, all right," he said. "I'm leaving. I won't mention it again—until tomorrow."

The next evening, Regina waited for Søren outside the theater with her father. The wind billowed his evening dress coat and the black opera cloak flung over his shoulder. The rest of the family had gone in already. The wind made a whistling noise as it blasted unopposed through the vast circle of the palace riding ring. As the last few theatergoers rushed past them, her father looked at Regina. "You know how he is, my dear. Perhaps the anticipation of the event was sufficient for him."

Regina felt her face set into a cold angry stare. She looked straight ahead. How dare her father try to justify Søren's rudeness with Søren's own twisted logic. Whose side was he on, anyway? Her own mind was so adept at defending him that she resented hearing it from someone else.

"Come," her father said. "The play will make you forget."

"I don't want to forget," she said, the skin around her mouth feeling slack in comparison to the tightness of the rest of her body.

She strode away from her father, knowing he would let her go. She wanted to punish somebody, anybody, for her hurt. She crossed the bridge leading away from the palace and headed toward home. The streets smelled of urine. A rat slipped under a gutter plank, making her jump. It was growing dark. Her skin felt cold from the wind, yet she was sweating. She couldn't walk fast enough because so many people were in her way. Street lamps affixed to the walls distorted the people and carriages into strange, sharp shapes. A noisy crowd approached. Night watchmen strained under the weight of a drunk they carried on a wooden plank. A gaggle of boys trailed after them, jeering. Regina skirted the crowd and at last stepped back onto the sidewalk.

Two middle-aged women now ambled ahead of her, blocking the sidewalk. *Move over!* she heard a voice in her head spit at them. She glared at the women's backs. *You're too fat*, the angry voice said. *People so fat should not walk side by side. Someone should tell you.*

She rounded a corner onto an open square and was almost blown backward by a rush of wind. She forced her way through it. Normally, she might have raised both arms and playfully rested in the wind gust to test how helpless she was in its embrace, but this evening she headed on, determined to discover and then be upset by Søren's newest excuse.

Finally she reached her parents' home. When she turned the handle, the front door blew inward with a bang. Why was it unlocked? She passed through the door and threw her weight against it to force it shut.

As she had expected, a letter—probably hand delivered while she and her father had stood in the wind—was waiting for her. It lay in the claw-footed silver tray on the hall table. The sickly sweet scent of lilies from the vase behind the tray made her feel like gagging. She dropped her opera glasses on the table and reached to pick up the letter.

The envelope felt heavy in her hand. Something round, metallic, and slightly sharp rested in the corner of it. As she tilted the envelope to open it, the metallic object rolled to the other corner. Had Søren included a gift, perhaps even a ring, to try and appease her?

Regina ripped open the wax seal. She tipped the metal object out of the envelope and gasped as it rolled into her hand.

Søren's engagement ring looked wide and heavy in her palm. She wasn't used to seeing it detached from living flesh.

She slipped it onto her own finger and clenched her fist. When she tried to force herself to breathe normally, her breath refused to cooperate. It came in quick, loud huffs as she read the letter:

> *"In order not to put more often to the test a thing which after all must be done, and which being done will supply the needed strength—let it then be done. Above all, forget him who writes this, forgive a man who, though he may be capable of something, is not capable of making a girl happy.*
>
> *To send a silken cord is, in the East, capital punishment for the receiver; to send a ring is here capital punishment for him who sends it."*

Regina's heart pounded against her chest. A pit formed in her stomach. She reread the letter. *Forget him who writes this.* The words reverberated inside of her. *Forget him.* The *tick tock* of the grandfather clock set the pace for the words repeating themselves in her head. *Forget him, forget him.* Her chest heaved. She seemed to be standing still for a long time.

The ink looked so black and permanent. The two paragraphs stood alone on the page as if they were an excerpt from some larger work. Had he written the letter quickly or slowly? No words were crossed out. The writing was neater than usual. He must have written multiple drafts before sending this one. She imagined him at his music stand, writing a ten-page letter, and then dropping it on the floor. Every time he rewrote the letter, it became shorter, until at last he had distilled it down to two paragraphs—paragraphs that cried out in their brevity, paragraphs that refused to reveal all the things he had dropped to the floor.

Once she had concluded that Søren must have spent a long time composing the words, her hands began to shake so much that she almost dropped the letter. She had to put it down. She folded and refolded it trying to reproduce its original creases. She slid it back into the envelope, folded the envelope, folded the envelope again, and folded it even smaller.

She turned Søren's large ring on her finger, and its unfamiliar looseness made her realize she had been standing in the hall for what felt like a very long time. She looked down at the envelope, now a small, bulky cube with sharp edges. She unfolded it, smoothed it out, and stuffed it deep in the pocket of her pelisse. She had to hide the envelope because what it said wasn't going to happen. She stuffed the envelope deeper into her pocket.

When Regina pulled her hand from her pelisse, Søren's ring almost slipped off. She caught it by curling the tip of her finger around it. It was a sign. She had to make him take the ring back. She pictured the ring, secure and safe on his finger. This was what must be done. The ring must be returned to Søren's finger.

Regina tried to quell the hysteria rising within her. She pictured Søren sitting by his window, confused, feeling betrayed that loving her had not been enough to save him from depression. He needed her—desperately.

She looked up at her parents' empty staircase and realized she needed to do something to help him. *Lord, it's not wrong. I just want to help him.*

Gripping her fist around Søren's ring again, she forced open the front door and ran down the steps. She heard the front door bang twice in the wind, and part of her knew she should not leave the home of her trusting parents open to the forces of evil, but the rest of her was already halfway to the bridge. She silenced the voice of responsibility and clawed her way through the wind.

After what seemed like no time at all, she reached Søren's apartment on Norregade. She rang his doorbell and waited.

Finally Anders answered. She pushed past him into the hall. "Where is Mr. Kierkegaard?" she demanded, looking around as if he might be lurking in the shadows.

"He is out, Miss Olsen," Anders told her.

For a moment, she didn't believe him. Her mental image of Søren at the window in his house had been so vivid, it had to be true. She tried to picture him somewhere other than his window, but that image began to crack and his smile fade, and she wondered if she had any idea what Søren was really thinking at all.

"I need pen and ink," she said. "Please."

Anders led her into Søren's study. She marched straight to the music stand but kept her eyes from the papers that littered the floor. She didn't want to see any earlier drafts of the letter she'd received from him—drafts that said: "I never loved you. It was all a game—a scientific experiment in passion. You made me feel a little happier but not anymore. It's over."

She dipped the quill in the ink, and then held the pen an inch above the paper, poised for attack. What could she say? She had to undo whatever wrong thing she had done. Should she tell him her heart was breaking, that she couldn't bear to live without him? Every time she drew the pen closer to try to write this, her heart beat so furiously she stopped.

So she summoned forth an image of Søren's stern father and wrote, "*In the name of Christ and your deceased father, do not leave me. This is but a symptom of your melancholy. Your Regina.*"

It was done. She felt calmer. She left his house and was even able to walk home at a measured pace without growing angry at anyone who blocked her path. When she reached home, her entire family was congregated in the front hall.

Don't tell them.

The moment she saw the concern on her parents' faces, she told them everything. She felt desperately hopeful that somehow they could fix the situation and make everything all right again.

When he heard it, her father's face creased in anger.

"Oh, my darling," her mother said, reaching out to hug Regina. "I wish there was something I could do."

"I could kill him," Jonas said. "I don't think I really understood hate until this moment."

Regina stiffened in her mother's weak clasp.

"Whatever you do," Olga said, "do not beg."

Regina felt a stab of panic. She already had.

"I will go to him," the Councilor announced in a menacing voice.

"No," Regina said. "Not yet."

"Oh, Regina," Cornelia said, "I feel so sorry for Mr. Kierkegaard right now."

What about me?

She started to reprimand Cornelia but stopped herself. She, too, felt sorrier for Søren than for herself. It was easier that way.

Regina suddenly felt exposed standing in front of her family, discussing what to do about her rejection. She saw their sympathetic eyes focused on her, but realized that none of them could really help her at all.

27

The Return

"She fought like a lioness."

Søren Kierkegaard

"The insight into the power that melancholia exercised over Søren's soul in fact increased my sensitivity, so that I felt the need to make every effort to remain with him—precisely for his sake."

Regine Olsen

The next morning, Regina lay fully clothed on her bed. The morning light seemed to mock her with its ordinary texture. It had the clean freshness that proclaims a new day is here, new beginnings are upon us, there is a chance to start over.

Regina's back felt sore from lying in the same spot. She rolled on her side. The waistband of her skirt pinched her stomach and her corset prickled her skin. There didn't seem to be any air in the room at all. *No wonder I spend so little time here*, she thought. *It is as stifling as a cabinet.*

She threw herself onto her stomach.

Her mother came into the room, closed the door gently behind her, and sat on the edge of the bed. The bed dipped, and Regina felt as if she were losing her position, her hollowed out self, on the down mattress. Her mother waited. Regina said nothing.

Regina felt her body grow tense. She felt anxious about keeping her mother so long in her room. Her mother had other things to do. The urge to explain began to gnaw at Regina, but she was stifled by an image of the satiny, gold-colored plate containers that her mother had given her—the ones her grandmother had given her mother. The containers seemed so practical and thoughtful a gift for a wedding, and they'd been stored in the attic for so long with such love, that Regina couldn't bear to talk to her mother about how she had ruined it all.

"Is there anything I can do?" her mother asked. Regina looked at the thin, ruddy lines that coursed across the surface of her mother's cheeks. Her mother's blonde hair was shot through with streaks of white. The corners of her mouth creased downward with concern. The creases made her mother's face appear, momentarily, unhappy. Regina felt guilty. She wanted to restore her mother's face to its usual places.

"No." Regina turned her face away from her mother, to the window. "But thank you," she added.

Her mother stood up.

Wait, Regina wanted to cry out. *Stay with me.*

She turned round to engage her mother. But it seemed to Regina that a look of resigned inevitability had taken over her mother's face and hardened it.

"I will call you if he comes," her mother said.

An hour later, the call came. Regina sprang to her feet, then slowed herself down. She patted her hair, smoothed her long violet gown. *A lady makes a gentleman wait,* she told herself. Then she thought, bitterly, *Not this lady.* She headed straight for the stairs.

Søren stood at the bottom of the staircase. Anna hovered beside him. Regina wished Anna would leave. Even from the top of the staircase, Regina could see how pale he looked and how dark shadows had overtaken the soft pads beneath his eyes.

Her hand slid down the polished banister as she descended. Anna scurried away down the hall. From the lowest stair, Regina tore his ring off her finger and held it out to him.

"I do not accept it," she said. "I refuse to take it back. It's yours."

He did not reach for the ring.

She did not drop her hand.

"If you don't take it back," she said, "I will hurl it into the street." She pictured it flying through the air and landing in the murky waters of the harbor.

He took the ring back.

She began to tremble, deflated. Regina had achieved her purpose, the thought that had obsessed her since she had read the letter, and she had no idea what to do next.

"Don't be angry with me, Regina," Søren said. "Believe me, this is harder for me than it is for you. Don't raise your eyebrows like that. I am the most wretched of men. No one in the history of mankind is more misunderstood than I."

"I'm having trouble feeling sorry for you right now."

His eyes wandered past her. "Regina, I love you more than any man has ever loved a woman. To break with you is a horror. You are only sad for yourself, but I bear the pain of knowing I've hurt you, that I'm responsible for your pain. I may never recover from it."

She stepped down onto his level. "I'm not worried about you," she said.

"I only take the ring back because you invoked the name of my father," Søren said. His hands were trembling as much as hers. "You had no right to do that. You must have known how that would affect me."

"Good," she said. "Someone had to make you see reason."

"Reason," he said.

"Yes," she said. "If you break with me, you will be lost."

"My brother said the same thing," he said.

"You told Peter Christian?" She was shocked. It made it seem so final.

He nodded.

"The next time you want to communicate something important to me," she said, hearing her voice speak as if from a place outside herself, "at least grant me the courtesy of doing it in person."

"All right," he agreed. "But there will be no next time. I must break with you. You must let me go."

"I won't. This is just your melancholy speaking."

"I am my melancholy," he said. His face became even more haggard, if possible, as if he were trying to prove his words. "She is my mistress."

"Today perhaps," Regina said, "but not tomorrow, or the day after. And I will wait. I will win."

"How can you wait," he said in a low voice, "when I myself cannot stand it, when I imagine doing away with myself every time I start to get better, just so that I will never have to dwell in the abyss again?"

"You love yourself too much ever to kill yourself," she said.

His smile looked tired. "Perhaps."

"And Christ could cure your depression if you trusted Him, if you let others pray over you, if you repented and asked God to forgive your sins. He'd cure you if you loved Him more than all your false idols."

"No," he said, "that's not the problem. It's not possible to love God *and* be happy in this world."

"That's your pride speaking. You could be happy, Søren, if you believed God could forgive you, if you believed in grace. Really believed—passionately—not just intellectually. You like to think of yourself as this melancholy, clever man. What if God is calling you to wholeness and you're just too enamored of this melancholy image of yourself to listen?"

"And marriage to you is part of the cure, Regina?"

"Well, yes."

"I'd be a terrible husband, Regina. You have no idea."

"Isn't that my choice? Besides, I don't want a perfect husband. You put too much burden on yourself." She could tell he was thinking. She waited.

"Perhaps this is not the best way," he said as if to himself. Then he looked at her. "All right. I relent."

She turned on her heels and ran back upstairs. *Don't look back*, she told herself. *Don't look back.*

In her room, Regina threw back her yellow curtains and peered out the window, watching Søren's stooped figure retreat from her house. From where she stood, he looked so small and bent over that she despised herself for loving him.

28

The Silken Self

"In her desperation she overstepped her limit and would compel me to overstep mine. The situation became dreadful."

Søren Kierkegaard

Two months later, Regina was exhausted. She and Søren sat side by side on the sitting room sofa, the late afternoon sun slanting dusky rays of light on his shoulders. And she could feel, in the way she leaned toward him and the way he leaned away, that it was over.

She told herself to calm down. Søren wasn't going anywhere. She just needed more sleep, that was all.

Her eyelids drooped. She'd stayed up all night pouring over his love letters, soaking them in. The candlelight had shrouded his words in a burnt sienna shadow, making even the way he wrote her name—*our own dear little Regina*—seem bathed in darkness.

If only she could relax around him, she wouldn't keep saying the wrong thing. She stared at the fireplace. It didn't seem real. Nothing in the room seemed real. Was she going mad?

She sucked in her stomach, but he didn't look her way. She was being ridiculous. Two inches off her waist, a straighter back—

a corset couldn't make him love her more. There was something else wrong with her—something fundamentally wrong.

Søren shifted beside her. He had wrapped his black cravat so tightly around the neck of his shirt that the two points of his white collar cut into his cheeks. It pained her to look at how tightly he had tied his cravat. Two opal studs glimmered from the shirtfront bulging out from beneath his white damask vest. One stud was a round amber yellow, and the other a hexagon of turquoise.

"Did you know you were wearing two different studs?" she asked. She reached over and touched the amber yellow one.

"Yes," he said, leaning further away from her, onto one elbow. The fingers of his right hand splayed over his chin and cheek like the overextended arms of a starfish. She let her hand fall away from his button.

"I must go," he said. He drew his watch out of his pocket. "I am meeting Emil at the Royal Theater tonight. *The White Lady* is playing. I don't want to be late." A muscle in his cheek quivered. He sprang off of the sofa, walked away from her, and leaned against the window sill.

Don't follow him.

She felt herself rise from the sofa and close the distance between them. She knew that the self doing this walking was the ephemeral, silken self, the one over which she had no control. She felt this shadowy self turn him round, slip its soft arms around his neck, drape itself around him, and hang off of him, while the muscle and bone self shuddered.

"Why don't you love me anymore, Søren?"

He looked away. He shrugged. She watched the rise and fall of his narrow shoulders, and felt it match the rise and fall of her breast.

She gripped his collar. "Who?" she asked. "Who is it? Who have you fallen in love with?"

"No one," he said. His face seemed to settle into stone. "Not yet. But there will be someone. My irony has something extraordinarily seductive and fascinating about it. It lifts women up out of their immediate existence. They like that. Enticing, yet always at a distance, never unmasking itself."

"Will you ever marry?" she whispered, wanting to know the answer but feeling that if he said yes, the shadowy ephemeral self that hung onto his neck would lose its grasp and fall to the floor.

His jaw tightened and his eyes narrowed to the shape of crescent moons. "First, I shall sow my wild oats. Then, perhaps in ten years or so, I shall marry some young girl to rejuvenate my blood."

The muscle and bone Regina recoiled, lurching away from him, dragging the ephemeral, shadowy self by the waist. The arms of the silken self dangled along the floor as it went.

"Don't look so surprised," he said, stepping close to her. "Seducing women runs in the family. My father—that bastion of severe Christianity—seduced his maid while his first wife lay dying in her bedroom. That maid was my mother. But then, you met him. You saw what he was, didn't you?"

"No, I didn't know," she said. "But you're not your father. You're not doomed to repeat his mistakes—that's only Satan whispering melancholy lies in your ear."

"Are you calling my mother a mistake? That's not very kind?"

"Stop it," she said. She walked away from him. "Just stop it."

"Don't be upset. I'm not worth it."

She spun around. "Is it because of the prostitute?"

"How do you know about that?" His eyes bore into hers, as sharp as a letter opener.

"I read about it in your journal entry that day I came alone to your apartment." Her face grew red. Her body tensed for the attack she knew she deserved.

He shrugged. "Yes, I ran with a bad crowd before my father died. We went. Once. But nothing happened. I was too drunk."

She recoiled. The image she had of him grew brighter and yet more tarnished at the same time. If only she'd confessed sooner. Maybe she would have acted differently, been more herself, more relaxed. She jabbed her fingernails into the palms of her hands.

"Don't worry," he said. "You will marry someone else, someone kind and good who loves you. You'll recover. You are just suffering from the illusory eternity of first love. It had to end eventually."

"I will never marry. I'll become a governess to eight children," she said, hating herself for the self-pity she was revealing. "I'll watch children who will hit me and tell me they don't have to listen to me because I'm not their mama."

"If you have anything else to say, please hurry. I'd hate to keep Emil waiting." His face closed in on itself, giving him the hooded look of a lizard.

"Søren! Why are you doing this?"

"Well," he said, pursing his lips, "the problem is, you love me too much. Don't you?"

"Kiss me," she said.

He moved to her, a mechanical stiff walk. She realized immediately that she'd made a mistake, that she shouldn't have asked. But it was too late. He closed his lips on hers with a cold, perfunctory compression.

She wrenched herself away from him. *Don't let him see your face. Don't let him see how much you love him, despite everything.* She pushed open the front door, ran down the steps, along the edge of the harbor, and over the bridge—as far away from him as she could get. She knew that if she kept running, she would not give in to the despair, the sobbing, wrenching despair that was trying to flatten her as completely as if she'd leapt from a window.

Interlude

"From her I went immediately to the theater because I wanted to meet Emil Boesen. (In time this gave rise to a story that I looked at my watch and asked her please to hurry if she had anything more to say, as I had to go to the theater). The act was finished. As I left the stalls the Councilor came from the first parterre and said: 'May I speak with you?' We went together to his home. She was desperate, he said: 'It will be the death of her; she is completely in despair.' I said: 'I shall calm her down, but everything is settled.' He said: 'I am a proud man and find it hard to say, but please, I beg you—do not break off with her.'

He was indeed a fine man; he had shaken me. But I held my course. I had dinner with the family and spoke with her when I left.

The next morning I got a letter from him saying that she had not slept all night and that I must come and see her. I went, and tried to persuade her . . .

So we separated. I spent the nights crying in my bed but the days as usual, wittier and in better spirits than ever. It was necessary."

Søren Kierkegaard

29

The Approach

"In those days, the step of breaking of an engagement was much more unusual than it became later on, and it was more likely to cause bitterness than a divorce between married people nowadays. It was an insulting break, which not only called forth curiosity and gossip but also absolutely required that every decent person take the side of the injured party."

TROELS FREDERIK TROELS-LUND
(SØREN KIERKEGAARD'S NEPHEW)

"She did not have the strength to survive the breakup."

SØREN KIERKEGAARD

Two weeks later, Søren left for Berlin. He didn't even tell Regina he was leaving. The finality of it, the coldness, flattened her. She became ill. Part of her was relieved. It gave her an excuse to stay at home, wallow in her pain, and lie in bed like Peter Christian's first wife had done, like Peter Christian's second wife now did. It almost made her feel like Søren Kierkegaard's wife.

Her illness began with strange aches—stings in her joints, especially her knees and elbows. They were such transient pains that she wondered if she was imagining them, if perhaps they were symptoms of her bereavement the way a man who has lost an arm feels the sensation of pain in his missing limb.

But soon the fleeting pains were accompanied by an overwhelming fatigue, a faintness in her limbs. She would try to rise from her bed, but after half an hour at the breakfast table, it was all too much and she would creep back upstairs. There was no end to the pain she felt. Life was hopeless. Everything was hopeless.

Then one bitter January morning three months after the final break with Søren, Olga came into her bedroom and told her that Thrine Dahl was engaged to a Frenchman.

Regina lay completely still for a long time. *Fritz.* His name didn't even move her.

"Regina? Are you all right?"

Regina propped herself up on one elbow. Hope stirred. "Isn't there an exhibition opening today, Olga?"

"Oh, Regina. You're not ready. Leave the poor man alone."

Regina could barely hear her. All she could hear as she slid into a dark green damask gown with a heavily pleated skirt was the urging in her head: *Fritz is free. Fritz will set you free.*

A few hours later, Regina strolled through the gallery. The memory of Søren strolled beside her.

All around her she could see only couples. She clenched her fingers. Being alone felt so uncomfortable. She felt out of place being here all by herself. She longed to shed the barren feeling inside her.

A woman in black bore down on her. It was Mrs. Rordam, her sharp eyes assessing Regina. Bolette hovered beside her mother, a pitying smile on her beautiful, married lips. "Regina," Mrs. Rordam said. "Darling. You poor dear. Of course, I shouldn't mention it. But . . ." Mrs. Rordam leaned closer. "It was dreadful what that man did to you. Dreadful. If he returns from Berlin, I shan't invite him to my ball."

"Mrs. Rordam. He hardly deserves so harsh, so capital a punishment."

I even sound like him now. She wished there were someone to tell Søren this.

Bolette smiled.

"Nonsense," Mrs. Rordam said, patting Regina on the hand. "We women must put these villains in their places." She swept out of the gallery.

Villains. Regina felt like someone had punched her in the stomach. It was true. Søren was a villain. He was evil, totally evil. He'd only pretended to love her. He wanted to see what it felt like. He probably just wanted to write about love.

"He's very good at falling in love, isn't he?" Bolette's voice was kind. Then she followed her mother.

Regina stared at Bolette's back. *No*, she thought, *that can't be right.* Regina walked through a doorway into the outer room. If Søren hadn't been in love with her, if he hadn't meant what his eyes said when he had looked at her, then the whole world as she knew it was an illusion. *But if he loved me*, *then why did he break up?*

Her shoulders felt crooked. Her right elbow jutted out. Irrationality was infecting her mind, heaving on the corner of her consciousness, urging her to buy a ticket on a steamship and appear on Søren's doorstep in Berlin in the middle of the night. She imagined screaming at him, explaining all the reasons he couldn't break up with her. But she couldn't quite force her imagination to envision him taking her back into his arms.

And yet, she thought. *And yet*, *if I had to do it all over again, I wouldn't be able to change a thing*. Her shame made her want to sob.

She strode back through the doorway and planted herself on a bench in the cupola room. Soft, warm, winter sunlight flooded the room. She looked out the French windows. What drew her gaze was not the courtyard below, but the red tiled roof of the palace and the hopeful, bright blue sky above.

What is wrong with you? I thought you came here to look at the art. You haven't looked at a single painting.

She looked at the paintings. In the closest, children skated on a small pond, heads bent low against the onslaught of wind and snow. In a second painting, two tiny figures of men walked along a wide dirt road beneath overpowering, tall trees. In a third, white-crested waves rolled onto a deserted beach. All the paintings were so bleak and sterile. Like her life. Like her heart. Like her faith.

She rose to go, and it was then that Fritz Schlegel walked in. She sank back down onto the bench. Fritz froze, averted his eyes, then kept walking toward her.

Regina felt a small sweet pinging in her stomach, like the rocking of a child inside her. She smiled at him—at his earnest face, his tidy coat, his neatly folded cravat, and his vulnerable, brown eyes.

He sucked in his lower lip. He reached her, hovered over her, then sat down beside her.

They surveyed the art in silence. After a long while, he shook his head ever so slightly.

She cast her eyes upward, outward.

The corners of his mouth stretched wider, higher.

Her lips felt fuller, warmer.

He tilted his head to the side, and he smiled. He smiled. And she smiled back.

The tips of Regina's fingers began to feel light and graceful. She longed to spin in a circle, to leap, to dive. She reached for him and squeezed his hand. His face softened. Perhaps he, too, felt as if the tips of his fingers had evaporated and instead of being flesh and blood were now something far more expressive, far more alive.

Regina looked away. She suddenly noticed that a soft pastoral light infused the paintings. The skaters' cheeks glowed rosy red. Sunlight poured through the trees in the forest, illuminating the path where the two men walked. Sandpipers hopped on the beach that had looked deserted just moments ago. How had she not noticed that she was in a room filled with warmth? The pastoral scenes, the soft sunlight, and the blue sky all whispered that Regina could live in this world of warmth and beauty, that she could love again, that she could bask in its light and be part of its hope. She was free. Fritz had set her free.

Only a vague uneasiness lingered near where the painting of a moonlit bridge once had hung.

Saint Croix, 1856

30

New Year's Day

"Life out here is very monotonous, but thank God we both tolerate the climate very well. Schlegel has a great deal to do and I have nothing whatever."

REGINE OLSEN

"If she found out for certain from me how I did love her and do love her, she would repent of her marriage."

SØREN KIERKEGAARD

Regina searched for her husband all over the Government House on the Danish island of Saint Croix. It was New Year's Day, and already she'd broken her only resolution about a hundred times.

The Government House was a grand, honey-yellow building in the middle of town, filled with the noise and bustle of the streets surrounding it. Covered walkways and steps strung together its eighty-five rooms. Its beauty was marred, however, by a large courtyard that lay like a gash in the middle of the palace. For Regina's new home was really two mansions, joined together, with a large cavity at its heart.

Regina stopped in the east walkway and peered down into the courtyard. She saw servants and soldiers attending to the horses and carriages, but no sign of Fritz. She sighed. The courtyard was so ugly. It needed a garden, trees, plantings—a woman's touch. If only it weren't always so hot here. She could do so much more if she could just get used to the heat. Instead, she felt dizzy all the time, useless.

She began walking again. Sweat dripped between the ox-horn busks of her silk corset. She envied the servant girls their loose cotton dresses and colored turbans. Her own red and green tarlatan dress fit tightly around the sleeves and bodice, then belled out in frills from her waist down, around reams of wide, stiff petticoats. How women's fashions had changed in the past fifteen years. The sleeves had tightened, the waists had dropped, and the skirts had ballooned. Sometimes Regina felt that she could no longer carry the load.

Lord, she moaned silently, *why can't I stop thinking about Søren Kierkegaard?*

Of course, she understood why Søren had haunted her thoughts in Copenhagen. Her sin had fueled it, her dreadful sin. She and Søren had engaged in an elaborate, painful dance, passing each other at ten o'clock on the same street, day after day, year after year. Always looking. Never speaking.

Thinking about it now brought the same sharp wrench in her gut. And yet in Copenhagen she hadn't been able to stop her feet from walking, her eyes from looking. It was as addictive as a drug. Each day, just before the unspoken but appointed hour, she would grow agitated, restless, unable to concentrate. And before she knew it, she would drop whatever she was doing, manufacture some excuse, and dart along the streets toward Langelinie in order to pass Søren. And after she had passed him, after their eyes had met, she had always felt a fluttering sweetness and a sharp loss. He cared enough to look for her. Not enough to speak.

But why was she still thinking of him here on Saint Croix?

She and Fritz had been here for nine months now. They had no plans to go back. She might never see Søren again.

She stopped walking and shuddered. Of course she would see him again. She had to. She wasn't complete without him.

Stop that, she told herself. *Lord*, she moaned quietly, her lips moving, *please help me love my husband. Make me love him more than I ever loved Søren Kierkegaard.*

She forced herself to keep walking, nodding to Danish officials who worked on this floor of the palace. She kept her chin up, her eyes straight ahead.

Why was she still enslaved by Søren? Why? She'd done everything she could think of. She'd repented. She'd prayed. She'd read every passage in the Bible she could find about fidelity and promises and marriage. Yet she couldn't stop betraying Fritz.

She didn't even need to close her eyes. All she had to do was picture Søren's sorrowful eyes staring at her, and she was fifteen again, back in the Rordams' front hall being introduced to Søren Kierkegaard for the first time.

The memory had seared itself into all of her senses. The shuttered doors of the Saint Croix hallway disappeared, and instead she could see her long ivory dress and her dark hair piled high, reflected in the mirror. She could smell the beeswax rising from the Rordams' gleaming floor. She could taste the aroma of the bitter coffee drying out the inside of her mouth. She could hear the laughter bubbling forth from the girls beside her. And she could almost feel the softness of Søren's face just below the place where the crow's-feet were beginning to creep out from the corners of his eyes.

She tried to thrust the memory away because it seemed more vivid than that of any other experience she'd ever had. The realization of this filled her with guilt.

Regina continued her march around the Government House. She needed to see Fritz smile at her. She sped along the long, stone-tiled gallery. Out of habit, she kept her eyes averted from the great hall. What overwhelmed her about her ballroom was not so much its size, nor the gilt mirrors that lined its walls, nor the multiple doorways that gave it a gracious, cooling feel, but the floor. The floor was made of thick planks of polished mahogany. Hand rubbed with coconut oil, it glowed more warmly than the most beautiful dining room table. The governor and his lady were to walk on a material that Europeans reserved for their finest furniture.

The ballroom floor made Regina feel unworthy. The whole mansion made her feel unworthy. She didn't deserve such luxury, especially since the only reason she was living here was because of Fritz's dedication, Fritz's talent, Fritz's skill. For Fritz had worked his way up the ranks in the colonial office to become the governor of the Danish West Indies.

Had Søren picked up on the irony? When they'd broken up, she had pathetically whined that she would become a governess. Now she had fulfilled her own prophecy.

Stop thinking about him. Who cares if he notices the irony?

She was sure he had.

Regina passed the thirteenth door of the ballroom, her eyes still averted. Governor von Scholton, the man who had ruled here until eight years ago, had made all these fancy renovations. Maybe the same grandiosity that had led von Scholton to invite free coloreds to his ball and his table, and that had eventually inspired him to proclaim all the slaves on the three Danish islands free before he'd even procured the authority of his king, had also fueled his extravagant redecorations. Maybe he'd been just like Søren. After all, one's greatest strength was always one's greatest weakness. And the same zeal that had enabled Søren to renounce the world and devote himself to writing masterpieces about Christianity for the past fifteen years had made him able to renounce her.

If only she could find Fritz.

The cabinet room beyond the hall was empty. Fritz's personal guards, standing in the reception room, told her that the governor was upstairs. Her heart pounding, she mounted the staircase, heading for their private apartments on the third floor.

Regina walked through the reception room and her sitting room and ducked her head into the master bedroom. The carved mahogany, four-poster bed lay vacant, draped beneath mosquito netting. A planter's chair sat empty in the corner, beside a blanket chest. A mahogany stand held a dry ceramic ewer and washbasin. A large armoire stood fastened shut. And the memory of how she'd given birth in this room just four months earlier made her knees buckle.

❖ ❖ ❖

The contractions were soaring on top of each other, the pain splitting her insides. She imagined herself as a wishbone, being torn in two. She moaned and thrashed her limbs around on the bed struggling to find a position free of pain, but there was none. The thrashing only made her more desperate. There was no way she could escape this pain, no place she could hide from it.

The black-suited doctor, his face bathed in sweat, ordered her to lie still. She couldn't do it. She tried to throw her body off the bed. "Stop it," the doctor yelled as he grabbed her arm, but Regina shook free of his grasp. *The floor*, Regina thought, *it won't hurt on the floor*. But she landed with a sharp thud, and it hurt just as much. Moaning, she fought against the hands that lifted her body back onto the bed. Then, just as she thought that she could not bear it any longer, that there was no reason for pain like this to exist on the earth, she heard the doctor yell at her to start pushing, and she pushed as hard as she could. It hurt just as much as before, but at least she could do something about it, at least now she was close to the end. Then the doctor told her to stop pushing, and moments later, he told her to push again.

"Breathe now," the midwife said.

"Now?" Regina asked in desperation. "Now?"

"Yes," the midwife shouted, and Regina breathed. They told her to stop and then to push again. There was a terrible aching pain in her back that would not go away. And then she heard the midwife cry in delight, "It's coming. I can see the crown of the head." As she spoke, Regina felt it, she felt an object emerge from inside of her, she felt the head come out.

She struggled to comprehend it. Her body told her that a baby, a real baby, her own baby, was actually emerging from inside of her, but her brain told her that such a thing was not possible, that a head could not emerge from inside another person's body.

"Push again," the doctor ordered, and Regina forgot her shock and tried to push again. "Push hard." Then Regina heard alarm in the midwife's voice, and she heard the doctor say something about the cord, the umbilical cord wrapped around the neck, and panic struck Regina and she pushed harder, harder than she had ever pushed in her life, and she fought more than she had ever fought, and she strained until she knew her own insides were forcing their way out of her body in order to bring the rest of the baby along with them. Then the baby slithered out in one long, quick, wet slide, and Regina didn't wait for the pain to subside but shot her head up to look at the doctor and midwife and knew immediately from their faces that the baby was dead. It had died, it had died, it had died, and she screamed like an animal.

Regina shut her bedroom door tight and walked further down the hall into the room Fritz used as a study. There he was at last, seated at the grand mahogany desk commissioned by von Scholton. The stiff collar of his red military coat stuck into his cheeks as he bent over a letter, his mouth open, his eyes half shut.

"Fritz," she cried, her voice louder than she intended.

He held up one hand to halt her. His face hardened. He turned his back further away from her and continued to read his letter.

Regina turned to go, feeling a heaviness in her limbs as if her feet were nailed to the floorboards. She picked up her feet. She'd been wrong to interrupt him. She'd been wrong to speak so loudly. It was probably a very important letter, maybe even from the king.

A back turning away from her.

Stop being upset, she told herself. *That's what marriage is all about. Watching your husband turn his back on you, then picking up your feet, picking up your head, finding something else to do, telling yourself you should expect it because no human could give you all his attention all the time, telling yourself you were expecting too much.*

What are you, Regina, a fool? The question slotted into her head like a letter dropped by an unseen hand.

She walked down the hall, through the dining room, and into her sitting room. She shut the door and sat in her rocking chair. She rocked and rocked. No breeze came from the adjoining porch. She stared at the serpentine back of the sofa beside her. She picked up the Marie Antoinette shawl she was beading for her sick mother. She let it fall to her lap.

Where was he? Why didn't he come and apologize?

Regina looked out the windows at the beautiful blue waters in the harbor of Christiansted, but it brought her no peace. The Lutheran church next door tolled the hour. The bells tolled and tolled, louder and louder, as if they pealed inside her.

A man walked into the room. His blue eyes were animated and adoring. "My darling," Søren said. He seemed to be taller than before, more handsome. "I've come to take you home to Copenhagen. I love you, Regina. I've always loved you. I was wrong to break up with you. What a terrible mistake."

"I know, Søren," she said, standing to meet him. "I've always known. I knew you'd come back for me."

He wrapped his hands around her waist. "I can still almost encircle you, my love. How do you do it? You are still so beautiful. You are more beautiful at thirty-three than you were at eighteen."

"Thank you," she said. "You always know what I want."

"This," he said. "You want this." And he leaned in and kissed her.

"Regina!" Fritz strode into the room.

Regina leapt backward, away from Søren's embrace.

"I'm so sorry," Fritz said. "I'm sorry I was so rude." He wrapped her in his arms. She stiffened, for the imaginary Søren hung in the air between them, as he always had. She returned to Fritz like a person clambering out of a misty lake of half-wanted dreams.

31

The Letter

I shall take her with me into history. There I walk by her side. As a master of ceremonies I introduce her in triumph and say, "Please be so kind as to make a little room for her, for our own dear little Regina."

SØREN KIERKEGAARD

I certainly expected some explanation from Søren Kierkegaard, although I must admit that I did not expect it in quite the form in which I received it.

REGINE OLSEN

"I'm furious," Fritz said, releasing her. "The mail packet arrived today, but our letters seem to have been scattered all over the island. I was reading a letter from Mother when you came in; it was stinking of rum from the cretin who misdelivered it."

"Maybe the rum was your mother's," Regina said. "Maybe she misses you too much."

Fritz eyed her.

Regina grinned. "Sorry. I couldn't resist. You were saying?"

"I was saying I'm sorry." Fritz looked out the balcony. "The truth is, Regina, I'm frustrated. I'm having trouble—

criticism from all sides. I think it's because everyone here still idolizes von Scholton. And I could never live up to a man like that, even though he's been gone for so many years."

She looked at Fritz's worried face—the stray locks of brown hair that hung low over his cheekbones, his thin, pointed eyebrows, his stiff, red coat. He looked so scared. *Why don't I have more sympathy for him?*

"These things take time," she said. "We've only been here nine months. Besides, not everyone liked von Scholton. I think you're reading too much into things."

"You're right," he said, coming closer. She stiffened.

Why can't you be nicer to him?

"Will you forgive me for my rudeness, Regina?"

"There's nothing to forgive."

"You are a darling. What did you want to tell me?"

She shrugged. "Only that the Fieldings will be here any minute."

He hit his forehead with the palm of his hand. "Today?"

"Fritz, we asked them weeks ago. I've been looking forward to it all morning."

"Of course," he said. "I'm sorry. I know how you adore Eleanor. Come. Shall we wait for them on the terrace? Is the table ready?"

She nodded and followed him back through the reception room onto the shaded terrace. The teak, West Indian table lay buried under a starched, white linen tablecloth, lace napkins, monogrammed silver, and Regina's best Danish china. Past the table, she could see down King Street to the Scale House, the busy wharf, the sprawling fort, and the old Lutheran Church. Ladies paraded with parasols, workers rolled barrels to the water, and uniformed soldiers moved easily about, chatting with each other. Women sold fruit, meat, and vegetables from trays balanced on their heads. The songs of sailors, sung in languages from all over the world, drifted upward.

She walked to the edge of the portico roof. Not a breath of wind. The blue and white Danish flag above her draped around its pole like a lady's cloak. She wiped her brow with her lace handkerchief. She could almost see the heat prowling along the periphery of the porch. Even the pink hibiscus that climbed up the delicate handwrought, ironwork railing looked wilted. Regina looked at where the shade ended, barely a foot away from her, and she found it hard to believe that if she were to take one step, just one small step, she would be in complete agony.

The portly doctor rode past, holding a bright red umbrella above him while a half-naked boy ran behind him carrying his medical kit. Regina turned away.

"No sign of these famous Christmas winds," she said.

Fritz rang a silver handbell and gave orders for coffee, fruit, and pastries to be brought out. No sooner had three servants delivered the food on silver trays and lit the flame under the silver samovar, than Ophelia stepped onto the veranda to announce the arrival of the Fieldings. Ophelia's voice was lilting, charming. Her dark skin glowed with health and youth despite the oppressive heat.

How does she do it? Regina thought.

"My darlings," Eleanor Fielding cried in perfect Danish, with only a trace of her English accent. "Have you seen this?" She strode onto the veranda, holding out a copy of the *Saint Croix Avis* in front of her like a sword. Regina grinned at the sight of her. Eleanor's hair was steel gray and wrinkles hooded her small eyes, making them appear even smaller. Her large nose was hooked and regal. She carried her weight well. Her dutiful husband, Alistair, followed. He was thin and graying and always reminded Regina of her family's old greyhound.

"Bad news?" Regina asked, in her heavily accented English.

"The opposite," Eleanor said, switching over to English for Alistair's sake. Smiling, she peered at the newspaper and read aloud:

> *"We have among us a new governor, of pleasing report, in the person of His Excellency, Johan Frederick Schlegel, who, we are glad to find, takes a lively interest in the welfare of the Colony, and who, we rejoice to say, is already gaining the affection of the community, and promises to be exceedingly popular for his courtesy, activity, and zeal."*

She looked up. "Fritz! Isn't it marvelous?"

"The writer's on my payroll," Fritz said in English.

Regina laughed. She looked at Fritz, and pride swelled inside of her like the fanning of a peacock tail.

"You dreadful man," Eleanor said, swatting the air in front of Fritz with her newspaper as if the governor-general of the Danish West Indies were a naughty puppy. "How does your wife stand for it? Regina, darling, you look pale. Where's the coffee? This heat's putting me to sleep." Looking anything but tired, Eleanor headed straight for the table. Her husband darted to pull out her chair.

Fritz pulled out a chair for Regina with a flourish and sat between the two women, grinning. Alistair slid into the chair beside his wife. His huge, wiry eyebrows stuck out at such sharp angles that Regina longed to brush them flat. She busied her hands with passing the food and filling the empty coffee cups from the silver spigot of the samovar.

Ophelia stepped back onto the veranda, apologizing with her mouth while her body stood upright and proud. "Another stray letter from the mail packet, your Excellency."

"I asked Ophelia to bring any letters up immediately," Fritz explained. "Something's gone seriously wrong with the mail today."

A yellow bird landed on the railing and eyed their sugar bowl.

Ophelia placed a thin, white envelope on the table in front of Fritz.

Fritz thanked Ophelia, glanced at the letter, and frowned. His eyes seemed to cloud. He turned, and his eyes followed Ophelia as she pranced off the veranda. His shoulder blocked Regina's view of the letter. She leaned forward to see.

"Ophelia was born free," Eleanor Fielding said the moment Ophelia closed the door behind her. "You can see it in the way she holds herself."

Regina straightened her back.

"It can take a lifetime to heal from the effects of slavery," Fritz said. "That's one of my challenges here."

He glanced at Regina.

"Who's the letter from?" she asked with her eyes.

"Later," his eyes replied. He gave his head a tiny, almost imperceptible shake.

"Why was Ophelia born free?" Fritz asked Eleanor. "It sounds like there's a story there."

"Ah ha!" Eleanor said. "Ah ha! You're certainly asking the right people. Ophelia's black grandmother was the, shall we say, *friend* of the man who used to own the plantation beside ours. Poor woman. She was lovely. It's such a shame your Danish law won't allow marriages between the races." She gave Fritz a significant you'd-better-do-something-about-that-law look.

"Our neighbor gave his mistress her freedom in his will," Alistair added hastily.

"Why didn't he give her her freedom during his lifetime?" Regina asked.

"Probably afraid she'd abandon him if she weren't his slave," Eleanor said. "Since he couldn't lock her in with marriage."

Regina laughed, and Eleanor's tiny eyes gleamed with pleasure.

Fritz picked up the letter and began to tap it against the table.

Regina studied his profile. He looked so irritated. Who was it from? She leaned forward again, but the back of the letter was facing her. All she could see was a black wax seal. Fritz loosened his cravat. Sweat formed lines of beads across his brow. Regina longed to take her thick, white napkin and wipe the sweat from his brow and smooth the angry lines from his mouth.

Fritz flipped the letter over, and Regina read the return address.

The name *Kierkegaard* shimmered in the air. A strange feeling of hope sprang into Regina's throat. Then the rest of the name came in focus. *Peter Christian?* Why was *he* writing? Did it have a secret message from Søren?

Regina squashed down her hope. Impossible. Peter Christian would never write to them about Søren. He was far too proper for that.

Still, Regina's heart fluttered. Second after second ticked by. When would Fritz open the letter? She couldn't stand waiting a second longer. Her hand itched to pluck the envelope off the table and rip it open. Instead, she skewered a piece of mango and glared at the Fieldings. Who had asked them here, anyway?

"So what are you going to do about the worker situation?" Alistair asked. "The colonial council wants to know."

Who cares? What's in that letter?

"There is so much unrest among the workers," Fritz said. He frowned. "Even after eight years, they seem unable to get used to the idea of having money deducted from their wages for food and beds."

"Who can blame them?" Eleanor said. "Those in the lowest bracket get paid five cents a day, but they have to pay five cents a day for room and board. Only now they also have to pay for things like doctors' visits."

Alistair shook his head. "My wife is very popular among the other plantation owners with these views, as you can imagine."

Eleanor grinned with pride. She fingered the huge gold cross around her neck.

"Yesterday," Regina said, nodding toward Eleanor's cross, "I saw a colored woman by the water wearing a large blue cross woven into the fabric of her white dress. It was so poignant. I couldn't help wondering if she realized she was wearing the Danish flag. It was as if she were proclaiming, 'I'm still the property of Denmark,' as if her slavery is a cross she's worn for so long, she no longer notices it."

"That's very eloquent, Regina," Fritz said.

"Thank you," Regina said. He smiled at her.

Eleanor's tiny eyes darted around the table. Every few seconds, she glanced at the letter. Was she scooting her chair closer to Fritz?

Regina wanted to snatch the letter away from Eleanor's inquisitive eyes.

Fritz lifted both hands off the table and flexed his fingers.

Eleanor leaned closer. "So what will you do," Eleanor asked, "to change things?"

"Education," Fritz said. "Education is the key. As my first step, I've embarked on a tour of the schoolhouses for the workers' children."

"Fritz was once a teacher," Regina said.

"*Regina's* teacher," Fritz said.

"A long time ago," Regina said.

Fritz grinned.

He suddenly looked so happy. Regina wished he could always look that happy.

"Take my advice, Fritz," Alistair said. "Don't listen to a word my wife says. Forget the workers. Your only mission out here is to keep up the steady exports of wood, rum, cotton, and cane."

Fritz laughed. "That's where you come in, Alistair. Although I know you don't mean a word of it, you're as soft-hearted as your wife, at heart."

"Don't tell anyone. You'd ruin my reputation," Alistair said.

Eleanor yawned and leaned over her gilded red coffee cup. Her shrewd eyes landed on the letter and then lit up. She read the return address out loud. "'The Reverend Parish Priest, Dr. P. C. Kierkegaard.' What a coincidence! By any chance, are you acquainted with his brother, Søren Kierkegaard?"

Fritz's lips twitched.

Regina tilted her head to one side as if fascinated by the sapphire blue ocean.

32

Fiction

"Perhaps her whole marriage is a mask and she is more passionately attached to me than before."

Søren Kierkegaard

"Fritz harbored no petty distrust of my old memories."

Regine Olsen

"Yes, we are acquainted with Søren Kierkegaard," Fritz said.

"Do you know him well?" Eleanor asked, watching Fritz closely.

"Eleanor," Alistair said, "stop prying."

"I'm interested," Eleanor said. "I've read everything Søren Kierkegaard has ever written—and I can tell you, that's no small accomplishment. Especially for an uneducated old woman like me. What is it—fifteen or so books, not counting the sermons? What a genius he is! Such an original thinker!" She raised one eyebrow, clearly wanting the Schlegels to be impressed.

"I didn't realize Søren's work was so well-known outside of Denmark," Fritz said. He glanced at Regina. His eyes looked worried.

"Eleanor reads Kierkegaard the way some people read the *Saint Croix Avis*," Alistair said. "Her Danish cousins send her his books from Copenhagen. Personally, I can't make heads or tails of the man. Whenever Eleanor translates bits for me, my brain feels like someone has put it through a sieve. I find listening to him harder than trying to swim through a seawall."

"I read Søren Kierkegaard," Eleanor said, pursing her lips, "when I feel depressed about being stuck out here in this dreadful heat. I've never met a man who understood doom and gloom so perfectly."

"That's Søren Kierkegaard all right," Fritz said. He looked at Regina. "Doom and gloom."

Eleanor threw up her fleshy arms. "Just as I've decided he must be the most narcissistic, vacillating, self-centered man who ever walked the planet, just then—almost as if he knows he's gone too far—he says something so profound and beautiful that I feel sympathy for him and keep going. Do you know what I mean?"

"Well—er—yes," Fritz said. He cast another worried glance at Regina.

"Fritz, why do you keep looking at Regina as if she's going to break in two?" Eleanor asked.

"Eleanor!" Alistair clamped his veined hand on Eleanor's large one.

"It's all right, Alistair," Fritz said. "I suppose it's no secret. My darling wife was engaged to Søren Kierkegaard once." Fritz gave a strange laugh.

"Really?" Eleanor's mouth fell open.

"Don't look at me like that, Eleanor," Regina said, trying to smile.

"But my dear," Eleanor said, "then it's you. You're the one."

"What one?" Alistair asked.

"The one Magister Kierkegaard's been writing about his entire life. The woman he talks about spying on. The woman in the green cape he followed around. The one he snatched out from under her earnest fiancé's nose! Ha, ha! It's you—you're the mystery woman, the Unnamed Person he's been dedicating his books to. How does it go? 'To an Unnamed Person who shall one day be named.' How fascinating. I always wondered if she was a real person."

"Oh, no—I hardly think. There was a Bolette—," Regina said, running her hand along the tablecloth.

"Yes," Fritz said. "It's Regina. It has to be. The man became a virtual recluse after they broke up. There's been no one else in his life."

"A recluse?" Eleanor said. "Why?"

Fritz's voice hardened. "He chose to live alone. He had all these grand aspirations, and I suppose he knew he couldn't live up to them if he had to engage with other human beings. Nothing shipwrecks good intentions quite so spectacularly as being in a relationship. Just ask my wife." He reached over and caressed Regina's hand. "But it's worth it. Well worth it."

"No wonder he was so tortured, poor fellow," Eleanor said.

Regina felt the edges of her face harden slightly.

"There's more to it than that," Fritz said. His voice grew intimate, as if he were relishing sharing the news of Søren's defeat. "Five years ago he crossed pens with a journalist who retaliated by publishing cartoons of him—caricatures. He depicted him as a skinny, bent over man wearing one trouser leg shorter than the other, things like that. For the last five years, I'm told, Søren has been taunted by youths everywhere he goes."

Regina exhaled. Thank God Fritz hadn't mentioned the cartoon showing a tiny Søren with a whip, riding the back of a large woman with hoop skirts—the cartoon of Søren training

Regina into submission, drawn after Søren had published that dreadful piece called *The Seducer's Diary.*

"The poor man," Eleanor said.

It serves Søren right, Regina thought. Where did *that* thought come from? Regina drained her coffee cup.

"So," Eleanor leaned closer, "if he's kept on writing about you like this, Regina, you must have broken his heart."

"Well. That's ironic. Not exactly." Regina looked at Fritz. Fritz raised his eyebrows.

"Nonsense," Eleanor said. "No one stays obsessed with someone if they did the breaking up. We only obsess over the people who leave us by the wayside."

Regina felt a blush rise to her cheeks. "No, no. I'm sure you're wrong."

"You're just being modest," Eleanor said. "But how awkward for you to have had an unrequited love around. Copenhagen is a small city. You must have run into him all the time, Regina."

"Oh, no," Regina said. She smiled. The muscle memory of her deception was perfect.

Fritz glanced at her.

"Hardly at all," she added.

"But didn't you speak to him? Tell him to stop writing about you?" Eleanor said.

"I haven't spoken to Søren Kierkegaard in fifteen years," Regina said. A quick clasp of guilt consumed her. If only she could tell Fritz. But the truth would kill him.

"So you had no contact?" Eleanor said. Regina glanced at her. Eleanor's jaws and neck were clenched like a pit bull clamped around a stick.

"I wouldn't say that, exactly," Fritz said. He leaned forward. His voice was conspiratorial, confiding. "He wrote to me once, after Regina's father died."

"Good heavens," Eleanor said. "How inappropriate." She leaned forward, too. "Why?"

"He wanted me to pass a letter on to Regina," Fritz said.

"No," Eleanor said with a thrill in her voice. "What did the letter say?"

"We'll never know," Fritz said. He leaned back. A self-satisfied smile played on his lips. "I returned the letter, unopened, with an indignant reply."

"Good for you," Alistair said.

"Weren't you dreadfully curious, Regina?" Eleanor reached her head behind Fritz's so that she could read Regina's face.

"Oh, no," Regina said, looking down. "No. I'm quite impervious. I was very young when we were engaged. Very impressionable. I'm so much stronger now. God can work such miracles—no?"

Eleanor eyed her.

"But what about his books?" Eleanor asked. "What did you think of them?"

Regina shot a quick look at Fritz and said, "Those? We enjoyed some of them. We used to read Søren's sermons together in the evenings."

"Really? Even *The Seducer's Diary*?" Eleanor said to Alistair, "*The Seducer's Diary* is part of a larger work where Magister Kierkegaard wrote about a man who follows a young girl in a green cape all over Copenhagen, seduces her, and then ditches her."

"It was fiction," Regina said. "Pure fiction."

Keep your face still, Regina ordered herself. *Don't let her guess that you promised to do anything, anything, if you could keep him.*

"But hang on a minute," Eleanor said. She knit her brows together. "If Regina was engaged to Peter Christian's brother, then why in heaven's name is he writing to Fritz? Here, in Saint Croix?"

Fritz and Regina exchanged glances.

"How fascinating," Eleanor said. "A mystery! Unveiling before me! Do let me know. Of course, I'm dying for you to open the letter this very second. But don't let me bully you. You know I'm a dreadful bore that way. Alistair can vouch for that."

"Thank God I'm not in politics like you are, Fritz," Alistair said, raising his pointed gray eyebrows. "I'd never survive a minute with a wife like this."

"Yes," Fritz said, "I'm lucky to have Regina as my wife."

Regina's mouth twitched into a painful, guilty smile.

Eleanor grinned. "All right, all right! I can take a hint. I'm leaving. Until this weekend—when we expect you to visit us on our plantation. You work far too hard, young governor. You *do* know that."

Fritz escorted the Fieldings off the porch. Then he returned to Regina. For a moment they sat side by side at the lavish table.

The letter lay between them.

33 The Opening

"Fritz did not pass judgment on Søren and bore no rival's hatred toward him."

Regine Olsen

"Should we open it?" Regina asked.

"We don't have a choice," he said. "Do we?"

Regina shook her head. She was glad they were here when they read the letter—on the openness of the porch with the sweep of emerald ocean beyond them, not shut up in a small room, its walls closing in on her.

One quick slice of his knife, and they'd be in.

If only it weren't so hot.

Fritz picked up the knife and slid it under the black seal. His movements were cautious. He slid out three single sheets of paper and shook them open. His eyes ran over the first sheet. Regina could see only a few splotches of sepia ink through the back of the thin paper.

Fritz compressed his lips, and Regina frowned. Fritz compressing his lips was the same as another man slamming his fist through a wall.

She felt her hand reaching for the letter. She dug her nails into her palm. The questions tried to force themselves from her throat. She clenched her mouth shut.

Fritz jerked the first sheet out of the way and scanned the second. His eyes raced over the words. He ripped the second sheet away and read the third.

She could hold back the rising tide of questions no longer. "What! What is it, Fritz? Tell me! Why is he writing to us?"

Fritz let his hand fall on the table. He looked at her. His warm, brown eyes held some strange emotion. Was it compassion? Pain? Anger?

"There are some letters that you wish you hadn't opened," he said, his voice thick and hoarse.

She clamped her mouth shut again. *Don't beg him for the news. Don't let him know how desperate you are.*

"Regina, I hate to tell you this—"

Fear clutched at her stomach. She bit her lip.

"Søren Kierkegaard died six weeks ago."

"What? Oh, no," she said. "No." Her lips trembled. "How did he die? Did he—" She broke off. She couldn't voice her deepest fear.

Fritz touched her hand. "He fell ill on the street. He was in the hospital for about six weeks. He died in the hospital. Alone."

Don't cry, Regina. Whatever you do. Don't cry.

"Sweet darling," Fritz said, clutching her over her chair. "Don't hold it in. It's all right."

She could control this. She was stronger than her weaker self. She could fight back the trembling in her mouth. She lifted her coffee cup, watching her hand. It shook so much. She stared at it angrily. *Stop trembling.* It was giving her away. She tried to place the cup back on its saucer without spilling any coffee, but the cup trembled. One thin trail of liquid leaked over the rim. Regina watched the slow drip of the murky coffee.

She had control now. She had complete and total control. "I-I'm fine," she said. She steadied her voice. "It's just the heat—the—you know—being so far away from home. Mother being sick. The—you know. The—" She couldn't say the word. *The baby. Our dead baby.* "Everything's getting to me here. And I just feel sorry for him. For Søren."

Fritz sucked in his lower lip. He looked angry.

"What? What is it?"

He looked down and she clutched his hand. "Don't be angry with me, Fritz." *I didn't mean to shake so violently. Really, I didn't. I did my best.*

He shook his head. "There's something else I have to tell you."

She stared at him.

"There's a reason Peter Christian wrote to us." The muscles of Fritz's face hardened. "He had to write to us in his capacity as executor of Søren's will."

"Søren's will? Why? Does he want to return my letters?"

"There's more to it than that, Regina."

Her hands clawed the sides of the chair.

"You see, Søren Kierkegaard left everything he had to you."

"What?"

Fritz gave a bitter, ironic laugh. "Well, you'd better read it for yourself." He held out the third sheet.

Regina plucked the paper out of Fritz's hand. The will, copied out in an unknown hand, was brief:

> *"To: Reverend Dr. Kierkegaard*
> *To be opened after my death.*
>
> *Dear Brother:*
>
> *It is of course my will that my former fiancée, Mrs. Regina Schlegel, should inherit unconditionally what little*

I leave behind. If she herself refuses to accept it, it is to be offered to her on the condition that she acts as trustee for its distribution to the poor.

What I wish to express is that for me an engagement was and is just as binding as a marriage, and that therefore my estate is to revert to her in exactly the same manner as if I had been married to her.

Your brother,

S. KIERKEGAARD"

34

The Closing

"If I had had faith, I would have stayed with Regine."

Søren Kierkegaard

"Fritz's chivalry, his rare sensitivity, and his sensible conversation were always my sole help."

Regine Olsen

Regina's eyes grew wide. She drew her eyelids down, slamming shut the window to her screeching, painful joy. *Søren thought our engagement was as binding as marriage? He left me everything? Then he must have loved me.* "Impossible," she said. "Søren was mad." Her hand crumpled to the table.

Fritz watched it fall. His lips seemed to slacken slightly.

A sharp knock fell on the veranda door. Ophelia stepped out again and announced that lunch was ready.

"Are you sure you don't want to be alone?" Fritz asked Regina.

She shook her head. "I'm fine."

"Let's discuss this after we eat," he said. "Shall we?"

She nodded. He held her arm to steady her as they walked down the hallway. She excused herself to freshen up. "I won't be a minute," she said.

She shut the door to their bedroom. For a moment, she fell against the door. Then she righted herself. From a white jug she poured water that lapped against the sides of the washbasin. A moan rose from her throat, catching on the raveled edges of her sobs. In the mirror above the washbasin stand, Regina saw red angry blotches filling in the white spaces on her cheeks, her forehead, and around her eyes. She splashed water on her face.

She found herself on the floor. The mahogany floorboards felt cool and smooth against her cheek. Her red and green skirts ballooned up above her. *Get up. Don't let Fritz find you lying here like this.* But she couldn't move.

After what seemed a long time, but not long enough, she hoisted herself upright and wandered down the hallway into their private dining room. Joshua, her husband's most indispensable servant, stood waiting, a look of resignation on his ancient face. Fritz sat alone at their polished dining room table. His eyes moved to her, then away. He didn't mention the red blotches, didn't mention how long she had taken.

The heat seemed to be rising. No breezes blew in from the open balcony overlooking King Street. The turtle stew made Regina's stomach turn. She looked away as Fritz slurped large gulps of the stew from the base of his silver spoon.

Joshua cleared away Regina's untouched stew without a word. He served the second course, a clean white grouper. It tasted like sawdust in her mouth. She could barely swallow. She looked at the watercolor on the wall beside her, a picture of slaves holing a cane piece.

"How's the fish?" Fritz asked.

"Good," she said.

"Then why aren't you eating it?"

She unclenched her lips. She severed one tiny bite of grouper and placed it in her mouth.

"I'm sorry it's not everything you hoped for," he said. His face looked so vulnerable that she took another bite, and another.

"It's better now," she said. Her face felt lumpy and disfigured as the swelling cooled and began to subside.

Fritz let his silver fork fall with a clatter against the rim of his china plate. "How dare he! So desperate to redeem himself, he does this! No matter what it means for us, for your reputation."

"I know, I know." Her voice was soothing.

Fritz's voice rose, as if to mimic a deathbed scene. He held out one shaking hand and made his face quiver. "Regina—I loved you—we are still engaged—remember me always—ignore that tiny detail of me breaking our engagement."

"Fritz!" A tiny smile stole onto Regina's face, then disappeared.

"You know I'm right. The coward."

"I thought we were going to discuss this after we ate," she said.

"Sorry." They resumed eating in silence. Finally, when Joshua retreated behind his screen to the place where he hung the silver above and the linens below, she pushed her plate away.

Fritz lifted his crystal punch glass to her. Was his hand shaking? "This was always my dream, you know." His voice punctured the air. "To have you here, beside me. The governor part is irrelevant."

Something tugged at Regina's heart. She looked down.

"We cannot accept Søren's bequest," Fritz said. His voice was gentle. "You know that."

"Maybe we should accept it and give everything to the poor," Regina said. She opened her eyes wide. "Just as Søren said. Wouldn't that be the right thing to do?"

"Regina! We're miles away. Think of the logistics! It would be an administrative nightmare." Two muscles twitched, simultaneously, at the hinges of his jaws. She stared at the places on his skin where she had seen the twitches. Why was he so angry at her?

Fritz sprang out of his caned chair. He paced around the table. He turned his back to her and stared deep into the empty marble fireplace.

"What is it, Fritz?"

"I'm hurt you even suggested it, Regina."

"It's not my fault! I didn't ask for this. I'm as shocked as you are."

He spun around and stared at her. He didn't speak, but his look accused her.

"Why are you acting like it's my fault?" she said.

"You know what it would mean, don't you? If we accepted it?" His face was tight with rage. She shrank back against the sharp spines of her chair. "It would be like saying that we agree with Søren that the engagement still stands."

"Of course I didn't—of course it doesn't—I never imagined for a moment—" She broke off and looked down at the ravaged remains of the fish, the delicate, life-threatening fish bones. "You're right," she said. "Of course you're right. How thoughtless of me."

But that was exactly what she wanted—to prove to everyone, and to herself, that Søren had loved her. *Now no one will know.* The thought kept hovering, welling. *Don't cry. Whatever you do, don't cry.* She twisted her cloth napkin into a tight ball on her lap.

Fritz sat beside her and pulled his chair close to hers. He was so comforting and stable—so real. Why wasn't he enough?

"Regina," he said, "Peter Christian doesn't think Søren had any money left. He spent it all on publishing books that hardly anyone bought. It's just the principle of the thing. You do see that. I know you do."

"Of course I do. I don't know what I was thinking. It's all such a shock. We must refuse it. You're right. The implications are entirely unacceptable."

He stood, looking relieved.

"But," she said, smoothing her face into an unbroken whole, "I'd like my letters back—the letters I wrote to him. And maybe a few other things that I gave him. My brooches. A ring—"

"Write Henrik Lund yourself," Fritz interrupted. He turned his face to the shuttered window. "Dr. Lund has all Søren's papers and personal effects."

Regina pressed her mouth shut and nodded. Why was Fritz acting like it was her fault again? What had she done wrong?

Fritz walked to the door. "I will write to Peter Christian immediately. I think we should put this whole thing to bed. The sooner we forget about it, the better."

Regina nodded. "You're right. Of course you're right."

That was the way. Just forget.

35

The Green Cape

"In the stillness, when the soul is all alone, the eternal power itself appears and the I chooses itself."

Søren Kierkegaard

"Since his death things have come to me from another point of view."

Regine Olsen

Two days later, Regina awoke late in the bedroom of their plantation estate outside town. An emptiness lay beside her on the mattress. She heard the crack of a whip and the creaking of wheels. She threw off the sheets, parted the mosquito netting, and ran to the window. Outside, she caught a glimpse of Fritz's carriage rolling away between the grand gates and turning into the road that skirted the sea and wound like a ribbon through forests cut through with fields of waving sugarcane. She watched the carriage disappear. Peacocks strutted in the empty wake of his carriage.

On her mahogany bedside table lay a note explaining that he had been called away on business, that there were rocks that needed blasting in the harbor, that he hoped she had a relaxing day. He also said he hoped she approved of his letter to Peter Christian. Beneath his note, lay the letter:

"The Reverend Mr. Parish Priest, Dr. Kierkegaard,

On New Year's Day I received Your Reverence's honored letter of November 23 of last year, and I am using the first departing steamship in order to send you my reply.

First and foremost, on behalf of my wife and myself, I wish to thank you and your honorable relatives for the discretion you have observed in a matter that, for many reasons, we do not wish to become an object of public discussion.

Next, with respect to the surprising information contained in your letter, I have the following to say to Your Reverence:

In the beginning my wife had some doubt as to whether, for her part, she had an obligation to fulfill with respect to the sort of thing implied in the second portion of the declaration of the deceased's will, which you have brought to our notice. She has given up this doubt, however, in part because of the great difficulties occasioned by our absence from home, and in part because of a consideration that both of us view as decisive: namely, that she absolutely does not dare to consider herself justified in accepting an offer that, according to what has been said, is motivated by views she finds totally unacceptable. This has been made even clearer in the private note you included for me, a note with which I acquainted her because I believed that I ought to leave the decision in this matter entirely in my wife's own hands. She therefore has asked me to request that you and your co-heirs proceed entirely as if the above-mentioned will did not exist; the only wish she has expressed is that she retain some letters and several small items found among the property of the deceased, which she assumes formerly belonged to her, concerning which she has written to Dr. Henrik Lund.

I have directly informed attorney Maag of my wife's decision.

With the greatest of esteem, I remain Your Reverence's
Most respectful,
F. SCHLEGEL"

It was a good letter. Of course it was. Kind, thoughtful, elegant. Extraordinary, really. She read the letter as if someone else were reading it.

She got out of bed and stood still. She stared at her old cape, left out by mistake by one of the maids. The cape, now threadbare, its emerald green faded to the sage of sea grass, hung over a chair. The back of the chair suspended the cape in its middle, like a woman held aloft over a man's shoulder. She knew she should throw the cape away, burn it. It was only when draped over chairs that the cape took on dangerous, suggestive shapes.

She picked it up. The worn silk almost slipped through her fingers.

Put it in the armoire, she told herself. *Now.*

Instead, she wrapped herself up in the cape and wandered down the arched hall. The high ceiling, designed to catch the prevailing winds, reminded her of a church. The church where she and Søren were being married. Søren lifted the cape off of her shoulders and twirled it around the length of the hall. "I'm so happy," he cried. "I've never been happier."

The wide mahogany stairs creaked, and Regina jumped. It was the housekeeper, Louise, a dignified elderly black woman, asking her where she wanted to have her morning coffee.

"On the veranda, thank you," Regina told her. She fingered her unkempt hair. "Lovely morning," Regina added with a bright smile.

The housekeeper stared at the tattered cape dangling over Regina's flowing white nightgown. "I'll send Susanne to help you dress," she said.

"What a lovely idea," Regina said. She scurried back to her room and thrust the cape into the bottom of the armoire. It lay in a crumpled heap, wrinkles forming on wrinkles, just as it deserved. A sound in the doorway startled her. Regina whirled around.

But it was only Susanne, standing outside the open door. She was a young girl of fifteen, her coffee colored skin so smooth it was hard to believe she would ever age.

I used to look like that, Regina thought. *When he first met me.*

Regina sat at her dressing table and Susanne began to brush the tangles out of her long brown hair. Susanne gathered her hair into a knot of curls high up at the back of her head and arranged a side curl in front of each ear. Regina crinkled up her face and stared at herself in the mirror. Were those really wrinkles? Perhaps mosquito bites. She leaned closer. No, they were definitely wrinkles. She frowned.

On the chair beside her, she saw a beautiful brown eye staring at her, and then she realized it was her own eye. It was her engagement portrait, recently sent by her mother, lying half buried under a shawl. She detached Susanne's fingers from her hair and unburied the portrait. She looked so young in the portrait. Innocent. Wrinkle free.

Was it possible for a woman to be more beautiful at thirty-three than at eighteen?

"For you, yes," Søren told her.

Regina smiled at herself.

"The green dress today, your Ladyship?" Susanne asked.

"No!"

Susanne cringed. "I'm sorry," Regina said. "I didn't mean to speak so sharply—I was thinking of another green dress." She tried to smile into Susanne's reflection in the mirror. "The green dress would be lovely."

Susanne's image disappeared from the mirror as she walked to the armoire.

"Oh, look," Susanne said, her voice muffled now. "This must have slipped off a hanger. I'm so sorry. Shall I iron it for you?"

Regina sighed. She didn't need to turn around to see what Susanne was talking about. It was inevitable that she couldn't lose the cape. There was no escaping it.

"Thank you," she said. "Yes."

A half hour later, Regina drank her coffee sitting on a rocking chair on the veranda overlooking the sweeping lawn, the rose gardens, and the cliffs leading down to the ocean. The ocean wore its waves like a lady's cloak. Today, small, choppy white breaks on top of sun-filled turquoise made the water look thicker than velvet, deeper than satin.

She looked out and tried to picture Fritz dutifully blasting rocks. But the betrayal had already begun. She leapt out of her chair and strolled through the gardens. Blue doves cooed from the tamarind trees. A parrot streaked by in a flash of green. Lizards lazed on the brick pathways. Hibiscus sent streaks of yellow, coral, and red shooting around her. A huge, silk cotton tree stood in the middle of the lawn, its roots sprawling above the ground and twisting around its trunk.

Regina turned around and surveyed their estate house. It was a lovely, two-story, cut-stone house with a red roof. Simple but elegant, just as she and Fritz liked. It perched on a promontory overlooking steep bluffs. Tree-covered mountain ridges rose behind it. The house seemed to nestle in a place of danger—of vertical drops, jagged rocks, crashing waves.

To her right stood a separate building for the kitchen and cookhouse. Beyond that lay the old mill, now fallen into disrepair, where slaves once walked in a circle pushing two poles attached to a roller that pressed the sugar out of the cane. Windmills dotted the tops of the adjoining hills, and in clearings among the trees, fields of cane bowed in the wind.

Still, Fritz did not return. A servant arrived with a message saying that he had been detained, that there were more rocks in the harbor, that she should go visit the Fieldings.

He was right; of course he was right.

She stayed put.

That night she slept fitfully. A sharp breeze banged open the shutters, startling her. African drums beat from the bushes, the sound of discontent, of unrest. A conch shell blasted. Were the former slaves mounting another rebellion? She was too tired to investigate. Regina shifted upon the white sheets and realized she had been dreaming about Søren. She rolled back toward the window, trying to find the same place in her bed, the exact indentation on her pillow where she had been lying, as if the dream waited there for her to slip into like a skin. But he was gone.

She parted the mosquito netting and pushed open the French windows that led to a porch. The depth of the heat outside shocked her. The scent of cinnamon and vanilla drifted upward from the night-blooming flowers. Tree frogs sizzled from their lairs. A swath of ghostly white moonlight coated the dark rippling water beneath the cliffs. Regina looked down the trail of moonlight and let herself silently cry out to Søren as if he could hear her: "I love you."

And she wondered if somewhere, sometime before he died, Søren Kierkegaard had been consumed with thoughts of her and had whispered the same thing to a moonlit sky.

Something inside her exploded. She swung round and strode back inside, slamming the French windows behind her.

It was pathetic. She was dreaming about a dead man. A man who'd never loved anyone but himself, who'd been as tormented and sick as she now felt. What was wrong with her?

Her heart condemned her with loud, finger-pointing thrusts. She was sick. Sin sick. Hers was a sickness unto death, just as Søren had once written in one of his books.

She crept back onto her bed. She felt so lethargic. Her nightclothes felt heavy; even her sheets felt thick with humidity. The wet air clung to her skin and her hair. It seemed to penetrate her muscles, weighing her down, and pressing upon her chest. She fell into the hollowed out place, the impression of her body on the down mattress. She knew she should get back out of bed, leave the mattress filled with the feathers of twenty-four Danish geese, do something—anything. Anything but give in to despair.

But it was hopeless. She was a failure. Her life had been nothing but a string of failures: a broken engagement, a dead father, a sick mother, a dead baby, a dead marriage. And now a dead fiancé—the only one who'd ever really loved her, the only one with whom she'd ever felt completely alive.

She should leave Fritz. She should return to her dear, sweet, sick mother. She pictured herself going home on the same steamboat that had brought her. She pictured Olga greeting her with a sarcastic, "I knew you couldn't stand that heat." She pictured Fritz, moping, Fritz, his head bent over his mahogany desk, Fritz alone. With the beautiful Ophelia.

She sat straight upright on the bed. No, on second thought, perhaps leaving was not the solution. She fell back again against the mattress. There was nothing she could do to fix this by herself. Nothing.

The moon cast a white cloak upon the dark floor, carving out a cross of windowpane. Her curtains billowed, sending a shadow through the moonlight, which then withdrew as if a prince had bent over her and embellished her moonlight colored skin with the colors of the moon.

The air shifted. Stillness. And truth stole into her heart so quietly that she was hardly even aware of it. There was only one person into whose arms she could leap. She'd tried everything else. There was only one leap left. The leap of faith.

"Lord," she said out loud. "I give up."

Tears filled her eyes, her eyelids. Pain coursed through her cheeks, like tears on the inside.

"I give up. Whatever You want me to do, I will do."

And in that moment of casting herself down, she felt a sweetness, a hope lift her up. She felt comforted by something, someone she could not see. Someone who loved her. Someone whose presence filled the room with more majesty, more love, and more intimacy than she had ever felt. Someone who longed to wipe the tears from her eyes, to heal her, to make her laugh with joy the way Regina Olsen Schlegel had tried to make others laugh all the days of her life.

And as she recognized herself as nothing, she became something. As she emptied herself, she became full. She became the beautiful, marred, perfect, flawed, sinful, beloved daughter of the Most High Lord. She became, for the very first time, her one true self.

It was subjective. It was objective. It was truth.

She was Regina.

And as rain fell on the hipped roof, she slept like the baby she never had.

36

Pirate Treasure and a Sea Witch

"If I had had faith, I would have remained with Regina."

Søren Kierkegaard

"Dear Henrik . . . God tempts no one, so if it were not his will that I should have come to know what I now know, it would not have happened."

Regine Olsen

Late the next morning, Regina walked onto the porch of their plantation house to find Joshua waiting for her. Beside him lay a small, battered trunk. "His Excellency asked me to hand deliver this trunk to you. He promises to be here by lunch." He handed her a letter.

"Why all these messages from my husband, but not the man himself, Joshua?"

Joshua's dark-chocolate eyes met hers. "You know what men are like when you put a stick of dynamite in their hands, don't you, your Ladyship?"

"Yes," she said. She smiled. "I have a brother."

As Joshua turned to go, she averted her eyes from the trunk. She stared at the flickering flames of the torches on either side of the door to the house. She considered having them blown out. But something made her stay her breath.

Joshua walked so slowly that it was agony to watch. She wandered onto the edge of the porch, lifting her pink muslin skirts and picking her way around the urns waiting to collect the rainwater. She waved to the five gardeners who bent over the rose gardens at the end of the lawn. A thrush called from the thorns of an inkberry tree. Butterflies darted among the long trails of the red and purple bougainvillea. Enticing scents rose from the herb garden edging the porch. An egret, slender and white, landed and then took flight.

She glanced over her shoulder. Joshua was still shuffling through the torches. Far off, a rooster crowed.

The moment she could no longer see Joshua's back, Regina flew to the chair at the round table and examined the trunk. It was curved at the top, with leather straps, like the sort of trunk that contains pirate treasure in children's books. She tore open the wax seal of Fritz's letter.

My darling Regina. This trunk arrived just after Peter Christian's letter. I knew it was coming because Peter Christian mentioned it. But I withheld it from you for two days because I thought it best. I was wrong. Forgive me. Your Fritz. P.s. You should know that I read only the first two pages of the trunk's content.

Behind Fritz's letter lay another letter, in a different hand.

The rustling of linen skirts behind her made Regina jump. Susanne stood shyly between the lit torches, her hair caught up in a brightly colored kerchief. She curtsied. "Louise sent me to see if you wanted breakfast, your Ladyship."

"No, thank you," Regina said. "I don't wish to be disturbed."

The moment Susanne left, Regina shook open the second letter. It was from Henrik Lund, Søren's nephew. Regina's heart began to pound. Her eyes took in the words before she understood what she was reading.

> *Dear Regina. Søren left a rather extensive journal. It was all inside of a small rosewood cabinet. It will take me years to cull through and catalogue it, but here are some of the pages that relate most obviously to you. Many of them were in a white envelope marked "About Her." As you are now the owner of all of it, I wanted to send these to you as early as possible, away from prying eyes. I leave to your discretion what you would like to do with these pages from his journal. I think you will quickly see why I thought it best to send these to you. Your friend, Henrik Lund.*

Søren's journal? His soul? His secrets? Within her grasp?

The trunk compelled her, twisted her, scared her. She snapped open the straps and lifted the lid. Inside lay piles of quarto sheets covered in spidery ink handwriting. They were just like the ones she'd seen on Søren's music stand. Regina began to smile. It was here, all here. The truth at last. She dipped her hands into the trunk and let the sheets ripple around them like gold coins.

She lifted the first sheet. Søren was writing about the irony that Regina, who had complained during their break-up that she'd have to become a governess, was now truly a Governess.

I thought the same thing. Pride swept through her, followed by sorrow. *If only he had known how attuned we were, he would never have broken up with me.*

She turned to another sheet. A line jumped out at her. *"If possible, she shall be my wife."*

When had he written these words? When? She scanned

the paper, her hand shaking. The entry was dated after their breakup but before her engagement to Fritz. So Søren *had* wanted to reconcile.

If only she hadn't accepted Fritz. *No*, she thought. *No. Søren broke it off. You couldn't wait forever. But* why, *Søren?* she said to the cloudless sky. *Why break my heart if you didn't have to?*

She realized that Fritz must have read this. No wonder he'd wanted to keep the trunk hidden.

She flipped to another page. *"The Seducer's Diary was written for her sake, to repulse."*

What was he talking about? Why would he want to repulse her? She read further. *"To extricate myself from the relationship as a scoundrel, if possible an arch-scoundrel, was the only thing to do to buoy her up and give her momentum for a marriage, but it was also studied gallantry."*

Søren had only been acting the part of a scoundrel? She let the sheet fall to her lap. He had loved her all along. No, it couldn't be. Jonas would have made such fun of this.

But what if it was true? The cold words Søren had spoken to her that last terrible day in October came back to her like so many rose petals. *He loves me. He loves me not.*

She plunged her hand back into the trunk and found the sealed document entitled "About Her." She ripped it open, reading faster and faster, her heart beats matching her pace. Søren explained that the "Unnamed Person," the one to whom he had dedicated the latter half of his books, was both his father and her.

So she was the Unnamed Person. Of course she was. And how typical of Søren that she had to share the honor. Only in Søren's kind of brain could one person be two.

The trade winds picked up, blowing the ends of Regina's hair up around her white matron's cap. She lifted her eyes to the lines of blue, aquamarine, and violet stretching out into the reaches of the ocean. And she let herself think the thoughts that crowded in on her.

Søren loved me. He was obsessed with me, obsessed with his guilt, obsessed with whether, because he had given up the one thing he loved, God would restore it to him. She had always suspected this, ever since Søren had examined the Abraham and Isaac story in his book *Fear and Trembling*. But until now, she had never dared believe.

She picked up another sheet. The journal was more addictive than love.

> *"When I lived in the second-floor apartment at Norregade I had a tall palisander cupboard made. It is my own design, prompted by something my beloved said in her agony. She said that she would thank me her whole life if she might live in a little cupboard and stay with me. Because of that, it is made without shelves. In it everything is carefully kept, everything reminiscent of her and that will remind her of me."*

"No!" Regina cried out loud. Not her cabinet request. Shame rose red hot in her face. She dropped her hands to her lap and looked wildly around. She stamped her foot and threw the page on the table in front of her. The trade winds picked it up and sent it billowing down the lawn. Regina watched the sheet fly and did not run to retrieve it. *Let it blow off the face of the planet*, she thought.

She thrust her hand into the trunk and leafed through some more pages, cringing. Søren had recorded in detail how Regina had mocked Fritz during their engagement. "*Anyone who knows how she talked about Schlegel in the past, that is, how disparagingly . . . will always have misgivings.*"

Her mouth quivered with fury. It was cruel. Søren was punishing her. He had to know that Fritz might one day see it. If Søren had written this, he was capable of anything.

She flipped to another sheet. She screwed her face up into a tight, fearful ball. In a paragraph called "About Her," Søren wrote how, during the years of her marriage to another man, he'd encountered Regina every day at the same time and the same place. "*It happened each morning at ten o'clock when I went home along Langelinie.*"

Regina's breath came in short quick bursts. Her eyes scanned the rest of the page. Søren wrote about how he'd encountered her in narrow passageways when leaving church. Every look, every raised eyebrow, was recorded.

She would have to tell Fritz. There was no other way. She'd have to confess.

But wait. Fritz hadn't read this yet. And hadn't Henrik said that the journal was hers, to do with what she wanted? Wouldn't it be better to destroy it? All of it?

The thick orange flames of the torches on either side of the door seemed to deepen. Black angry curls of smoke surged out of them, marring the white paint behind.

She could burn it all, right now. No one would ever know. The idea filled her with quick, cold excitement. The page revealing the truth about the cabinet fluttered further down the lawn. It caught on a hedge and rolled upward, flattening itself against the manicured edge. She leapt out of her chair and ran down the lawn holding one hand over her cap. She plucked the sheet off the hedge and returned to the table. Her heart pounded inside her corset.

She picked up the quarto sheet that described how she had met Søren on the street every day. Her hand shook. She drew closer and closer to the torches. She stole a glance all around the wide veranda, the white pillars, the sweep of lawn, the flower garden.

No one was here. No one at all. Even the gardeners seemed to have disappeared.

It was as if she were all alone in the entire world. Alone with a single piece of paper. And two flaming torches.

She held the paper closer to the torch. Closer. A corner caught on fire. Orange flames drew upward. The paper crackled. The flames devoured the thin sheet until there was more flame, less paper.

And a sword pierced her heart. "No," she cried out loud. She blew on the flame. It rose higher, then quenched.

Shaking, Regina fell back in her chair and stared at the charred remains of the page. The printed words accused her. *Every day. At ten.* She had not burned the incriminating details.

She put her back to the torches, slammed the lid of the trunk shut, and slammed her eyelids shut.

Lord, she prayed. *I promised to submit to You.*

Only because you had no other option, she thought.

Silencing herself, she returned to her prayer. *Lord, why is this so hard?*

Knowing filled her. *It's so hard because your ways are not God's ways. And God's ways are so much better.*

She opened her eyes and laughed out loud. She was still on the same porch, looking out over the same stretch of lawn and rose garden and ocean, but everything felt better. Almost.

All right, Lord. I obeyed. I won't burn it. But what do I do next?

"Do I smell smoke?" a husky female voice asked.

Regina leapt out of her chair.

"I'm terribly sorry, Regina," Eleanor said. "I didn't mean to startle you."

Eleanor's tiny eyes gleamed from beneath a huge, foam-green turban. She wore a matching foam-green dress with tight gauze sleeves and a wide skirt.

Oh, Lord. I wanted You, not Eleanor Fielding.

"Eleanor," Regina said. She smiled.

Where did *that* smile come from? She must have mustered it from memory alone. She hoped it looked authentic. Wasn't that how smiles were supposed to feel?

"Welcome," she added.

Eleanor's eyes swept over Regina's face, the trunk, and the blackened sheet in Regina's hand. "Burning something? The letter from your former fiancé's brother, perchance?" Eleanor's eyes sparked with intrigue.

Regina blushed. "Oh—I—it's—" She sat down in her caned chair. "Please, join me," she said. She rang a small silver bell. Susanne returned, and Regina requested two breakfasts. While Eleanor prattled on about how Alistair had caught their chief overseer sliding down one of the gutters meant for the sugar water, Susanne set two places, laid out the strawberry jam, passed a tray of pastries and fruit, and then withdrew.

Regina poured the coffee.

"Well?" Eleanor scooted her chair closer to Regina's and lowered her voice. "I'm simply bursting with curiosity. You must tell me what the letter said. I do hope you admire my restraint in waiting this long? Although, truth to tell, it was only because I thought you were still in town, and Alistair refused to drive me back."

Regina couldn't help grinning.

"I see you do have news," Eleanor said. "Tell me all. Please. Of course, you don't have to. But if I die suddenly in my sleep tonight, it'll be on your conscience."

Regina eyed Eleanor. "I thought the English were supposed to be reserved."

"Why do you think I left England?"

Regina laughed. It felt like smoke clearing from her brain.

"Besides," Eleanor said. "I'm half Danish."

"Well . . ."

After all, it could hardly be a coincidence that probably the only other person in the Danish West Indies who'd read all of Søren's books had shown up on her porch that morning. And so she told Eleanor everything. She told her about the will, the journal, and her dilemma.

"My goodness," Eleanor said when Regina was done, her eyes popping open. "My goodness. You poor dear. What a lot of forgiving you have to do."

"Oh, as for that . . ." Regina made a sweeping gesture with her hand. "I already forgave Søren. Long ago. Of course."

A small smile played on Eleanor's lips. A small smile that seemed to say, "I am *so* much more mature than you."

"What," Regina said. "What?"

"You poor dear child," Eleanor said, taking Regina's slender hand in her own large, soft, wrinkled one. "Forgiving doesn't work like that. You don't just forgive once and it's done. You have to forgive over and over again, every time a memory pops into your head. Now that I know about forgiving, it feels to me as if the Holy Spirit puts memories in my head, just so I can forgive and have the chance to heal from past hurts. And this wretched Søren Kierkegaard has just tormented you from beyond the grave—God rest his soul—and so you have to start all over again on the forgiving."

"Oh, well. I'm sure poor Søren didn't mean to torment—"

Eleanor shut her eyes and held up her hand like Regina had just said something painful.

Regina broke off and waited. She waited, holding her breath. Because in saying it, in saying that Søren hadn't meant to torment her, she had felt the lies wrapping themselves around her words, dragging them down, and dragging her down into the dark place she was sick of inhabiting.

"My dear Regina," Eleanor said, looking heavenward. "Søren Kierkegaard was one of the cleverest, most self-involved, selfish men who ever lived. You can't read a single one of his books without understanding that. And if you want to forgive God's way, you have to admit that. You have to stare the truth in the face. It's hard—oh, yes—it's hard. You have to admit that someone who loved you actually chose to hurt you—deliberately. You have to open yourself up to the pain. To suffering. It's the only way forward. The way of the cross. You have to throw yourself on God's mercy, and say, 'Lord help me to forgive. Help me to give up my desire for revenge. Help me to release this person into Your justice system, not try him according to mine.'"

Regina stared at Eleanor's face—at her wrinkles, the gray, wiry strands of hair, her sharp nose, thin lips, and tiny eyes. She realized that Eleanor had just given her something beautiful and precious and warm, like a present wrapped in homespun cloth, but shining with a golden glowing light inside.

"Eleanor. I think you're an angel!"

"Actually," Eleanor said, her eyes gleaming, "I feel more like a sea witch in this foam-green number, but my seamstress insisted." She rose to her feet. "I'll be on my way," she said. "Believe it or not, I do know when I'm not wanted."

Regina opened her mouth to say, "Oh, no, please stay." But she shut it again. "Thank you, Eleanor," she said. "I appreciate your thoughtfulness. I do need to be alone."

And Regina felt herself grow and expand as she spoke the truth.

37

Red Shoes

"Dear Henrik . . . Who knows but whether these many serious thoughts, which I have recently had in my head, are destined to save me from becoming lost in the petty things that are part of small-town life."

REGINE OLSEN

Regina walked Eleanor to her two-seated phaeton and then raced upstairs to her sitting room. When she reached her room, her ladies' writing desk beckoned to her in a soft, seductive voice. "Write a letter to Henrik," it called to her. "You can write about Søren to your heart's content. You can indulge in daydreams." The faded rose chintz curtains waved softly.

Regina held up one hand. No. She had work to do. This minute. She eased down onto her knees in the middle of the room. The mahogany floorboards were so hard. Her poor knees. Why not slip up into her rocking chair? She could pray just as well from there, for heaven's sake.

Regina Olsen Schlegel, she told herself. *This prayer is so overdue, you ought to be face down. You stay put.*

Her needlework rested nearby displaying more unfinished white canvas than threads. The Marie Antoinette shawl she was beading for her sick mother beckoned.

She slammed her eyes shut. Why was this so hard?

She prayed. She felt as if each prayer were being dragged out of her. And yet, once forced out, the prayers seemed to soar above her in a shimmering, almost visible stream, like the heat that rises from a sugarcane field on the hottest of days.

An image rose in her head of Søren lurking in darkened doorways, trailing behind her, running into her on the streets, following her when she'd been only fifteen years old. The image was clear, vivid, true. What Søren had done was manipulative. It was wrong.

Pain flooded her. *Lord, help me to forgive.*

Another image of Søren came to her. This time he was in the parsonage at Lyngby, talking about being a pastor, waving his hand dismissively at the idea of taking care of his flock's physical needs. He'd been wrong, dead wrong. He was selfish and afraid. She felt a stab of pain in her stomach. *How could I have let him deceive me?*

Lord, help me to forgive him.

She saw Søren at her parents' house, felt him touching her back.

Lord, help me to forgive.

She saw him proposing, then walking away from her, ignoring her at the riding ring. He'd mistreated her.

Lord, help me to forgive.

Where were these memories coming from? They were shown to her so sweetly, so gently, she felt sure the Holy Spirit had to be guiding her to give her an opportunity to heal, just as Eleanor had said.

She couldn't bear anymore. She was through. But as she lifted herself up, another image rose in her head. It was an image of herself at the door of her parents' house, lying to Fritz. "Stay for dinner," she had said. "Stay because I love you," she had implied.

Forgive me, Lord. Forgive me.

She saw herself nodding to her father, opening her eyes wide. "Of course Søren is a Christian. Of course." The truth was, she hadn't cared. And now, finally, she was sorry. Why had it taken her so long to feel sorry? Was her heart really that hard?

Another image came into her head, this one of herself on the ramparts. "Søren, I will do anything you want," she had said. "Anything. Because you, Søren, are more important to me than anything else. Even God."

Shame spun thick heavy ropes around Regina's heart. The shame felt so dark, so desperate, she wanted to drown in it. But drowning wasn't God's way.

Lord, I am so sorry. I am so very sorry. And she wept. She wiped the tears away with the back of her hand.

God could never forgive all that I've done. Never.

She lifted herself up to her rocking chair and rocked, and rocked. She put her hand on a book on the side table to steady herself. It was the New Testament, the Bible Søren had given her. All this time, she had treasured it because Søren had given it. She hadn't even told Fritz why she kept it with her. Maybe it could help her now. Even if she'd kept God's Word for the wrong reason, it was still God's Word.

She flipped it open. Where was the passage she needed, where? It was something to do with forgiveness, something she had marked because Søren needed it. Not her of course, not her. She swam through the pages, through the turned back corners, until she found the verse that sang to her a new song. "If we confess our sins, he is faithful and just and will forgive us our sins."

She tilted her head back over the top of the rocking chair. She just didn't believe it. She couldn't believe it.

She had only one option. She had to give back to God the very words He had given her: *Lord, You are faithful and just. You promise to forgive my sins if I confess them. I confess them. So I must believe I am forgiven. Not because I say so. Because You say so.*

She sprang to her feet and paced around the little sitting room. Light danced on the ocean outside, light danced on the hand she put on the white windowsill, light danced on the heart she opened up to the living Lord.

And she was free.

Outside, she heard the creak of carriage wheels, and she rushed to the window. Fritz eased his lean, strong body out of the carriage, holding onto the brim of his black hat with one hand. He dipped forward and looked absently around. Her heart sank. *Lord, why don't I love him the way I loved Søren? Why?*

Prayers surged out of her—old prayers. *Give me. I want. Get for me.*

She silenced herself. *Lord, help me seek Your face. Your glory. Only You. And don't listen to me if I ask for anything else.*

38

Trade Winds

"The few scattered days I have been, humanly speaking, really happy, I always have longed indescribably for her, her whom I have loved so dearly and who also with her pleading moved me so deeply. But my melancholy and spiritual suffering have made me, humanly speaking, continually unhappy—and thus I have no joy to share with her."

SØREN KIERKEGAARD

"I would be very ungrateful if I did not call myself happy—yes, indeed, happy as very few are happy."

REGINE OLSEN

Fritz was waiting for her beneath the silk-cotton tree, his white shirtsleeves rolled up to his elbows. The tree's leaves and branches cast a deep shade over him that seemed to penetrate his skin, transfiguring him into an image of mellow warmth, in contrast to the glare inhabiting the rest of the garden. He looked so relaxed. She couldn't tell him now. It wouldn't be fair to ruin his good mood. Her green slippers seemed glued to the ballast floor of the veranda.

Slowly, Regina stepped out of the shade of the veranda to join him. The sun bore down through the pale green silk of her parasol as if the parasol were a magnifying glass. Fritz watched her fumbling progress down the lawn, the heels of her green slippers sinking into the soft earth. She joined him beneath the tree and lowered the parasol.

"You were gone a long time," she said.

"I was angry."

"Are there any rocks left in the harbor at all?"

"Very few." He gave a sheepish grin. His smile faded and he stared at her, his face serious, questioning.

"Did you read it?" he said.

She nodded.

"And?"

"I learned a lot of things," she said.

He waited. A kind, encouraging voice inside her urged her on. *Tell him. Tell him the truth.*

No, she told the voice. *I can't do it.* She spun her parasol, round and round. He watched her carefully.

"Are you mad at me, Regina?" he said. "For keeping the journal away? Do you forgive me?"

"Of cour—"she stopped.

In the distance, a peacock wailed like the cry of a child in pain. "No-oh! No-oh! No-oh!"

A memory slipped into her brain. It was a memory of Fritz turning away from her after their dead baby was born, of him telling her that it was better to forget, that she was wrong to feel so desperately miserable.

"Will you excuse me?" she asked.

She left her parasol leaning against the tree and walked away from him. She walked past the rose garden, past the sun-dial, past the edge of the lawn, through the brush, to a clearing on the cliff. A line of coconut trees fringed her view. Jagged rocks led down a thirty-foot incline. A bare patch of earth, purple like a bruise, lay on the opposite hill of the bay.

Waves crashed beneath, and shimmering swatches of emerald, aquamarine, and violet led directly to the horizon.

For a moment, Regina imagined Søren's arms sliding around her, his cheek brushing against hers, his mouth whispering into her ear. But a verse rose in her mind—a verse about false gods and eyes that couldn't see, mouths that couldn't speak, ears that couldn't hear. The image of Søren cracked and faded, leaving only pain etching harsh, deep lines into the crevices of her face, into the cavities of her chest.

The pain was so great she summoned back the image of Søren. But she didn't want that. She shut her eyes. *Lord, forgive me for my sin. Help me be free of this.* She imagined hoisting Søren's image onto an altar. He rolled off and stepped closer to her. She opened her eyes. She knew what she had to do.

Help me forgive Fritz, Lord, she whispered. *Help me forgive him for leaving me alone after my baby died, for telling me to forget, for not being the husband I want. Help me forgive not because he deserves it, but because it's the better way.*

Seagulls circled and cawed. The wind picked up, flooding her with air, with salt, and with light.

"May I join you?" Fritz asked. He lifted the green silk parasol over her head.

She looked up and smiled at him. She took the parasol in her own hand and twisted her lips. In that way of holding her lips she felt a maturity she could not have had when she was eighteen, a maturity born of suffering and pain, of loss and joy.

"Yes," she said. "Yes, you may join me. And yes, I forgive you."

He smiled back, his eyes softening so that they seemed to grow warmer. His eyes gleamed. And his ears, why, they were the most perfect ears she had ever seen. Joy filled her, the joy of knowing that this was the right place for her to be, the right man for her to love.

"I am lucky to have you as a husband," she said.

Fritz shifted his weight from one dusty boot to the other. His eyes lit up. He tried to look away. "And I am lucky you made me suffer so much," he said.

"What?"

"How else do you think I became a Christian? After you broke off with me not even Thrine Dahl was enough."

She smiled. The sea sparkled and glimmered below her. "You never told me about the timing of that."

"I had to retain some modicum of dignity," he said. "I was desperate. I'd never been rejected before. Not like that. And it was just as Søren said, although I shudder to admit it. I threw myself at Christ's feet for the first time in my life. You know, the picking up was so sweet, I'd go through the despair all over again."

"I know what you mean," she said quietly.

"Søren was right about a lot of things," Fritz said. "But he wasn't right about everything." Fritz's serious, earnest eyes examined her. "He was right to say you find your identity standing alone before God and that you don't stand alone before God until you've reached rock bottom, until you've heard the howling of wolves. But he got stuck there—standing alone before God." Fritz leaned closer. "You have to take risks in life, Regina. If you want love."

She twisted her eyes upward. *Lord, You answered my prayer. I do love this man. But it's too late.*

She had to confess. And it would ruin everything. She would love Fritz, and he would hate her. It was easier when she despised him. A flock of pelicans swept past. She wished she could go with them.

Lord, can't You just swallow me up in the earth so I don't have to say this?

She looked down. No crack opened up. She sighed. She looked away, down the rocky pathway at the wan roses that wilted in the thorny underbrush—the only kind of roses that can grow in sandy soil.

"Fritz," she said, "I have something to tell you."

He looked ashen, terrified. *He probably thinks I'm going to leave him, to return to Copenhagen like so many Danish wives do. But for once I have to let him wallow in his misery, until I can explain.*

"Fritz, I used to run into Søren in the streets of Copenhagen. All the time. Even after you and I were married." She felt her body growing smaller, flatter. He would hate her now. She knew he would.

"Of course you did," he said. His voice took on a forced heartiness. "You couldn't help it. It's a small city."

"No, it's more than that. I met him deliberately. As he did me—" She broke off and gripped Fritz's wrist with her hand because his face was horror-struck and she realized what he was thinking. "No, it's not like that," she explained quickly. "We met on the streets. On Langelinie. At ten o'clock. We never spoke, only looked. And in church our eyes often met."

"Well then," Fritz said. "Well then. Thank you for telling me." His face smoothed back into a mask.

There. She had done it. She was finished.

But a small, gentle voice urged her on. She looked away.

"Until the day we left Copenhagen. And I looked for him all over the city. On purpose. And I wished him well."

"You mean the day we were all packed?" he asked. His voice sounded strained. He was trembling. "The morning Mother was visiting, and you ran out the door mumbling something about your gloves?"

She nodded.

Fritz's face narrowed. Pain appeared behind his eyes.

Regina cringed. She let her hand fall from his wrist. "I'm sorry," she whispered. "You must hate me."

His arms went around her, and she let the point of the parasol fall into the soft earth. "I don't hate you, my darling," he said. "I couldn't." His voice cracked.

"And Fritz," she began again, her cheek pressed against the warm cloth of his coat. She forced her mouth open, forced the muscles to comply even though she wanted only to remain silent. "I have one last thing to tell you, and it's the worst part. But I think I have to say it, even though it's going to hurt you, because I want to be free of it, and I don't know how else to do it."

She felt Fritz's torso stiffen. She wanted to sink into the earth, to be swallowed up by a bottomless sofa, to never have to speak again.

But there was a more excellent way. A way of pain.

"Fritz. I still think about Søren. All the time. I don't know why. I'm so sorry. I'm so very sorry." Tears leaked out of her eyes. Pain in her eyelids, her cheeks, her mouth, her stomach. "I'm so sorry."

His arms dropped. He turned away from her. She watched his back. It was straight and unyielding. He was silent. Above him, the fronds of the coconut trees began to rock in the Christmas winds beginning to stir above the sea.

She steeled herself. He was going to walk away from her. She lifted her chin and began to talk herself out of the tired, tearing-down feeling of regret. *Oh well, not this time. But there will be another time, another day. He'll forgive me eventually. Isn't that what marriage is all about?*

She didn't even see it coming. His hand engulfed hers. The angles and sinews and veins of his hand poked into her like nails protruding from the palms of his hands. And yet his skin against hers felt supple and graceful. She gripped his hand in return, tightly, and she could hardly breathe. All she could think was, *He's holding my hand! Oh, dear God! He's holding my hand. Oh, dear God, yes!*

Her heart was so full, she could not speak at all.

Sources

In researching this novel, both in New York City and also in Copenhagen and the Danish West Indies (now the U.S. Virgin Islands), I was blessed by the fact that so very many books on the subject have been translated.

As Søren Kierkegaard and his fabled love affair with Regine Olsen have garnered something of a cult following, I will confess the following two inaccuracies: (1) from an obscure footnote buried deep in a volume of Søren's journals, I learned that the Olsen family lived in only half of a town house at Borsgade 66. By the time I learned this, however, it was too late; I'd already imagined scenes taking place in every room in the house (now destroyed). (2) The second inaccuracy was deliberate. While Regina had access to Søren's journals, and while she did correspond with Henrik Lund after receiving Peter Christian's letter, I sped up the sequence of events in the interest of pace. The journal entries in chapter 36 are authentic, therefore, but the two letters in that chapter are not; they are the only fictional letters in the novel. Those are the inaccuracies of which I am aware. There could be more, for which I apologize in advance.

Regine Olsen's entire version of the story can be found in *Encounters with Kierkegaard: A Life as Seen by His Contemporaries*, collected, edited, and annotated by Bruce H. Kirmmse; and translated by Bruce H. Kirmmse and Virginia R. Laursen (Princeton, N. J.: Princeton University

Press, 1996). This is a wonderful book to which I am entirely indebted. All of Regine Olsen's epigraphs, Henriette Lund's epigraphs, Troels Frederik Troels-Lund's epigraph, the will, and Fritz Schlegel's reply thereto are taken from this book.

Søren Kierkegaard's affair with Regine Olsen figured prominently in roughly the first half of his works, also known as his "aesthetic" writings. She also occupies much space in his journals, as he remained obsessed with her throughout his life. Søren Kierkegaard's epigraphs, his letters, and some of his dialogue are taken from the following of his works:

The Last Years: Journals, 1853–55. Ronald Gregor Smith, ed. and trans. New York, N. Y.: Harper, 1965.

Søren Kierkegaard's Journals and Papers, vols. 5 and 6. Howard V. Hong and Edna H. Hong, eds. and trans., and assisted by Gregor Malantschuk. Bloomington, Ind.: Indiana University Press, 1978.

The Concept of Anxiety. Reidar Thomte, ed. and trans., in collaboration with Albert B. Anderson. Princeton, N. J.: Princeton University Press, 1980.

Fear and Trembling. Alastair Hannay, trans. New York, N. Y.: Penguin Books, 1985.

Philosophical Fragments/ Johannes Climacus. Howard V. Hong and Edna H. Hong, eds. and trans. Princeton, N. J.: Princeton University Press, 1985.

Stages on Life's Way. Howard V. Hong and Edna H. Hong, eds. and trans. Princeton, N. J.: Princeton University Press, 1988.

The Concept of Irony. Howard V. Hong and Edna H. Hong, eds. and trans. Princeton, N. J.: Princeton University Press, 1989.

The Sickness Unto Death. Alastair Hannay, trans. New York, N. Y.: Penguin Books, 1989.

Concluding Unscientific Postscript to Philosophical Fragments, vol. 1.

Howard V. Hong and Edna H. Hong, eds. and trans. Princeton, N. J.: Princeton University Press, 1992.
Either/Or. Alastair Hannay, abridged and trans. New York, N. Y.: Penguin Books, 1992.
The Point of View, Howard V. Hong and Edna H. Hong, eds. and trans. Princeton, N. J.: Princeton University Press, 1998.

Other sources I found helpful include:

Cain, David. *An Evocation of Kierkegaard.* Kobenhavn: C.A. Reitzel, 1997.
Lowrie, Walter. *A Short Life of Kierkegaard.* Princeton, N. J.: Princeton University Press, 1942.
Palmer, Donald D. *Kierkegaard for Beginners.* New York, N. Y.: Writers and Readers Publishings, Inc., 1996.

Kierkegaard lived during the Golden Age of Danish painting. In addition to the beautiful paintings hanging in Copenhagen's museums, the illustrations in the following book provided a wealth of social detail: *The Golden Age of Danish Painting*, catalogue by Kasper Monrad (New York: Hudson Hills Press, 1993).

The St. Croix Avis, available on microfiche in the public library at St. Thomas, supplies a plethora of intimate detail on life in the Danish West Indies. Governor Schlegel, as well as his wife, are mentioned several times. One of the epigraphs and the quotation about Fritz Schlegel in chapter 31 are taken from this paper.

The details on the Danish West Indies were also enriched by the following works:

St. Croix St. Thomas St. John: Henry Morton: Danish West Indian Sketchbook and Diary 1843-44. Copenhagen, Denmark:

Dansk Vestindisk Selskab & St. Croix Landmark Society, 1975.

Haagensen, Reimert. Arnold R. Highfield, trans. *Description of the Island of St. Croix in America in the West Indies*. St. Croix, U.S. Virgin Islands: Virgin Islands Humanities Council, 1995.

Lawaetz, Erik J. *St. Croix: 500 Years: Pre-Columbus to 1990*. Denmark: Poul Kristensen, 1991.

Watkins, Priscilla G. *Government House St. Croix*. Greensboro, N. C.: Friendly Desktop Publishing, 1996.

York, Nina, trans. *Islands of Beauty and Bounty*. St. Croix, U.S. Virgin Islands, 1986.

Acknowledgments

My profound gratitude and thanks go to:

Barbara Bellows for saying, "Caroline, why don't you write about *that?*"

Mally Cox-Chapman, Jennifer Bancroft Kelter, Michele Wijegoonaratna, Jennifer Ash Rudick, and Regina McBride for reading my early drafts, for brainstorming with me, and for all your encouragement and kindness.

Bob Svenson for saying, "God help you if you *don't* write."

Alice Ross, Tory Walsh, Boo Van Ingen, Liete Eichorn, Liz Cooke, Tory Baker, Christie Maasbach, Katie Norton, Meredyth Smith, Chris Diefendorf, Lieta Urry, and Joan Kaye for your weekly prayers.

Melanie Riggs, Mary McNeil, and Barbara Ernst Prey for being such enthusiastic cheerleaders when I needed it most.

Jan Coleman for writing the pitch that sold this book. We must be related somehow.

Betsy Pierce for your expert legal advice.

Beth Moore for all your Bible studies, but especially *Breaking Free*, which underlies Regina's spiritual growth. I am especially indebted to you for the Jesus-as-Prince-Charming theme.

Tim Keller for your inspired preaching at Redeemer Presbyterian Church, especially your many sermons on identity. You truly have a gift from God.

Laura Dail for believing in me before anyone else did. Your enthusiasm means more than I can say.

Ramsey Walker, Tony Schulte, Eddie Auchincloss, Greg Gilhooly, Megan Jessiman, Patricia Haas, and Abby O'Neill for trying to help me on the twisting, turning road to publication.

Steve Laube for handling the business side of things.

Gary Terashita, my editor, for giving me the Phone Call At Home From An Editor and making my dream come true.

My brothers, Struan, Alex, and David Coleman, for wrestling with Søren Kierkegaard's philosophy with me—or at least Dad's version of it—throughout our childhood.

My parents for lavishing such attention on us, and for teaching us about the love of Jesus Christ, not only by your words, but so much more by your actions.

Peter for supporting and encouraging me and never, once, asking why I didn't get a real job.

Luke and Sheila for making me laugh every single day that I have had the supreme pleasure of being your mother.

And finally to my Lord and Savior, without whom, truly, this book would never have happened. Thank You for not letting me be published until I learned to put You first of all.

All of the author's after tax royalties are going to
Hope for New York, a conglomeration of approximately
thirty faith-based charities in New York City.

www.hfny.com